T0245427

Noah's Rights

Noah's Rights

Kenni York

www.urbanbooks.net

Urban Books, LLC
300 Farmingdale Road, NY-Route 109
Farmingdale, NY 11735

ISBN 13: 978-1-62286-798-1
ISBN 10: 1-62286-798-X

First Trade Paperback Printing March 2017
Printed in the United States of America

10 9 8 7 6 5 4 3 2 1

This is a work of fiction. Any references or similarities to actual events, real people, living or dead, or to real locales are intended to give the novel a sense of reality. Any similarity in other names, characters, places, and incidents is entirely coincidental.

Distributed by Kensington Publishing Corp.
Submit Orders to:
Customer Service
400 Hahn Road
Westminster, MD 21157-4627
Phone: 1-800-733-3000
Fax: 1-800-659-2436

Noah's Rights

Kenni York

www.urbanbooks.net

Urban Books, LLC
300 Farmingdale Road, NY-Route 109
Farmingdale, NY 11735

ISBN 13: 978-1-62286-798-1
ISBN 10: 1-62286-798-X

First Trade Paperback Printing March 2017
Printed in the United States of America

10 9 8 7 6 5 4 3 2 1

Distributed by Kensington Publishing Corp.
Submit Orders to:
Customer Service
400 Hahn Road
Westminster, MD 21157-4627
Phone: 1-800-733-3000
Fax: 1-800-659-2436

Dedication

In life, there are some situations that are hard to live through, much less revisit. For me, penning this book greatly based on my own testimony and truth evoked so many tears, emotions, and fears. Although I'd long since found my voice and have sought comfort in speaking out about sexual abuse, it was only after meeting you that I found the strength to actually write what was in my heart and highlight what rests in my darkest memories. During our short time of acquaintance, it was through listening to some of your stories and witnessing your endless support of my craft that gave me the nerve to say, "Now is the time!" That saying that everyone comes into your life for a reason or a season holds true—perhaps your brief presence was to give me the push I needed to make this story come to life. For that, I thank you . . . for helping me find my voice in literature in order to share this powerful message with the world and for forcing me to look at myself and realize that despite what's been done to me, NOTHING is wrong with me. For that, I dedicate this novel to you, Lawanda Sims. May this serve as the epitome of affection and learning to let go of the hurt in order to move on and inspire.

~ Penned in loving memory of my literary idol, Jackie Collins ~
1937–2015

Acknowledgments

My sincerest thanks goes out to all of the individuals who have allowed me to share my testimony in order to impact the community, as well as those who have partnered with me to do the very same. Speaking up, being a voice for the voiceless, and encouraging others to raise their voices isn't an easy task. I thank you all for breaking barriers, working to end the silence, and supporting me in my mission to encourage any abused individual to "Let Your Voice Be Heard." A few in particular who I'd like to give honor to:

Phyllis Miller, Director of Day League (Decatur, Ga.)
Dj Sed, host for annual Let Your Voice
be Heard Benefit Event
Kris Barnes, Senior Consultant at
Voice Today (Marietta, Ga.)
Angela Williams, Founder of Voice Today (Marietta, Ga.)
Tamiko Lowry, Founder & Director of
The Still Standing Foundation (Atlanta, Ga.)
Elizabeth Eichelberger, Producer for Atlanta Live
(Norcross, Ga.)
Sheila Wells, Columnist for *Glamour* magazine
Heather Jarros, Producer at
Trinity Broadcasting Network
The founding honorees for Teal Stilettos:
Samantha McVey, Betty Reeves, Elena Robinson,
Sheri Harrigan, Misty Holt, Wyvette Jones,
Allison Grace, and Shanell Banks

Prologue

"Kennedy! Kennedy!"

She could hear his deep baritone calling for her across the distance of the hall and the office that separated them. She lay still for a moment on top of the plushness of her comforter, debating whether she should feign sleep and ignore his calls. She thought better of that when she heard him call out for her once more. It was as if he had a sixth sense about these things and knew good and well that she wasn't asleep. Never mind the fact that she'd stayed up late cleaning the kitchen from the mess a family of seven often made around dinnertime. Never mind the fact that she had to get up for school in the morning. He didn't care; he'd call her at any time to do anything. She was beginning to feel more like Cinderella than herself.

"Kennedy!"

"Ugh!" she huffed as she dragged her tired, slim, four-teen-year-old body from her queen-sized bed and exited the darkness of her room. As she stepped into the hall, the light cascaded from the living room to her right. She knew that Carmen, her older sister, was still awake doing homework, no doubt. It perplexed her why he didn't call for Carmen, instead, knowing that she was still up.

Her bare feet moved along, across the carpeted hallway into the office that he used as a recording studio. The lights were out as she felt her way along the familiar path through the myriads of equipment in the room. She approached the one step that led down into the open door of her parents' bedroom and was greeted by only the glimmer of light radiating from the television set. She continued a straight path to the right side of their king-sized bed—his side of the bed—where her father sat propped up against his pillows with his eyes glued to the television screen.

"Yes, sir?" she asked politely, ignoring the low murmur of his television and the steady snoring coming from her stepmother's side of the bed.

"I want some candy," he stated. "I want peanut brittle in the brown wrapper."

Kennedy winced. "But I don't think we have no more of that."

"Go look. If not, bring me some chocolate."

"'K."

She trotted out of the room, back through the studio office, and up the hall into the living room where, sure enough, Carmen was staring into a book. Their eyes met, but neither said a word considering the argument they'd had earlier in the day. Kennedy entered the kitchen and pulled the candy bucket from the top of the refrigerator. She scoured through its contents and was only able to retrieve two pieces of his first choice of candy. It'll have to do, she thought as she replaced the bin and headed back to his room.

She reapproached his bedside and handed him the two pieces of peanut brittle candy. He took the treats, and she turned her attention to the black-and-white movie still showing on the screen. It was beyond her why he continued to sit there and watch those old, colorless films day in and day out. They had cable with good, current shows in color. Why did he feel inclined to remain stuck in the olden days? "Why do you watch this stuff?" she asked, totally uninterested in the western playing out before her.

"It's classic," he said in a low tone.

She continued to stand there staring at the screen, trying with all of her might to feel the sense of intrigue that he obviously felt . . . but nothing happened. She felt nothing—until a light touch against the back of her right leg caused her to flinch. Astonishment kept her silent as she felt his hand rise up to cup her ass through the fabric of her tiny, pastel night shorts. Her spirit then jumped out of her body, screaming at her physical being in a pantomiming manner. But Kennedy was stuck. Her brain no longer functioned normally as it was crowded by fear, shock, and the ultimate question of why. The neurons couldn't fire off to alert her body to move and her feet to flee. She was rooted to the spot.

Her eyes never blinked as the black-and-white film carried on with seemingly happy faces staring back at her as if nothing in the world was wrong. As his hand slipped inside the leg of her shorts and panties simultaneously, her stepmother's steady breathing continued to play the soundtrack for her moment of violation. Kennedy's heart stopped as her father's thick, calloused fingers toyed with her juvenile clitoris as if it was a normal action. From there, he slid one finger into her feminine opening, and Kennedy's throat become lodged with the sobs she couldn't seem to get out. Her world was shattering with each devastatingly incestuous thrust he made as he forced himself inside of her tight walls.

Sweat rolled down her back under the pressure of the moment. The movie continued to play with the jovial characters carrying on with their cinematic lives. Her stepmother lay unmoving, oblivious to the crime and torment occurring less than ten feet away from her. So convinced that his actions were okay, and taking Kennedy's silence and stillness to mean that she enjoyed his molestation, he reached for her right hand with his free one and pulled it toward his growing hard-on. The second her fingertips neared the lump covered by the very comforter she'd washed for her parents the day before, life returned to Kennedy's body. Her feet found their purpose, and she was filled with the slightest bit of energy needed to escape.

She yanked her hand away from his embrace and broke into a sprint, causing his hand to abruptly slip from within the confines of her womanhood. She stumbled over the one and only step as she exited her parents' room, never once looking back to face the monster that had taken possession of her father's body. She tore through the studio office, went to her room and pulled her door shut as if she'd retreated inside her room for the night, then quickly, she ascended the hall and stood at the threshold of the living room, staring at Carmen with the light complexion of her face flushed with anguish, tears gushing at full speed, and her chest heaving in fright.

Carmen looked up, prepared to tell her sister to go away, but her mouth hung open as it became apparent to her that something was horribly wrong. This had nothing to do with the argument they'd had earlier. No. This was something tragic, and the signs were written all over Kennedy's trembling body.

Kennedy motioned toward the back, and Carmen understood. She was summoning her for a meeting. Afraid that he'd find her in the living room instead of locked away in her room, Kennedy hurried back to her bedroom and softly opened the door to enter and wait for Carmen to appear. Within seconds, they were locked behind the safety of the bedroom door, and Kennedy collapsed on the floor in front of her bed, unable to contain her sorrow any longer. Carmen fell to her knees and held her younger sister in her arms, unsure of exactly what it was that had the young girl so upset.

"What is it, Ken?" she asked. "What happened? Tell me what it is."

Kennedy's sobs grew harder and louder as she tried to compose herself, at least long enough to tell Carmen what had just happened. She couldn't find the words to express the terrible thing that she knew would change her and their family forever.

"Talk to me," Carmen urged. "I can't help you if you don't talk to me."

"He . . . He touched me," Kennedy stated frantically. "He touched me . . ."

"Huh?"

"He asked me for candy . . . I took it . . . He touched me . . . he was feeling on me . . . and he tried . . . he tried to make me . . ." She couldn't do it. She couldn't divulge the horrid details of the three minutes' worth of degradation she'd just suffered. Instead, she buried herself in Carmen's chest and cried relentlessly.

Nothing else needed to be said. Carmen understood completely. She hugged Kennedy even tighter. "It's gon' be okay. Shhhh." She tried to encourage Kennedy to stop crying. "Calm down, baby. Calm down. It's gon' be okay, I promise."

How could it be okay when the person who was supposed to love and care for her was the very person who'd just assaulted her? How was she supposed to feel safe and secure in the place that she called home, now knowing that the monster, the predator, the pervert that they warned you to be leery of when encountering strangers had turned out to be a member of her own family, a resident in her own home—her *father?*

A loud knock occurred at the door, and Kennedy's heart began to pound. Carmen rose from the floor, and Kennedy pulled at the leg of her lounging pants.

"No!" she begged of her older sister. "Please don't. Please don't let him in."

"It's okay," Carmen assured her. "Nothing's going to happen to you. I'm right here."

Against Kennedy's wishes, Carmen unlocked the door and opened it to find their father's large, intimidating build standing on the other side.

"We don't lock doors in my house!" he barked. "Why aren't you finishing your work, and why is she not asleep?"

"We were talking," Carmen explained. She looked over her shoulder at the frail, frightened image of Kennedy, and then turned back to face the bear of a man before her. "Can I talk to you in the other room?" she asked in a whisper.

"For what?"

She pursed her lips. At eighteen and a little more confident when it came to addressing their father, Carmen looked him dead in the eyes and whispered. "What did you do to her?"

"I didn't do anything to that child!" he replied defensively. He pushed Carmen to the side and entered the room, towering over Kennedy's sobbing body. "You saying I did something to you?"

Kennedy stared at him in fear, not knowing what out-of-character action he'd commit next.

"Ain't nobody did shit to you! You wanna wake the whole damn house up with your stupid allegations? Huh? You want me to go wake up ya' mama so you can tell her your little bullshit story?"

"That's enough," Carmen called out.

He shot her a menacing look. "I'll go get her up right now, and you can see what she has to say about this foolishness," he told Kennedy, knowing full well that the child wouldn't dare to call his bluff. "We can do it, but I'll tell you what'll happen . . . Your ass will end up with the county. You go around lying on folk, and they'll throw your ass in foster care where you won't know what kinda people or shit you'll end up facing. Is that what you want? *Huh?*" he yelled at her.

Kennedy began to weigh her options. She could either be homeless and at the mercy of strangers and whatever torment they forced upon her or stay quiet and risk living a life where she was susceptible to being molested or even raped at any given moment by her own father. It was a heavy decision for a fourteen-year-old to make, and all she could do was lie on the floor with her face now buried in her arms crying over her hopeless situation.

"That's what I thought," her father spat out in a vindicated manner with his chest poked out. "Nobody would believe you any-damn-way. Lying ass, fast tail girls." He shook his head and glared at Carmen as he turned around. "Don't lock my doors and I don't want to hear shit else about none of this." He walked away as if certain that he'd just instilled the fear of God into both of his daughters.

Carmen softly shut the door, and her own sense of fright forced her to keep it unlocked. Slowly, she eased down to the floor and covered Kennedy's body with her own. She could feel the shaking caused by Kennedy sobbing. Her own tears began to trickle out as she tried her best to comfort her little sister.

"It's okay," she whispered into Kennedy's ear. "I know how you're feeling, and I'm here for you."

Kennedy doubted that anyone knew the hurt and disgust she was feeling. She had half a mind to rise from the floor and throw herself under the shower to attempt to scrub away the memories of his sordid touches. But she knew that even the hottest water and the best soap would never clear away the pain that filled her body and spirit.

"If you want to go tell someone, I'll go with you," Carmen said. "I believe you, and I'll tell with you. I understand because . . . It's happened to me . . ." She caught herself and bit her lower lip. "But it wasn't Dad," she said in rushed manner.

Instead of feeling secure in knowing that Carmen had her back, Kennedy felt even more afraid and alone. How could Carmen help her when she wasn't even able to speak up for herself? It was a helpless situation, and she was stuck living in a house of ill repute, not knowing what to do or who she could turn to. She stifled a scream so as not to wake the others in the house, but it resounded deeply within the core of her being. Gone was the innocent fourteen-year-old girl who believed in security, trust, and love. In her place was now a forever frightened, badly damaged young woman who had no one solid to stand up for her.

Chapter 1

"What I'm supposed to do with this?" he half said, half cried silently to no one in particular. "Always making me do this . . . can't do this . . . sick of him. Why he can't do his own stuff? Stupid . . . I don't wanna go back to that stupid house."

Snot slipped from his nose, and suddenly, he realized that he was crying. That was no good—crying openly like that could easily get him beat up and picked on should anyone from his school or from the neighborhood—period—catch him. That was the last thing he needed—to give anyone any other reason to jump him or make fun of him. He did all right in that department just by being his regular, ordinary self on any given day. Not wanting to give any potential lurker any ammunition against him, he took the back of his closed, left hand and wiped it across his nose collecting the snot on his ashy skin. With his right hand, he used his fingers to quickly brush away the fallen tears that lingered on his bony cheeks.

The likelihood of someone he knew seeing him wasn't that great, but it was still possible. He'd purposely walked a block away from his apartment complex to one of the better-looking, gated communities in his neighborhood. There, he chose to hide behind a two-story apartment building, hidden away from any passersby making their way down the Bouldercrest Road. During this awkward period when the weather was beginning to change in mid-September, he sat in the middle of the stairwell slightly shivering against the cool temperature of the early evening while wearing tattered shorts and a faded, second-hand Polo-style shirt. Every time a car crept around the building, his head shot up, and he stared, praying that no one inside knew or noticed him, and that the car wouldn't turn into the parking lot directly to his right. He didn't want any of the residents of the building he was hiding at to come home and find him resting in front of their door. They'd surely call the police or notify their apartment manager. That was also unwanted trouble that he wished to avoid.

Looking down into his closed fist, a million thoughts ran through his head. The crumbled aluminum ball was torturing him beyond belief. He'd gone the whole school day with it practically burning a hole in his pocket. He hadn't been able to concentrate at all in class, and when his classmates engaged in their usual ridicule of his attire, demeanor, personality, and intellect, he was unfazed. His fear wasn't of them eventually beating the shit out of him on the playground as he was accustomed to. Instead, his fear was that they'd shove him around enough for the aluminum ball to fall from his pocket or someone would actually snatch it from his pocket in an attempt to rob him of whatever possession they felt he had. Either way, he feared that everyone would be privy to the contraband that he was toting around, and he'd ultimately end up in the principal's office, followed by the intake office at the juvenile detention center. Life at home wasn't great, but he certainly didn't want to see the inside of juvie again.

"I don't even want this," he said out loud to himself. "Why he give this to me? Why he do that?" He begged the universe for a clear understanding as to why he was being set up for failure. Wasn't it enough that he was already dealing with traumatic things that kept him awake at night? Why'd he have to be faced with such an adult type of situation? At that point, he would've given anything to have a life like the kids he would see on old-time television shows like *Leave It to Beaver* and *The Brady Bunch*. Those white kids didn't ever have to worry about bullying to the extent that he'd suffered it, and their greatest obstacles were bad grades and how to get some boy or girl to like them. They had bubble gum problems that were easy to solve and didn't threaten to land any of them in jail. But he knew better. This wasn't television. He wasn't some privileged white kid in suburbia, and his issues were far from easy to fix. Instead, he was an orphaned foster kid living in the hood of Atlanta praying day to day just for the opportunity to make it through the day alive and out of jail despite the hell he had to endure. This wasn't some far-fetched television show that could be turned off if, and when, it got too heavy—this was his miserable life.

In the midst of trying to talk himself into how he'd handle his current situation, he completely missed the opening and closing of the first door on the upper level of the building he was squatting at. The resident, a woman in her late twenties, stood at the top of the stairs with her arms folded looking down at him from the back. She'd opened her mouth to say something initially, but was caught off guard the moment she realized that he was speaking to himself. She looked around the parking lot for a car or any sign of another individual of whom he may have belonged to, but saw no one. Intrigued, she continued to watch him, unsure of what to do or say next. A part of her didn't want to disturb his apparent battle he was having with himself. Whatever he was going through wasn't any of her business, but he certainly did sound tormented for a little kid.

Olivia Collins had only stepped out of her apartment to get some fresh air. She'd spent the greater part of her day sitting in the office of her two-bedroom apartment trying her best to get through the climax of the manuscript she was working on. For some reason, she'd felt herself spiraling into a writer's block and knew that it was time to take a break. In doing so, she walked out onto her back porch with the intention of leaning over the rail and closing her eyes to meditate while looking up into the sky as dusk began to creep up. She'd done this countless times since living in the apartment, taking full advantage of her upper level unit. Only, this time, she wasn't so sure she'd have the opportunity to reflect. Not with this unknown character having a borderline schizophrenic spell on her back steps. The curiosity within her forced Olivia to slowly move forward, inching down to the second step. With her arms still folded, she crouched down a little and leaned forward before speaking.

"Are you okay?" she asked in the most gentle, soothing way that she could so as not to frighten him.

Her gentility was of no consequence. The boy practically jumped out of his skin at the sound of her voice, rising to his feet and turning around to face her with stunned eyes and a shocked expression on his tearstained face. He shoved his hands into the pockets of his shorts that seemed to be at least a half size too big for him. At this point, Olivia noticed how thin the child was and yet again, wondered who he belonged to.

"Hi," Olivia stated, giving him a smile to try to help him relax and know that she would not harm him.

He blinked but said nothing.

Olivia looked into his eyes noting the fear that was there and present in the way that he rocked side to side on the step that he was now standing on. "Are you okay?" she tried again, now lowering herself to a seated position.

He nodded, but remained silent.

"You out here alone?" It was a stupid question with an obvious answer, but it was the first thing that came to her mind.

This time he shrugged. Communication was clearly not his strong suit.

"You live around here?" she asked him.

He nodded slightly, and then lowered his eyes.

Olivia didn't know what to make of it. He couldn't have been more than eight years old, and it seemed odd to her that he was sitting on her back steps alone with no other children to play with and no adult in sight. She wondered exactly where his unit was and if his parents had any idea where he was. Remembering the somberness of his posture and the way he'd been nearly crying to himself when she first walked out, she had to ask herself if maybe he'd run away from home, making it only as far as her steps. It was a juvenile thing to do when you were upset because your parents wouldn't let you have your way or someone picked on you. Perhaps that was exactly what was going on now.

"Do you think maybe it's time for you to go home now?" she asked. "The sun's about to go down, and I'm sure your parents are gonna be worried about you soon." She pointed across his shoulder where a tiny beam of light sprung to life. "See there. The streetlights are coming on."

There was an unspoken Southern rule that once the streetlights came on, young children were expected to return indoors for the day. Olivia assumed that the child understood and abided by this. Pointing out the lights should have encouraged him to make his way back to the safety of his own unit.

She sighed, seeing that he was not going to respond no matter what. Rising from her seated position on the step, she looked at him and motioned her head toward the slew of other apartment buildings that rested behind hers. "You should head on home, okay?" She turned to walk away, hoping that he'd take her advice.

Abruptly, he reached forward and grabbed her arm. "Can I get a piece of paper?" he blurted out.

His request caused her to stop in her tracks. With him having said nothing else in response to any of her questions, she was shocked that he'd be asking for something so unusual for a stranger to request of another. "Uhhh . . . sure," she answered skeptically as she looked down at him, his small but mighty grip holding on to her. "Let me go and I'll get it."

He released his grasp and stared at her with huge eyes, wondering if she was really going to run inside and call the police on him for touching her.

"I'll be right back," she said.

Olivia hurried up the couple of steps and reentered her apartment in search of a sheet of notebook paper from her office. As he waited for her, the little boy stared out into the dusk of the evening and contemplated her previous words. *I'm sure your parents are gonna be worried about you soon*, he thought. Ha! He knew better than that. Where he was going, he was sure that the only reason they'd want to ascertain he was there was for the financial gain. His well-being and safety were of no consequence.

Olivia returned with a notebook and a pen. He hadn't asked for the pen, but if he needed the paper, she felt certain that he'd need the pen as well. Cautiously approaching him so as not to scare the child off, Olivia handed him the notebook with the pen clipped to it. "Here you go."

He looked at her and shook his head. "Naw, I just need one piece of paper."

"It's okay," she told him. "You can take the whole notebook. I have plenty of them, and this one's never been used."

He looked at her quizzically for a moment before reaching out to take the notebook with his right hand. There were a lot of thoughts running around in his head, things he wanted to say but didn't dare let out, not that he had anyone to confide in. He needed the paper to jot down his thoughts, thinking that he could then fold it up and hide it in his pants pockets so that no one would see it. His thoughts were private, and he kept them as such.

Olivia watched as he removed the pen and scribbled down a few lines in sloppy penmanship. She resisted the urge to rubberneck for a glimpse of what it was that he was so feverishly writing. For a second she wondered if maybe he had a story in his head. *At least one of us is able to write right now*, she thought. She hugged herself against the brisk air and once again looked out into the quiet of the complex. In the units around them, families were having dinner, winding down for the evening, and someone was maybe even already asleep. But, there she stood on her back steps with a strange boy, watching him write when she herself needed to be tapping the letters of her keyboard.

Soon, the boy stopped writing, closed the notebook, and reached behind himself to stick it into the waistband of his shorts and underwear. He promptly covered it up with his dingy shirt. He looked up at her as if he wanted to say something, but no words escaped his lips.

"Do you need anything else?" she asked, perplexed as to why he was still standing there instead of running off to return home. More and more she wondered why his parents were not looking for him by now.

He bit his lower lip. She was a nice enough lady even though she was a stranger. She seemed to want to help him, and that was something he wasn't used to. Maybe she was his answer. Maybe if he could just leave it with her for now, overnight, he could figure out what to do with it and how to get himself out of this situation. Slowly, he reached into his pocket with his left hand and pulled out the aluminum ball that had been giving him so much grief all day. He extended his hand to her and looked into her eyes pleadingly, though his voice remained small and even.

"Can you keep this for me?" he asked.

Her face frowned up as Olivia surveyed the crumpled aluminum in his little hand. She had no clue why he wanted her to hold on to such a weird object. Her initial thought was that maybe it was his good luck charm and he was offering it to her as a way of thanking her for her generosity. Absentmindedly, she reached for it, and once she felt the weight of it, she knew that it wasn't just about the foil. There was something concealed within in it.

"What is this?" she asked him. Curiously, she peeled back the layers of foil until her eyes fell upon the unmistakable baggies of white powder within. Her glance shot back up to him, and her eyes were questioning. "What is this?" she asked again, though she knew the answer. She only prayed that she was, by some chance, wrong. "What are you doing with this?"

"It—it's not mine," he said quickly, immediately caring what she thought about him. "It's not mine. I just—"

"Then why do you have it?" Olivia held the dope in her hand and stared at it as if it was about to burn a hole through her extremity.

"He said . . . he said if I didn't do it, he'd cut my feet off."

She gave him a look of disbelief at the sound of his explanation. Her common sense told her to give the child back his stash or call the police. Either way, she wasn't buying into the fact that someone was threatening to pull a Toby on him.

He sensed her skepticism and nodded his head with vigor. "For real! I'm telling you the truth! He made me do it."

"He who?" She cocked her head to the side and waited for his reply.

"If I go back home with it he'll know I didn't sell it like I was 'pose to," he responded, ignoring her question. "I'on know nothing 'bout selling dope and . . . and I was scared to do it . . . but I can't take it back. I gotta hide it somewhere."

It was the fear in his voice that made it real for Olivia. He was genuinely petrified that whomever had given him the coke was going to punish him for not selling it for them. The thought frightened her as well, and once again, she wondered who the hell this child's parents were. "Who is it?" she asked again. "Tell me who it is. You can trust me. Let me help you," she pleaded with him. She looked down at the drugs again, convicted in what needed to be done. "We have to call the police." She wrapped the coke up and turned to head back into her apartment.

Once again, he lurched forward and grabbed ahold to her arm. "No!" he cried out. "You can't do that. You can't do that!"

She looked at him and shook her head. "Do you know how dangerous it is for you to be carrying this around? Whoever gave this to you should be arrested."

"You can't do that." Tears began to well up in his eyes. "If you call the police . . . if you do that, then I'll get in trouble."

"You're just a kid," she reasoned with him. "All you have to do is tell the police the truth. Just tell them what happened and who gave it to you."

"The police don't care nothing about kids like me!" he hollered, releasing his grasp of her arm and stepping down a few steps.

Olivia's heart was racing, and she was jarred by his loud, harsh tone. She was sure that he was about to run off and leave her standing there holding enough coke to catch a case.

"If you call them, something bad will happen to me!" he screamed. "I just needa hide it for a minute . . . I just need some time to figure out what I'ma do. That's all!" He was on the brink of breaking down in front of this strange woman who'd been kind enough to entertain his drama for this long.

Olivia was confused. She knew what she needed to do, but watching the boy's reaction pulled at her heartstrings, and she just couldn't stand to put him through any more torment. It was clear that he was caught up in the middle of something that could end up fatally catastrophic, and she didn't want to cause him any more fear or place him in greater danger than he was potentially in already. She was conflicted, but one thing was for absolute sure—this child was in trouble. She swallowed hard and looked around them. Her eyes fell upon a tree with a small, yet hollow hole that she knew was there. She pointed to it while handing him back his property.

"Stick it in that tree," she advised. "In the hole. No one will notice."

She wondered if she was making the right move, but she knew that there was no way she'd keep an illegal substance in her home. She watched as the boy hurried down the stairs and followed her instructions. Slowly, she descended the steps while watching his figure in action. "What are you going to do?" she asked weakly, still battling with the decision she'd just made. There was still time to call the police. "When *he* asks about it?" she clarified.

The boy shrugged. "I'll come up with something . . ." He lowered his head for a moment, contemplating what he should say next. Coming up with nothing, although he was filled with gratitude which was instantly replaced with the new worry of what story he would exactly provide, he bit his lower lip. He blinked nervously as he took a final look at the woman before turning around and dashing off around the building and disappearing.

"Wait!" Olivia cried out, descending the remaining stairs and running in the wake of his path. "Wait!" But she couldn't catch him. By the time she made it to the closed iron gate at the complex's entrance, the boy's figure was nothing more than a memory as he vanished up the road.

"Damn it!" she cursed herself. After all of that, and she hadn't even gotten the child's name.

Chapter 2

"Girl, you gotta try this fried alligator," Shanice gushed, dipping the delicacy into its specified sauce and smiling as if she was in culinary heaven. "I'm telling you . . . It's nothing like what you'd expect."

Olivia shook her head and continued to nurse her cocktail. "I'll pass."

"You don't know what you're missing."

"And you don't know what swamp that alligator came out of. Trust me, I'm good."

They were seated at a small table inside of Pappadeaux's on Jimmy Carter Boulevard. They were supposed to be celebrating Shanice's promotion at work while also clearing Olivia's mind of the cobwebs that were keeping her from successfully completely the novel she was currently working on. Their friendship had originated at the Department of Family and Children Services in DeKalb County where Olivia once worked as a case manager in the office of financial independence. The two of them started out together on the bottom tier of the OFI totem pole where they tirelessly pushed papers in their lonely cubicles, ensuring that applicants received the food stamps, welfare checks, and Medicaid that they applied for. On several occasions, Olivia passed up the opportunity to advance to a case manager position in the Social Services Department, not wanting to expose her soul to the horror stories often heard on the news about foster care and the heart-wrenching circumstances of defenseless children. That was nearly seven years ago. After five years, having felt slighted, overworked, mentally, emotionally, and physically exhausted by simply maintaining a job at a place where she didn't feel appreciated or satisfied, Olivia walked away from her managerial position and decided that it was time to pursue her passion for writing full time.

Shanice Gordon still remained an employee at the DeKalb County Office. As of the month prior, she'd been awarded the administrator position, presiding over the county's OFI division and answering only to the county's director. Unlike Olivia, the job was enough for Shanice, and she planned to see it all the way through to retirement. The benefits were good, and she was well-versed in the programs that she oversaw. But, most importantly, at the end of the day when she went home, the job stayed behind, and she didn't have to worry about it again until she was on the clock once more. It suited her lifestyle, and today, she was proud of her accomplishment.

Olivia was happy for her friend, but couldn't shake the feelings inside of her or the thoughts running through her mind that had absolutely nothing to do with the occasion they were celebrating. Her despondent behavior wasn't lost upon Shanice.

"Maybe you need to go-ahead and guzzle that down so that you can get another one," Shanice said, nodding her head toward the now-watered-down drink that Olivia was playing with.

"Huh?" Olivia responded.

"Girl, you're practically in la-la land. What is it with you today? I'm gonna need you to perk up. All this good food and drink around us . . . I'm in a good mood, and you sitting over there looking all depressed."

"I'm not depressed," Olivia rebutted.

"Hmmm." Shanice took a good look at her friend and was sold on the fact that Olivia was attempting to mask whatever it was she was going through. "You might as well spill it, honey."

Olivia shook her head. "It's nothing." She didn't mean it at all. Her little voice was telling her that it was very much so something.

"It's something enough to have you over here all mopey-faced when we're supposed to be having fun, so you might as well tell me what the hell's going on. Is it Kasyn? Did he do something to piss you off?"

"No," Olivia answered softly.

"Girllll, if that dude did something to fuck with you, you better believe we can set his ass straight. I don't know why these brothers think that they can just mess over a good woman and we'll still be around to love on them. Erroll is the same way. Do you know that we were supposed to go to dinner last Saturday night, and I didn't hear from his behind all day, all night 'til two in the afternoon that *Sunday?* I was hot! I know he's messing around with somebody, but wanna convince me that he was just tied up with his mama, and then was tired. If Kasyn is on that same type of bullshit, then it must be some kind of a stupidity epidemic going around."

Olivia shook her head, almost amused by her friend's amped up behavior over the thought of seeking vengeance against a slew of cheating men. Were but it all that simple. "No, no," she said, waving her hand at Shanice to calm her down. "Relax, it's nothing like that."

"Oh." Shanice settled down and surveyed Olivia's body language and facial expression. "Then what is it?" Concern laced her tone, and she silently yet quickly prayed that she wasn't about to hear some heartbreaking news concerning her bestie.

"Well, something happened yesterday that kind of bothered me."

"Uh-huh . . ."

"I met a little boy."

"Excuse me? Like, are you saying you met a younger guy, or are we talking about an actual kid?"

Olivia rolled her eyes and shook her head once more. "This has nothing to do with men, 'Nicey. Stay focused. I'm talking about an actual child."

"Okay, okay."

"Anyway, I walked out of my apartment, and there he was just sitting there on the steps like he was waiting for someone or something. There was something so strange about how he was just there all alone . . . no friends, no parents. I'd never seen the kid in my life. And he was kinda jumpy when I approached him."

"So what? You think he ran away from home?"

Olivia hesitated before answering. "I don't know. I mean, the thought kinda occurred to me as it got later. I wondered who in the world would have their kid out so far away from their vantage point, you know? But, it wasn't really him being out at that hour alone that has me disturbed. It's that fact that he . . . It's what he asked me to do . . . It's what he had."

Shanice's right brow rose. "What did he have? A gun? Don't tell me this little boy tried to rob you, Livi."

"No . . . No, he didn't. He didn't have a gun. He had about a gram of coke wrapped up in foil."

"Whatttt?"

"And he asked me to hold it for him."

Shanice's hand slapped the table with a loud thud, causing other patrons to turn in their direction. "Shut up! How old was this child, and where the hell did he get some cocaine from?"

"I don't know. I didn't really get a chance to ask him many questions, but if I had to guess, I'd say he was about eight."

"Eight? My God! The dope boys are getting younger and younger these days. It's a damn shame. I hope you called the police."

Olivia simply stared at Shanice, unable to go on with the story.

Shanice reached for her glass, took a sip from her straw, and noticed that Olivia had yet to respond. She recognized the flicker of guilt in Olivia's eyes and knew that her friend had made a grave mistake. "You didn't call the police? What were you thinking? That child was out there hustling rocks, and you just overlooked it?" She paused for a second and gave Olivia a hardened expression. Her nose flared as she spoke. "Don't you *dare* tell me that you took that mess."

"No, of course not!" Olivia replied, slightly offended. She lowered her head and her voice. "But I did tell him where to stash it."

"Unbelievable. What the hell were you thinking, Livi?"

"He was telling me that some guy gave it to him and threatened to hurt him if he didn't take it, and I guess, sell it. I felt bad for the boy. I didn't want anything to happen to him, and I certainly didn't want to have the child sent to juvie if he was telling the truth about being bullied into this."

Shanice shook her head in complete disbelief. "There's more to this than meets the eye, Nicey. I know there is," Olivia stated, trying to plead her case. "The moment I mentioned calling the police he freaked out, asking me not to."

"Of course he did, honey. Who actually wants to get locked up? He's a street thug, Livi. Face it. Like I said, they're getting younger and younger these days. You got played. For whatever reason, he needed somewhere to leave his stash, a safe place, and all you did was help him out. Who knows how many li'l kids he's poisoning with that mess he's pushing."

Olivia adamantly disagreed. "It wasn't like that at all. If he was a dealer, and if he truly intended to sell the stuff, then why didn't he just run off the second I mentioned the police instead of begging me not to and asking me to help him? There's something else going on here."

"You can sit here and try to understand these people's street mentality all you want, but you're never going to get it. Apparently, he knew that you were a compassionate being and knew exactly what to say to wrap you around his finger. You got played. It's as simple as that."

Olivia wasn't so sure. "If you'd seen him you'd understand."

"I don't need to see him. I've seen enough thugs, dope boys, and con artists in my lifetime to be able to spot one a mile away, and, boo . . . You were played. I told you from the jump that staying in that apartment was a bad idea."

Olivia grimaced. She didn't want to hear her friend go into her rant about her residence anymore. Two years ago, when Olivia had quit her job at the DFCS office, she'd moved to Macon, Georgia, for a change of scenery. Despite the distance, she and Shanice remained good friends and saw each other at least once a month. But, when Olivia's mother died just three short months ago, Olivia left her condo in Macon to return to Atlanta where she buried her mother and took up residency in her mom's old apartment. It didn't make sense to Shanice because the complex was located in the heart of the hood where criminal activity was a frequent occurrence. It also didn't make sense to her fiancé, Kasyn Terrell, who still resided and worked in Macon but made the drive out to Atlanta four times a week to be with her.

"That has nothing to do with this," Olivia stated. "I'm telling you . . . I'm concerned about that child. Something isn't right with him."

Shanice was no longer interested. She picked up her fork and began to attack her entrée. "You're right about that . . . Something's not right. He's a li'l dope boy when his ass should be focused on school or being on somebody's Little League team. You're only feeling some kind of way because your conscience knows that you should have called the police when you had the chance. Now, all you can do is let it go and steer clear of this kid and any of his other hustling buddies. Next time you'll do the right thing."

The subject was closed. Olivia knew that there was no way of getting Shanice to see things from her point of view. She wasn't there. She hadn't seen the ragged appearance of the little boy or the fear in his eyes. How could she explain her longing to help this stranger to a person whose mind was already closed to the possibility of the child being innocent? It simply wasn't going to happen. Realizing that she was going to get no support or understanding from her friend at the moment, Olivia decided to drop the subject. Who knew if she'd ever run across the boy again. All she could do was hope and pray that whatever situation he'd gotten himself caught up in would work out in his favor. There was nothing else within her power that could be done.

Or was there?

The house was quiet as he entered. He knew that Ms. Mae, his foster mom, wasn't there since her old beat-up Buick LaSabre wasn't in the driveway. He quickly shut the door and locked it before making his way into the kitchen in hopes of finding something he could eat. They never had much. Ms. Mae wasn't much of a cook whenever she was home. Throwing open the refrigerator door, he stared at the nearly empty shelves wondering what he could possibly throw between two slices of the bread, even though he knew it was stale. He didn't care. Pulling out the loaf of bread, he had it fixed in his mind that he'd make only a peanut butter sandwich since they were apparently out of jelly.

The moment he closed the refrigerator door he jumped, startled by the intimidating figure standing there glowering at him with a scowl that read trouble with his hands behind his back. The boy dropped his bread and almost peed his pants as the thought of running didn't make it as far as getting the actual message to his feet.

"Fuck you doing?" Mikey, his twenty-year-old bully of a foster brother asked him.

The boy swallowed hard. His voice trembled as he spoke. "'Bout to make a sandwich."

"Didn't they feed you in school?"

The child didn't want to think about the way he often skipped lunch to avoid ridicule, or the times he'd eaten lunch tucked away hiding behind the stage of the auditorium or in the unlocked janitor's closet. Coincidentally, on that day, he'd eaten his square-shaped pepperoni pizza in the privacy of a pissy restroom stall, hiding from the other boys in his class because of the hole in his shoe that they'd been making fun of all morning. The energy he'd gotten from the pizza was long gone, and there was no telling if he'd have a real meal before heading back to his elementary school in the morning for another dose of humiliation from his peers.

He nodded in answer to Mikey's question because no sound would escape his throat. He wasn't sure what Mikey's next move would be, but he was certain that whatever it was wouldn't be pleasant.

"How you gon' come in my house and try to eat my food when you ain't brought back my money?" Mikey asked.

Now wasn't the time to ask Mikey when the hell he'd ever put food in the kitchen. The little boy was smart enough to know that Ms. Mae used her EBT food stamp card to buy food every month. She was always complaining about how the state was giving her little to nothing to feed him, but the truth was that Mikey and his other drug-dealing, ambition-less friends sat around munching up any and everything in sight, daring the boy to so much as inhale the scent of whatever they devoured.

Mikey hit the side of the refrigerator causing the young boy to jump. "Where's my money!" he screamed.

"I . . . I . . . I . . . I couldn't sell it," the boy answered meekly. "I don't got the money."

"You don't have my money?" Mikey cocked his head to the side as if the idea of the child being cashless was difficult for him to comprehend. "Then where's my dope?"

The child's eyes grew wide with fear. He knew that this next admittance would be the one to bring about some sort of brutal response. No matter how much he braced himself or how many deep breaths he took, he knew that he would never be prepared for the type of punishment that Mikey so commonly inflicted upon him. "I don't got it," he whispered.

Mikey took a step closer, causing the child to back up against the counter. "The fuck you mean, you don't got it?"

The child remained silent, waiting for the blow.

"You ain't do what I told you to do so you don't got my money. Now you telling me you ain't got my shit either?" Mikey asked, pretty much summing up the situation. "How the fuck you manage that?"

The boy stared down at his feet praying that a for-midable lie would seep out of his mouth, but nothing happened.

"Oh, you don't hear me talking to you now, sissy ass?" Mikey taunted. He dropped his hands from behind his back to reveal the tattered, wooden paddle that he kept in his room as his only reminder of his father, a former member of Phi Beta Kappa. "Fuck you gon' not have my money or my shit. You better be coming up off somethin' . . . explainin' why the fuck you roll up in here short."

"I . . . I . . . I couldn't do it at school," the boy tried to explain in hopes of buying himself a little bit of time before being assaulted. "I didn't want to get in trouble . . . They woulda took it."

"So what the fuck you do with it, sissy ass?"

"I hid it."

Mikey gave him a blank stare. "The fuck? You hid it? Where?"

Should I lie or tell the truth? The dilemma didn't really have much time to play out in the child's mind. "In a tree."

"In a tree?" Mikey repeated the words as if saying them himself would make more sense. The longer he stood there trying to process the information, the angrier he became. "I look like I'm fuckin' stupid? You gon' stash my shit in some fuckin' tree for some other nigga to come up on? You that stupid, nigga? I know yo' ass ain't that fuckin' stupid. All the fuck you had to do was get one of ya' li'l snot-nosed-ass friends to cop the shit. You can't even make money right. The fuck you gon' do with ya'self? Stupid ass!" He closed the space between him and child and gritted his teeth. "That shit's like stealing from me, nigga, and you know what I do to li'l bitch-ass, pussy-ass thieves?"

Mikey's bad grammar and bad breath were of no consequence to the boy. At this point, he didn't know which was louder or more disturbing—the growling of his nearly empty stomach or the pounding of his heart from the fear Mikey's presence evoked.

"I'm 'bout to whoop yo' ass, li'l nigga," Mikey seethed. "Drop ya pants and turn around."

The boy shook his head in a silent plea for his foster brother to spare him just this once. The thought of pulling his pants down never excited him because he knew that by the time he pulled them back up, he'd have another couple of physical and emotional scars to add to the collection of the ones Mikey had already caused.

"You wanna act like a bitch ass? I'ma treat you like one!" Mikey hollered, forcing the child to turn around by turning him roughly by the shoulders. "Hurry the fuck up, nigga!" he barked.

Tears streaming down his face and moving from side to side with nervousness, the child dropped his pants, purposely leaving his worn-out underwear on in hopes that Mikey wouldn't mandate him to remove those too. Mikey pushed him into bending position and held him down with his strong left hand as his right hand went to work smacking the child's backside relentlessly with the solid wood paddle.

"Oww! Owwww! I'm sorry!" the child screamed out, struggling underneath Mikey's restraint. "I'm sorry! I'll get it! I'll get it!"

His pleas mixed in with his sobs and sounded in unison with the smacks Mikey laid upon his small frame. At this point, not only his butt was getting the brunt of Mikey's anguish, but his legs and even arms were feeling the effects of the heated moment. The child eventually withered to the ground as Mikey released his grasp, but Mikey didn't cease in his torment. He stood over the child, locking his small, frail legs between his wide ones as he bent over and hit him wherever he was able to make contact. The boy's arms flailed about in an attempt to escape the blows, but it was no use. Mikey was dead set on beating the shit out of him over his crack, and there was nothing the child could do about it as he succumbed to the abuse on the dirty, stained, linoleum floor.

"What the hell?" Ms. Mae's voice sounded from somewhere across the room. "Mikey, let that boy up!"

The child's eyes closed tightly, sealed shut by his tears as he exhaled deeply with relief. He'd never thought of Ms. Mae as a lifesaver—truth was, he didn't really care much for her since their relationship mostly consisted of her ignoring him or complaining about him whenever she was home—but today, he was more than grateful to hear her raspy smoker's voice call out.

Ms. Mae placed a couple of Walmart bags on the counter and looked from her son, Mikey, down to her foster son who was now balled up half naked on the floor. She shook her head. "Hell you doing to that child?" she asked Mikey.

"Whooping his ass, Ma," Mikey explained as if it was the most natural thing in the world. "He always fuckin' some shit up. I don't even know why you let his ass stay here."

She waved him off. "I don't wanna hear that shit. He just a damn kid, and if his ass wasn't here, I'd be missin' out on my money. You done proved whatever point you was in here making, now get on. I'm tired, and I don't wanna deal with this shit."

Mikey stared down at the boy's body as he shook slightly from his light sobbing. He kicked his foot and grimaced. "You better get my shit back, or I'ma beat yo' ass every day 'til you get it." He threw a look at his mother as if daring her to ask questions before walking out of the kitchen with his paddle in hand.

Ms. Mae looked down at the boy again and shook her head. "You might as well quit that crying and get on up from there," she advised him. She hesitated for a while, watching as he failed to move. "Go'ne and get on up now!" she repeated with a little more authority.

Slowly, he peeled himself from the kitchen floor feeling every last one of the welts and blisters popping up on his bare skin. Ms. Mae examined him quickly as he stood before her pulling up his pants. She shook her head and pushed him toward the kitchen door leading to the hall. Together, they made their way through the house, and she pulled him into the bathroom where he stood quietly crying and staring down at his old beat-up shoes as she ran warm water into the tub. Ms. Mae added some Epsom salt to the bathwater and motioned for the boy to get in.

Feeling hesitant at first, the child avoided eye contact with his foster mother as he stripped off all of his clothing. Ms. Mae sat on the closed toilet seat and watched as he climbed into the heated water and eased his aching bottom down on the old porcelain.

"You'll be all right," she told him, never taking her eyes off of his small, bruised, naked body. "But you gotta stop pissing off Mikey if you wanna stay here. Now I'on know what happened, and I'on care. Long as you keep yo' mouth shut and don't go telling everything you know, everybody'll be just fine. Last thing you wanna do is make Mikey angry . . . You see how he gets."

The child said nothing as he used his washcloth to try to cover up his private package. He was uncomfortable with her presence, but was used to the dehumanizing way she'd often stare at his nudity.

"Noah," she called his name.

Reluctantly, he looked up into her tiny eyes embedded in her pockmarked face.

"If you wanna stay here . . . if you wanna stay out of county . . . you best not say nothing to nobody. You hear?"

He nodded slowly and quickly returned his glance to the ripples he created in the water with his index finger.

He felt the warm tears still making their way down his cheeks and wished that she would just go away and let him cry in peace. But, it was not to be so. Instead, Ms. Mae perched at the end of the toilet seat, reached for the soap, and then snatched the washcloth away from him.

"Here," she said, lathering up the cloth. "You just sit there and soak. I'll wash you up."

He was eight and old enough to wash himself, but he knew from experience that if he objected, his night would get a whole lot worse. So he sat there in the water staring at the ripples that his toes now made, trying to get his spiritual being to escape his physical body as Ms. Mae probed and caressed with the washcloth in places that he wished no longer existed so that she could no longer touch him. She continued to speak, but Noah didn't hear her. All he heard was the sound of the water sloshing from time to time and the sound of his spirit crying on the inside.

His butt hurt, but it was nothing compared to the bruise on his arm. He didn't even remember Mikey hitting his arm, but that tenderness was definitely there. Sitting in the cafeteria during breakfast the next morning, Noah tried to stick to himself. He sat at a back table with his head buried in his arms, trying to block out the commotion around him. But, just like any other day, his classmates just wouldn't leave him alone.

"Hey, Holey Noey," John-John, the biggest bully in the fourth grade, taunted him. He poked Noah in his side, sticking a finger in a hole in Noah's shirt. "Look, his holey shirt matches his holey shoes," he told several other kids surrounding them.

Snickers and giggles taunted Noah as he tried his best to ignore John-John.

"Holey Noey came up, y'all!" John-John called out. "He took a bath. He don't smell like piss today!" John-John shoved Noah a little, causing him to slip over the side of his chair. "Or did you run through a car wash?" he asked him.

Noah's nostrils flared as he raised his head up from the table and sat up straight in his chair. His fists clenched at his sides as he stared into the laughing faces of his classmates.

"Look, he getting mad," another kid called out.

"What you gon' do?" a fat kid asked, stepping up beside John-John. Noah knew him as Justin, but he was a fifth-grader.

"He ain't gon' do nothing," John-John commented. "Can't even put on matching socks. He's just a dumb, smelly kid. Holey Noey ain't gon' never do nothing."

"What you balling up yo' fist for?" Justin poked Noah in the chest. "Tryin'a act like you hard or something."

Noah huffed and bit his lip. His face turned red with frustration.

"Leave him alone!" Sonya Mims, a girl from Noah's class, encouraged. "He'on never mess with nobody. Why y'all always picking on that boy?"

"Ain't nobody picking on him," Justin lied.

"Yeah," John-John cosigned. "We just wanna know why he ain't got no clothes without holes. I bet even yo' drawers got holes in 'em."

The crowd burst into hysterics at the thought of Noah wearing holey underwear. He was tired of being the butt of everyone's jokes and standing idle while the school picked him apart. He lurched forward and shoved John-John with a burst of energy that surprised even him. The other students went wild with excitement over the anticipation of a cafeteria room fight while some egged John-John on.

"You gon' let Holey Noey punk you like that?" Justin was the main one stirring up trouble. "Bet you won't come for me like that," he said threateningly.

Before Noah could speak or react, John-John regained his footing, stepped forward, and swung his book bag at Noah's face. A hard object inside made contact with the corner of Noah's eye, causing a stinging impact. With all of the chaos and ruckus, finally a member of the staff hurried over to see what all of the fuss was about.

"Students!" Ms. Nelson, the assistant principal called out. "Students, please! What is the meaning of all of this?"

Before John-John could throw another blow, and before anyone could say exactly what was going on, Noah made a run for it. He pushed past the kids standing behind him and made a dash for the cafeteria door.

"No running in the halls!" a safety patrol called after him.

Noah didn't listen. He made a beeline toward the back hall and exited out of the back door leading to the back of the school. From there, he hurried down the stairs leading to the field and ultimately winding up on the street outside the perimeter of the school's grounds. Traffic was high as buses still transported students to school and adults tried to make their way to work. Noah maneuvered through the maze of activity and soon found himself on the path walking past his neighborhood and back in the direction of a quiet place where he felt he could seek refuge. Every once in a while, he looked behind him to make sure that no one was following him and that no truancy officer was scoping him. His body ached, but he pushed on. The farther away he got from the plethora of people that found pleasure in hurting him . . . the better.

Chapter 3

Olivia parked her car on the side of her apartment building, retrieved her groceries from the backseat, and rounded the corner to walk up the stairs to her unit. Her head was filled with the lyrics of the old Lauren Hill song she'd just hummed along with during her ride from Eastland Road to her apartment complex. Mentally, she marveled over how dynamic the female artist was and how it was a shame that she hadn't put out a sophomore album after all these years. One step after the next, Olivia bobbed her head to the sound playing in her mind until her eyes were drawn toward a slight and abrupt movement from the upper porch. She paused, hoping that there wasn't some crazed assailant crouching and awaiting her at the top of the stairs near her door. Cautiously, she took the next couple of steps up with her eyes peeled and her body ready to turn and flee at any second.

"Oh my goodness!" she exclaimed when she realized what was going on.

Balled up with his head between his legs rocking slightly sat the little boy whose memory had been haunting her since the day she'd met him. For the last two days, she'd wondered about him—asking herself if and when he'd ever come back. Just when she was about to let go of the whole thing and move on with her life, there he was sitting in a troubled demeanor by her door. With the way he was positioned, she assumed that he was crying. Immediately, she turned to face the tree that he'd stashed his product in previously. Her first mind said to her that some other curious or criminal-minded individual must have found it and taken it. Why else would the youth be so unglued and be sitting on her porch?

Olivia glanced down at her watch noting the time. Surely the child should have been in someone's classroom at this time of the morning. There was no way his parents knew that he was out and about during school hours. That thought seemed laughable considering she was also sure that his parents didn't know he was also out in the streets slinging dope. Not wanting to add to his distress and feeling her heart go out to him, Olivia set her bags down in front of her door and eased her body down into an Indian-style position on the porch in front of him.

As if sensing her presence for the first time, he looked up, and they locked eyes. No words were exchanged as each tried their hardest to read and figure out the other. His eyes were red and swollen from the many tears he'd shed. A tiny bruise was evident at the corner of his left eye. He shivered as if he was cold. His pants legs nearly stopped at the top of his socks which Olivia could see were clearly not mates. It looked as if a piece of masking tape was sticking out from the bottom of his left shoe. Everything about him raised red flags, but Olivia continued to sit there with an awkward feeling of obligation filling her spirit.

"What's your name?" she finally asked him. There was no way that she was going to let him get away from her this time without some form of identifying information.

He sniffed and consider his options, not knowing just how much he could, or couldn't, trust the woman. "247," was his response.

Olivia's eyebrow rose. "That's not a name," she told him. "It's just a number."

His eyes never broke their stare. "We're all numbers, aren't we? Even you. You're a number."

Olivia considered the statement. It was quite profound coming from such a young person. "I guess it depends on how you look at it," she admitted. "I'm a Social Security number legally speaking . . . an account number when it comes to bills and stuff like that. But, I have a name too." She paused for a moment, hoping he'd give in and tell her his. She sighed when he didn't take the bait. "My name is Olivia."

He said nothing.

Sensing that she wasn't going to get anything coming from that angle, Olivia decided to take another approach. She had so many questions and concerns, but it was clear that she was going to have to tread lightly with him. "What happened to your eye?" she asked him, noticing yet again the small shiner he was sporting.

His hand flew up to the spot where John-John's book bag had clocked him. He touched it gingerly, yet still winced from the pain. "Oh . . . this . . . I got into a fight at school . . . in the school yard."

"Yeah?"

He nodded.

"What happened?" Olivia inquired.

"Some bully was messing with some kid . . . some new girl . . . so I tried to get him to leave the kid alone," he lied. "And the dude socked me with his book bag."

"Ouch. That was pretty brave of you to stand up for someone else like that," she commented, wondering how the child could be so strong-willed in this instance, yet so passive by allowing himself to be forced into selling drugs.

He shrugged. "Somebody had to do it."

"Hmmm. So, did you get in trouble at school because of the fight? Is that why you aren't in school?"

"Ummm . . . I kinda ran off so that I wouldn't get suspended with the other kid."

"You don't think your parents will be upset about you running off like that? I mean, skipping school isn't exactly a safe thing for you to be doing."

"My parents?" He considered which direction to take his lie. "They won't be mad too much . . . I mean, I'm gonna tell 'em what happened, and they'll be proud of me for standing up to that kid. I just didn't wanna get a suspension put on my permanent record because I don't wanna go . . . I mean, I don't wanna disappointment my folks."

"But if they'll be proud of you for standing up to the bully, then surely they'd understand if the principal suspended you. It was a noble act." Olivia watched his facial expression grow rigid. "I mean, I doubt that the principal would have suspended you once he found out you were helping someone else."

The boy shrugged.

"Do you think you should maybe call your parents now?" she asked, dying for an opportunity to speak to them herself.

He shook his head. "Naw, I'm just gonna go home and wait until they get there." He rose from his spot on the porch. "They're . . . uh . . . they're at work so—"

"What do your parents do?"

"My dad's a lawyer, and my mom's a doctor. A really smart one," he stated quickly. "She cuts people's brains open and stuff."

"So your mom's a brain surgeon?" Olivia asked, pulling herself up from the ground as well.

He nodded. "Yep."

"At which hospital?"

His eyes searched the ground as if the answer lay in the concrete of the porch's foundation. "Uh . . . the big one downtown."

There was no point in questioning him about it further. She knew his story was shakier than a politician's campaign speech or a house on a fault line. "Where do you live?"

"We have a big house over off of Sky Haven Road. My dad had it built from scratch just how my mom wanted it. We have the biggest house on the street too. And I have my own room with all kinds of cool stuff . . . video games, toys, a brand-new laptop."

"Wow." She smiled at him, not wanting to burst his bubble. "Sounds nice. So why would you want to leave all that to sit all the way over here on Bouldercrest on my steps in the middle of the day?" Olivia asked, remembering the night they'd met.

He was done answering her questions. "I gotta go." He moved to walk past her.

Olivia quickly grabbed his arm and was dismayed by the earsplitting yelp that escaped his tiny body. Her eyes widened, and she immediately let his arm go. "Are you okay?" she asked, wondering what had set him off.

He nodded profusely and scurried by to make his way down the stairs.

She watched him flee. "Do you want me to drive you home?" she called after him. "That's an awful long way to walk . . . and you don't want a truancy officer picking you up, do you?"

She had a valid point, but after the picture he'd just painted for her of what his life and his home were like, there was no way that he could allow her to take him home and find out the truth. "Naw," he said over his shoulder. "I'm good." He walked off without another word.

Olivia remained standing at the top of the stairs. She could get in her car and follow him . . . or she could do nothing. It was clear to her that something strange was going on with the child, but she couldn't exactly put her finger on it. Maybe Shanice was right—maybe he was just a little punk street kid yanking her chain and messing with her. Maybe he was feeling her out and he and his street buddies would come back and rob her. It was a possibility, but her gut didn't tell her that it was so. Feeling no more certain about the boy now than she was initially, Olivia absentmindedly picked up her bags and let herself into her home. She didn't know when, but she felt almost certain that she'd see the little boy again.

"I can't believe that he actually thought I was going to change the grade. I mean, I give him credit for creativity, because, let's face it, it was a colorful lie, but at the end of the day, these privileged-ass kids need to adopt some sense of responsibility." Kasyn was going on and on as he dressed his baked potato to his liking.

Kasyn Terrell was an adjunct professor at a local college in Macon. It was customary for him to fill their dinner table chatter with talk about his students and his adventures in college education. Most times, Olivia clung to his every word, asking questions and paying attention to details on the off chance that something could inspire a story line. But, tonight, she was barely able to keep up as she took her time slicing her grilled pork chop into tiny pieces. Her appetite was nonexistent, but she was going through the motions for Kasyn's sake.

"Livi!" Kasyn called out. "Livi!"

She snapped out of the daze she hadn't even realized that she was in. "Huh?"

"The hot sauce, babe," he said, pointing to the bottle sitting to her right.

"Oh." She handed him the bottle and gave him a weak smile. "Sorry."

"Everything okay?" he asked as he doused his meat.

"Yeah, yeah," she lied. "Everything's fine."

"Come on," he said, forking a piece of chop into his mouth. "What gives? You're like a zombie over there. I practically gave you comedy gold a minute ago, and you didn't even crack a smile."

She chuckled in an effort to placate him. "No, no. I'm listening."

"Come on now. Don't try to fool me. What's bothering you? Still having trouble with the book? Maybe you just need to leave it alone for a minute and focus on something else." He looked around the eat-in kitchen. "Like packing this place up and moving in with me or planning something major . . . like our wedding."

Olivia put a forkful of potato in her mouth and chewed it without tasting its flavor. "I can't just abandon it. I have a deadline to meet," she said with a hint of edginess in her tone.

"Then what's keeping you from doing it? I mean, what's the cure for this writer's block thing if it isn't focusing on something else for a minute?"

"I'm not troubled about the book, Kasyn."

"Then what is it? And don't tell me it's nothing 'cause you're sitting over there looking like you've got the weight of the world on your shoulders."

She set her fork down and stared at him for a moment, wondering what his take would be on the matter. She'd battled with herself back and forth over whether to disclose her concerns about the little boy with him. She knew Kasyn, and she knew that he wasn't as compassionate as she was. If anything, his mind-set would probably be much like Shanice's, but the thought was so heavy on her mind that she had to get it off of her chest.

"Something happened," she told him, watching his expression as she made the statement.

He looked at her with seriousness and concern all over his face. "To you? Something happened to you? Did someone bother you, Livi? Was it here? Were you robbed?"

She waved her hands to calm him down. "No no no. Nothing like that. I met someone and—"

Kasyn dropped his fork on his plate. "*Excuse* me?"

She caught herself, realizing how her statement must have sounded to him. "Oh God, no. Bae, not like that. It's a child . . . a kid. I met a little boy who has kinda . . . grew on me."

"Ah. You trying to adopt someone's son, Livi? We don't have to do that when we can make our own."

"No, I'm not trying to adopt him. I met him outside . . . like on the steps." She sighed. "He was sitting there one evening and startled me. I talked to him for a second and come to find out that he was holding some cocaine for someone that he said forced him to sell it. He asked me to hide it for him, and you know I couldn't do that. So . . . I told him to hide it in a tree outside." She took a quick breath and forged on. "Then I saw him again this morning when I came in from the store, and he seemed like something was really bothering him. He was all shaky and jumpy . . . his face was bruised. I asked him about his parents and from what he told me, they sound like good, solid, decent folk but who in the hell would be that out of touch with their child, their eight-year-old, to the point where he's walking around in raggedy clothes, being bullied by some dope dealer, and getting into fights all willy-nilly? Then he just ran off . . . twice . . . without me getting any real information about him. I mean, I don't even know his name." She sighed at the end of her confession and lowered her head as if feeling fatigued from telling her story.

Kasyn contemplated the things his fiancée had just dumped on him. She'd spoken so quickly, and some of the things she'd said sounded so outrageous to him that, for a second, he wondered if maybe she was delirious and getting real life confused with her fictional story lines. "Soooo . . . you're telling me that you aided a drug dealer in stashing his drugs?"

"He's not a drug dealer."

"And how do you know that? You just said that you didn't get any information about this kid. No name, no nothing. You don't know him," Kasyn countered.

Olivia couldn't dispute that, but she had another angle to at least defend herself. "My gut tells me that he isn't a drug dealer, 'Syn. He's just a kid who obviously has some issues. I think something's going on with his parents . . . something he hasn't told me. But, for some reason, he keeps coming back to me. My gut tells me that's not an accident . . . like, it's fate or something. Like, I'm destined to help him or something."

"Help him what, Livi? Huh? The kid asked you to do something illegal, which you should have called the police on his ass. That's the only kinda help he's looking to get from you."

Olivia shook her head, dismayed that neither her best friend nor her fiancé understood her feelings about this situation. "No, I think you're wrong. I'm telling you, my gut says that something serious is going on with that child, 'Syn, and I just can't ignore what my conscience is screaming to me. I mean, what if whoever's bullying him into trapping is the one who is beating on him? What if his parents are so busy with their career endeavors that they don't really just don't know what's going on with their kid? What if—"

"Livi, stop! This whole 'what-if' game is going to drive you crazy. Look at you." He stared at her demeanor noticing the way her hands trembled and her breathing was irregular. She was really worked up over this situation, and Kasyn couldn't understand why. "I think most of this is in your head. If it's as bad as you're making it out to be, then his parents should be up on it. That kid's parents should be dealing with it, so just let them deal with it. Don't let your imagination run wild."

"It's not my imagination. I'm telling you, something's going on with this child."

"And I'm telling you that you don't know that. You've already admitted that you don't know jack about him. So just leave it alone. Stop stressing yourself out over something you don't know anything about. And if you see the kid again, steer clear. I don't really want you getting involved with unsavory creatures."

It was the most judgmental thing she'd ever heard him say, but his take on it was much like Shanice's. Popular opinion was luring her toward emptying her mind of the memories and thoughts surrounding her brief interactions with the child. Sure, she could busy herself and tell herself not to think about him or whatever problems he was experiencing. The problem was . . . how could she manage to empty her heart of the feelings that were drawing her nearer to this stranger that now had her so intrigued? She was stuck between a rock and a hard place. Now what was she supposed to do?

Chapter 4

An involuntary shutter followed by a quick toss over on his back characterized the fitful night that he was having as sleep tormented him. Perhaps it was his dreams that kept him gripping at his covers, or more to the point, his subconscious thoughts holding him hostage mentally as his body tried to relax before tackling yet another trying day of living the life that he'd been stuck with. Settling down, stretched out in his twin-sized bed with the old, lumpy mattress, he once again settled into another few minutes of silent slumber, hoping that this time, he wouldn't find himself tossing once more.

Moments passed, and as his mind settled back into a series of fragmented visions that were seemingly unconnected, the air in his lungs began to feel constricted. His eyes popped open, and his pupils stared into the darkness, struggling to focus in on the figure before him that was illuminated by the light shining into the room from the hallway. Noah's hands flew up to the larger more powerful hands engulfing his tiny neck. Understanding escaped him as he flailed away the stranger's fingers in his effort to reclaim the air he needed to breathe properly.

"Hurry up!" Mikey's voice called out from behind the man. "Don't let this shit take all night. Shit. Don't be a pussy about it."

Noah was confused. He hadn't done anything to this man to his knowledge and wasn't clear about why he was now being subjected to his brutality. Was this Mikey's form of payback? Did the dope that he'd failed to sell belong to this big burly man? Even if that was the case, this moment was a shocker because Noah had made it a point to return to the tree, retrieve the coke, and place it under Mikey's pillow in his room earlier that day. Nothing was missing . . . so why was he getting this treatment?

As he kicked and winced, the large man finally let him go and turned to Mikey. "I don't know about this, man."

"Fuck you don't know?" Mikey asked. He walked over to a stunned Noah who was now sitting upright in the middle of his bed, gasping for air and struggling to comprehend the danger he was in. Mikey gritted. "Fuck this." He pushed Noah down onto the bed and roughly tugged at the child's faded ninja turtle pajama bottoms.

Noah tried to fight him off. "No!" he cried out. "Mikey . . . Mikey, stop! Mannnn! Stop!"

His whining and begging did no good as Mikey ignored Noah and snatched the boy's pajamas and underwear free from his legs. He paid no mind to the fear in Noah's tone or the tears in his eyes as he looked back at the older, drunken man to his left and nodded in Noah's direction. "Go 'head." He looked at the petrified Noah. "You won't work my way, then I'll get my fuckin' money outta you another way." He stepped back to allow the man who was now unzipping his fly to step forward.

The man stared at Noah, and Noah backed up on the bed and quickly turned to make an attempt jump off the other side. Although there was nowhere for him to run because he would have had to pass both men to get out the door, Noah still didn't feel inclined to remain posted on the bed like a sitting duck waiting for whatever torture was coming his way.

Mikey leaped across the room and forced Noah back onto the bed. "Hell no! Be still, nigga, and shut up!" he demanded as he pinned the little boy down. He stared up at the man whose limp dick hung out of his pants expectantly. "Come on, man! Handle ya' business."

"B . . . b . . . but," the man stuttered. He nervously looked at Mikey holding down the terrified child in front of him. "It's a boy, dude."

Mikey was frustrated. "So, man?"

The oaf winced and ran his fingers through his short, stringy blond locks. "You said you had some tender young thang up here, buddy," he complained.

"What the fuck difference does it make?" Mikey asked, still struggling to keep Noah from breaking free. "A hole's a hole, man. You want somethin' tight to fuck, right? Handle ya' business."

Noah looked from Mikey to the big man who seemed indecisive about what he wanted to do. He prayed that the man would walk out of the room and abandon the idea of assaulting him. He wondered where Ms. Mae was while her son was back there whoring him out to some drunk white man he must have picked up in some bar. Just when he thought that he was about to be granted his wish, he watched in horror as the man neared the bed and dropped his pants to the ground.

"Well, turn 'em over," the man insisted.

Noah shook his head in horror, his kicking escalated, and his screaming could be heard at a resounding octave. "Nooooo! Nooooo! Please! Don't do it! Don't do it, Mikey. I'm sorry! I'm sorry!"

Mikey wasn't hearing it. "Shut the fuck up!" he boomed as he pushed Noah's head down into the cushion of his mattress to muffle his cries while lying on his torso to keep him from breaking free. "Come on, man!" he encouraged his customer. "Get this shit over with. You got ten minutes, then the show's over."

The man touched the smooth skin of Noah's legs in an eerie caress, causing the boy to flail his limbs and shake in horrified anticipation of the nightmare to come. The man sneered and felt a peak of excitement enter his body as he stroked his member to life. With his calloused free hand, he pulled Noah's left leg away from the right and held it in place at the spot just below his buttock in an effort to give him greater access to his only point of entry. Taking his right hand, he licked his palm and lathered his pink penis with fresh, liquor-tinged saliva so that it would act as a lubricant.

Noah's muffled cries and fidgeting increased and turned into shallow screams of agony and trembles of distress as the man's dick ripped at the delicate tissue surrounding the young child's anus. Even Mikey had to look away as the dirty son of a bitch tried to force his modest six-and-a-half-inch dick into an opening that wasn't equipped for such activity. Sure, the man had paid Mikey a good forty bucks thinking that Mikey had a fresh piece of virgin ass for him to fuck relentlessly—specifically, a female he was whoring out, but clearly that had been a lie—but never had Mikey really thought for a second that the dude would actually go through with it. He figured that he'd bitch up and demand his money back, at which point he'd planned to reiterate his no-refund policy. But there he was, standing watch and holding Noah down as the man he'd only known for two hours pumped away with only just past his head making its way inside of Noah's body.

After a while, Noah stopped moving. His body grew numb to the burning and searing pain, but his spirit was caught up in a gush of turmoil that had yet to settle down. His eyes were squeezed tightly shut as he stopped crying and concentrated on trying to breathe despite his involuntary grimacing and the fact that Mikey was nearly suffocating him by keeping his face pressed into the mattress. The seconds turned into minutes, and the minutes felt like eternity. By the time the man huffed and bucked, releasing a puddle of his slimy semen onto the back of the child's leg, Noah had grown completely limp, having passed out from the shock of it all.

Mikey released his hold on the boy and jumped up off of the bed as the man stood along the side of the bed, staring up at the ceiling in the afterglow of his orgasm.

"A'ight, man. You gotta roll!" Mikey rushed the man, pushing his arm and motioning toward the door. "Shit's over. Grab ya' pants and get the fuck outta my house."

The man blinked profusely and looked from Mikey to the kid's seemingly lifeless body, down to the crimson trail on his dick, and then back at Mikey. His heart began to pound as he realized the dehumanizing thing he'd just done. He tricked off on whores before, but never had he taken advantage of a kid, much less a boy. Quickly, he pulled up his jeans and dashed from the house which he vowed to never return to again. If he could get away quickly enough, it would be too soon. His thoughts attacked him as he feared being stopped in the street by the police and placed in jail for sexual abuse of a minor boy. How the hell would he ever explain that to his wife and daughter?

Mikey was glad to see the dude go. He was forty bucks richer and had it in his mind that surely there were other fucks just like that guy who would probably pay even more money for a few minutes with Noah's sissy ass. He looked over at his foster brother lying motionless on the bed and considered waking him up and cleaning him before his mom returned from her night out with her friends. After a second or two, he decided against it. If Noah had the mind to wake up and tell about what happened, he'd simply deny it. He figured the little nigga could make his own way to the bathroom and clean his own self up, so why should he? He studied Noah's body for a moment longer and ignored the urges stirring within him. Quickly, he closed the bedroom door and headed to the kitchen for a beer, leaving Noah to lay soaked in his own blood and broken spirit.

The sun barely peeked through the blinds of her bedroom as she lay with her back to the door listening to the muffled sounds on the other side. It was an early Saturday morning, and while she was certain that the rest of the neighborhood was asleep, it was obvious that her father and older sister were not. She could hear them speaking to each other, double-checking their packing list, as they walked back and forth from the living room past her bedroom into his studio space. The night before during dinner, they'd discussed how they were going to hit up the flea market about an hour outside of the city to sell some of the mixed tapes and knickknacks that he no longer had use for. The only reason he wasn't pulling her along on this boring expedition was because someone had to stay home and watch the smaller children since her stepmother had to work.

That was just fine with Kennedy. The last thing she wanted to do was to be stuck anywhere with her father for an extended period of time. Carmen could have it. Besides, it seemed to Kennedy that Carmen and her dad got along just fine these days despite the monster she now knew him to be. It ate her up on the inside, carrying around this secret about the ungodly things that were happening to her inside of the modest, yellow, three-bedroom home on the quaint and quiet country road in a town where everybody knew everybody's business. The only problem was that no one knew hers—

no one knew the truth about what happened behind her family's closed doors.

Kennedy sighed deeply, waiting for her father and sister to finally vacate the house so that she could relax. She was never comfortable in the house as long as he was awake and moving around. Just when she thought relief was coming, his deep voice fell hushed out in the hall just before her door creaked open.

"Ken," he said in a regular, nonescalated conversational tone.

She didn't stir. She figured that if she ignored him he'd just back out of the room, put the alarm on, and leave the house without bothering her. If she didn't budge an inch, maybe she'd escape being forced into looking into his deceitful eyes and holding even a brief conversation with the one person she privately wished would drop dead.

"Ken?" he called for her again. "You asleep?"

She stared at the wall, being sure to lie perfectly still on her side. As his feet shuffled across the floor to her bedside, she closed her eyes tightly and tried to wish him away. She felt his presence close to her and fought back the urge to swallow the lump that had rapidly grown in her throat. Her wish had totally not come true. She felt him touch her arm as if to tap her awake, but then his tap became more of a caress. She pursed her lips and forced herself not to make a sound or flinch.

Believing that she was in a deep sleep, her father quickly looked over his shoulder to make certain that no one was standing in the doorway or walking by. He turned back around and stared at the back of Kennedy's unmoving form. Gently, he reached for the top of her sheet which rested right at her waistline. Quickly, he pulled it back and took in the curve of her lower body as she lay curled up on her side. Biting his bottom lip devilishly, he dropped the sheet at her feet and slowly pulled up her gray nightgown to sneak a peek underneath.

Disgusted and feeling completely degraded, Kennedy couldn't remain still. She was devastated to know that even in her slumber he would have the nerve to take advantage of her. But she wasn't surprised. Since his initial misconduct, her father had taken every possible opportunity available to touch her inappropriately or say something to her that was completely out of line for any man to utter at a young woman, especially his own daughter. Several times she'd thought about running away, but the thought of being tossed in juvenile detention . . . or worse, being returned to this home of ill repute, put a damper on her plans. She'd been saving money just in case she got up the nerve, and every day she battled with herself mentally trying to figure out which adult would be the best person to tell what was happening to her. Unfortunately, everyone in their neighborhood was either intimidated by her father, because of his size and demeanor, or considered themselves his friend. Either way, Kennedy didn't expect much support from any of them.

Not wanting to lie there and allow him to violate her further, Kennedy stretched her arms out and made a loud yawning sound. Her father immediately removed his hand from her nightgown, yet did not step away from her bedside. Instead, he watched as she turned over and pulled her gown down self-consciously before grabbing the sheet to cover herself back up.

"We're leaving now," he told her. "Mom's already gone, so when the kids get up, make sure you give them breakfast and clean the kitchen."

She simply nodded, having nothing to say to him. Surely he knew that she realized what he'd just done and had her own assumption about how far he'd planned to take it.

"Don't open the door for anyone or go outside for any reason," he instructed her. "Y'all stay in this house and don't mess with nothing you're not supposed to." He studied her face with scrutiny.

Kennedy felt his stare and looked down at her covers uncomfortably as she sat up in bed.

"What's wrong with your face?" he asked her.

"Nothing," she replied, raising her hand to touch the cool flesh of her left check instinctively.

"You got all these little bumps all over your face."

I'm a teenager, *she thought.* I have acne, you asshole.

"Hmmm," he said, reaching out to touch her face himself.

Kennedy flinched and turned her head, urging him not to touch her.

"Those are either getting some bumps or needing some bumps," he observed with a sly smile as he leered at her. "Which one is it?"

"What?" She was mortified by the flow of conversation. Was he really standing there asking her if she'd been having sex or wanted to? Who has that kind of conversation with their daughter?

"You heard me. You been fucking?"

"No!" she snapped.

"Then you must want to." He stepped closer to her bed and spoke in a tone. "I know y'all women have needs. You probably be lying in here thinking about stuff and touching on yourself at night, huh? You probably need something for that . . . a vibrator . . . or something."

Kennedy failed to give him eye contact as she shook her head, denying his words. "Naw . . . I'm good. I don't need that."

"I can go get you one, and we can cut a little hole in your mattress so you can hide it in there. I can burn you a copy of a movie too, but you have to watch it with the

sound down so no one else will hear it. And I can show you how the vibrator works too . . . Would you like that?" He reached his hand up under the sheet to touch the softness of her stretched out leg.

Kennedy squirmed and shook her head feverishly. "No," she whispered. "No, I don't want that," she told him as she moved her legs close together and away from her father.

Forcefully, he grabbed her left thigh, pulling her back toward him, and then jammed his hand between her legs to stroke her feminine spot over the top of her cotton undies.

"No, please!" she cried, pushing at his hand and staring at his chocolate, bald head, unable to meet his dirty glare. "Don't . . . please . . . don't!"

"Okay, I got the keys!" Carmen's voice screamed from the hallway.

Kennedy's dad retracted his hand hurriedly and stepped away from her bed. Immediately, she drew her knees up to her chin, wrapped her arms around them, and buried her face into the sheet as her body shook with sobs. Her father said nothing as he exited her bedroom, closing the door behind him. She heard his voice correspond with her sister's as they made their way out of the house. The door closed, and she listened for his truck to start up and pull off before finally slumping her shoulders downward into her hunched over stance.

"I hate you!" she screamed with her head still down. Her tears soaked the sheets. "I hate you! I hate you! I hate you!"

"I hate you!" she screamed out into the darkness. "I hate you! I hate you!"

"Livi! Livi!" Kasyn shook her body relentlessly, trying with all of his might to pull her out of the nightmare that had her so disturbed. "Olivia, wake up!"

She gasped for air, and her eyes popped open in the darkness of the room. *Where am I?* she thought, confused about her surroundings. Reflexively, she pushed Kasyn's hands away from her body and sat straight up in bed, looking around and collecting herself. Within seconds, she recognized the bedroom and turned to look at the man beside her, recognizing her fiancé despite the confused look he was giving her in the dimness of the lamp light which he'd just flicked on.

"Are you okay?" he asked, staring at her. "You're crying and shaking, babe."

She nodded her head and raised her hand to wipe her tears away. Her heart rate was accelerated, and although she really wanted to scream, she held it together for the sake of not scaring Kasyn. "I'm fine."

He studied her before drawing her into his embrace. "You had one of those dreams again, huh?"

She nodded her head as she allowed him to comfort her.

Kasyn kissed her forehead and spoke in a gentle voice. "They're just dreams, baby. I'm right here for you. Nothing or no one can hurt you while I'm here. Especially from a dream. It's okay."

She closed her eyes and counted to ten silently before slowly retracting from his hold. Then she slipped from the bed and placed her feet into her slippers.

"What's the matter? Where you going, Livi?" he asked.

"Nothing's wrong," she lied. "I'm fine. Just going to get some water. Go back to sleep."

"I'll wait for you to come back so I can hold you, okay?"

She shook her head. "No, no, I'm fine. Really. Go on back to sleep. You have to get up early to drive back." She noticed his skeptical facial expression. "Really, I'm fine. Okay? I don't want to disturb you anymore than I already have. Please . . . go back to sleep."

She didn't wait for him to consent or further object before turning and walking out of the room, being sure to pull the door up behind her. She trotted to the kitchen and up to the cabinet that held all of her cups and glasses. Reaching for the knob, she felt a tightness in her chest and dropped her hands to press against the counter. Hot tears dripped freely, and her chest rose and fell rhythmically as she cried. Kasyn meant well, and she knew it, but he was wrong. They weren't just dreams, and they very well did hurt her. But that wasn't something that she could ever explain to him without him seeing her differently. Instead, she kept it all to herself and tried as much as she could to push it all to the back of her mind—every bit of the pain, hopelessness, fear, and injustice. No one had ever cared before, so there was no sense in expecting anyone to care now.

Her thoughts trailed to the boy who'd mysteriously come into her life and stirred up familiar emotions inside of her. The despair in his eyes, the tremble of his body, and the desperation of his tone were all familiar to her. It was true that she didn't know him anymore today than she did the first moment she'd laid eyes on him, but there was something about the child that spoke to her—some kind of connection that drew her in and made her feel invested in him. Shanice didn't understand it, and neither did Kasyn. Hell, she, herself, didn't truly understand it, but she was certain that it was no coincidence that the moment the child entered her life, dreams she'd long since repressed were beginning to torment her yet again. God was trying to tell her something, but what was it?

***

The afternoon traffic was killing her as she tried to maneuver her way toward I-20 from Moreland Avenue in pursuit of reaching her meeting spot with her publisher downtown. She'd run a few errands, including dropping Kasyn's laundry off at the cleaners on Moreland, and now, here she was bordering on being late to handle her own business. As she sat in the long line at the red light, her eyes ventured around taking in the scenery. She was right in front of McDonald's and found herself debating whether she had enough time to stop to get fries. Just as she was about to neglect the idea altogether, her eyes squinted at the sight of a familiar person. Walking into the fast-food establishment was the very image of the persona that had been stuck in her head for days. Guiding him along was a woman who looked to be middle-aged and was dressed in a brown and tan business suit.

Quickly, Olivia switched lanes, pissing off drivers behind her, and made the left into McDonald's parking lot. She couldn't believe her luck. She'd been wondering about the boy and his parents all this time, and now, as chance would have it, she had the opportunity to meet the child's mother face-to-face and inquire about his well-being. She found a parking spot, exited her car, and hurried inside to find the mother and son duo. Searching the order line, she was unable to locate them, so she turned toward the dining area of the restaurant. Seated near the window she spotted them and made her way over to say hello.

His eyes fell upon her immediately and a sinking feeling hit the bottom of his stomach. He shook his head with a smile on his face yet said nothing. Olivia caught his look of trepidation but dismissed it as him simply being afraid that she'd sell him out about the crack. It was a thought, but it wasn't her initial concern at the moment.

"Hello," Olivia said pleasantly to the woman sitting across from the boy.

"Um . . . hi," the woman replied confused.

Olivia held out her hand with a smile plastered across her face. "Oh my goodness. I can't tell you how happy I am to finally meet you."

The woman shook Olivia's hand with her mouth open, yet unable to find the words to express her confusion with the situation.

"I was beginning to wonder if you even really existed, but it warms my heart to actually see you in the flesh," Olivia went on. She looked over at the boy whose head was down with his eyes fixated on the empty table in front of him. "We . . . uh . . . we kind of met by accident a little while ago. He was actually sitting on the steps of my apartment building one evening, and I was wondering if you even knew where he was at the time. He, uh . . . he told me that you're very busy. You know, because of your job. By the way, which hospital do you work at? He seemed a little fuzzy about that the last time we spoke."

"Which hospital?" the woman asked, perplexed.

"Yes. He told me you're a doctor but didn't give me the name of the hospital."

"He told you that? I'm sorry . . . and who are you again?"

"Olivia Collins . . . like I said, I ran into your son outside of my apartment building one evening."

"My son?" the woman repeated, looking over at the boy and shaking her head. "He told you that too, huh?"

Now it was Olivia's turn to be confused by the way the woman was behaving so evasively. "I'm sorry, but did I miss something?"

"It seems that you've been misinformed," the woman replied. "I'm not Noah's mother. I'm his social worker. Noah's in foster care, and I'm really wondering now how he got to your apartment complex, wherever that may be, without the knowledge or consent of his guardian."

"Noah," Olivia said, repeating the child's name as she once again looked at him.

This time he met her glance and his facial expression was blank. He didn't know what to expect now or how much Olivia was about to share with his case manager. He knew it wasn't going to be pretty for him the moment she opened her big mouth to snitch on him. It was bad enough that she'd told that he was so far away from home. He could almost see the doors of juvenile detention now, and he had no one but himself to blame. Why had he ever thought that he could trust her with even the little bit of information and the lies that he had shared with her?

Olivia was stunned. Learning his name was a relief, but hearing that he'd basically lied to her was heartbreaking. She'd defended him to both Shanice and Kasyn when they'd both been adamant that he was playing her. If he'd lied about his parents and his living situation, then surely, any and everything else that had come out of his mouth must have been lies too, especially about the drugs. She stared at him, unable to understand how she could feel so in tune with him, yet so distant at that moment. Olivia didn't know what to think or what to say.

"I'm sorry that he's been a nuisance to you," the social worker stated. "But I'll make certain that his foster mother is aware of his . . . uh . . . disappearing acts . . . and that he doesn't bother you again."

Olivia looked away from Noah and refocused her attention on the woman speaking to her. She shook her head. "No, no. He was . . . uh . . . He was never a bother. It was kind of refreshing to have someone pop up who wasn't trying to sell me some Girl Scout cookies or teach me about Jehovah." She tried to make light of the situation, but she was fuming on the inside, mad at herself for allowing this con artist of a kid to have her emotions all wrapped up in him. "I'm sorry to disrupt your meeting or what have you, Ms. . . ." Olivia looked to the woman to fill in the blank.

"Hardy. Vanisha Hardy," the case manager introduced herself. "Here, take this." She handed Olivia a card. "If there's ever anything else I need to know about our little Christopher Columbus here who likes to explore the neighborhood, then please, feel free to call me."

Olivia looked down at the standard DeKalb County DFCS business card with the woman's name on it and nodded. "Thank you. I'm really sorry again."

"Oh, not a problem," Ms. Hardy assured her.

"Enjoy your day," Olivia stated before throwing a final glance in Noah's direction before placing the business card in her purse.

She turned and hurried out of the restaurant unsure of her feelings at the moment. Clearly, Noah had been dishonest with her, but what could she do about it? It saddened her to remember how passionate she'd felt about helping him and seeing him again, just to know that he was okay. But now that she knew he was a troubled foster kid with a habit of lying, she felt disgusted. The time she'd spent agonizing over what she should have done or what she could do for him could have gone toward finishing the book she was about to be chewed out by her publisher about.

"Damn it!" she exclaimed as she hit the steering wheel once inside of her car. She'd wasted a lot of time and energy on this kid, and now she was late for her meeting.

Chapter 5

The kitchen was filled with the scent of chocolate chip cookies. As therapy for the trying afternoon she'd had, Olivia had gone baking crazy. She nibbled on an oatmeal raisin cookie which she'd plucked from the mountain of others resting on the platter on the counter. The batch of chocolate chip cookies had just about seven more minutes to go in the oven before they'd be ready. She'd been given a stern talking to by Vera Power of Powerhouse Publishing because of the lack of productivity regarding her current literary project. Sighing, she bit into another cookie, resigned to drowning her sorrows in her dessert.

Her thoughts were disrupted by a series of radical tapping at her door. She knew it wasn't Kasyn. He had a key, plus he wasn't due home for another hour or so. Cautiously, she veered out toward the peephole and didn't see anyone immediately. The knocking persisted, and she stood on her toes and struggled to look downward seeing the top of a head she'd come to know. Sucking her teeth, she stepped away from the door and wondered why he was there. Was it a setup? Did he have some of his older cronies with him, waiting in the wings for her to open the door so that they could attack and rob her?

His knocking didn't cease and against her better judgment, she opened the door and looked down at him. "I don't think you should be here," she told him. "I'm sure your foster mom wouldn't appreciate you being this far away from home."

His look was sorrowful as he spoke. "Yea, I'm sure that Ms. Mae could really care less."

"Hmmm . . . Well, that makes two of us," Olivia replied, moving to close her door.

Noah grabbed the knob of the door and spoke quickly. "My name's Noah Maxiel, and I'm a foster kid. I live off Eastland Road with my foster mom Ms. Mae and her son Mikey. I'm eight and been in foster care since I was five. Ms. Mae is my third foster parent. I lied about my folks because I didn't want you to think I was just some street kid."

Olivia hesitated, listening to him trying to explain himself. Shanice and Kasyn's voices lingered in her head telling her to just close the door and leave the situation alone, but she ignored it. The pleading of his tone pulled at her heartstrings. She opened the door wider and looked down into his sullen eyes. They stared at each other in silence, each evaluating the other. The timer buzzed on the oven, and Olivia glanced back over her shoulder.

"Shoot!" she exclaimed. "I have to get my cookies out of the oven." She hesitated again for a second before stepping back and nodding toward the inside of the house. "Come in," she told him.

Noah wasted no time stepping inside and taking a seat at the table in the dining room attached to the kitchen. Olivia closed and locked the door and rushed over to rescue her cookies from the oven. Noah watched her and tried to ignore the rumbling inside of his belly. The thick aroma of cookies assailed his nostrils, and his mouth began to salivate.

Olivia took her time transferring the cookies onto the platter with the rest of them. "You know, you put me in an awkward position today. I didn't really appreciate that."

"Sorry," was Noah's reply.

"You don't have to lie to get people to like you or to help you, Noah. Telling the truth is always the best thing. I mean, I wouldn't have thought any less of you had you told me about your foster mom instead of painting that elaborate picture of the perfect family." Olivia fell silent, realizing that she sounded as if she was lecturing him. Now that she knew his name, she couldn't deny that she was intrigued to know more of the truth about him. "So, how'd you end up in foster care?" she asked, taking a quick glimpse over at him.

Noah shrugged. "My mom died when I was littler, and I stayed with my grandma for a minute," he said. "But then she died when I was four, so all I been with is foster families."

"You said this is your third. What happened with the other two?"

Again she looked over at him, but this time she noticed how his eyes were glued to the platter of cookies. In turn, she pulled out a saucer, filled it with oatmeal raisin and chocolate chip cookies before getting down a plastic cup and filling it up with milk. She placed the snack before Noah and took a seat across from him.

He looked at her in an unsure manner. "I can have this?" he asked as if he was unused to being given food or being extended a kind gesture.

Olivia nodded. "Of course."

Before the last syllable dropped from her lips, Noah began to shove cookies into his mouth. He munched away as if he hadn't had a meal in days. Olivia watched as he practically inhaled the entire plate of cookies drinking his milk only after there was nothing but crumbs left on the plate.

"My goodness," Olivia commented. "Either those cookies were really good, or you've just got a big appetite."

"Can . . . more . . ." Some of his words were gobbled
up as he tried to get the remainder of the food out of his
mouth and down his throat.

Olivia rose from her seat and retrieved his plate. "Let's
make a deal. I'll give you a few more cookies if you
promise to slow down because I don't know CPR, so if
you choke, I can't help you." She threw him a smile as she
refilled his plate.

Noah gave a half smile as crumbs fell from his mouth.
The display was genuine and warmed Olivia's heart. In
that instant, she couldn't understand how she'd ever felt
any ill emotions toward the child. She carried over the
new helping of cookies and took her seat once more at
the table.

"So, what happened with the other two foster homes?"
she asked again, getting their conversation back on track.

Noah tried to take his time chewing as he spoke slowly
with his mouth full. "At the first one, they said I was too
much . . . two of the other boys kept messing with me . . . we
kept fighting . . . so they gave me back. The last one . . . I ran
away."

"You ran away?" Olivia's eyes grew wide at the thought
of the young child venturing the streets trying to fend for
himself.

Noah nodded. "Three times."

"Why?"

"He was beating her, and nobody believed me . . . I kept
telling Ms. Hardy, and she wouldn't listen to me. The
lady, my old foster mom, said I was lying. But, he was
beating her, and I knew he was gon' beat me too . . . He
did it before."

Thinking of the horrible things the child had already
been exposed to at such a young age made Olivia's skin

crawl. His greatest worry should have been about what video game to play or passing his next spelling test in school—not protecting himself from getting beaten by a foster parent. The thought of him being physically abused then led to the remembrance of his partial black eye. Olivia studied it intently and spoke gingerly. "So . . . your eye . . ."

Noah focused on his cookies and failed to make eye contact with her. "Told you. I was helping that kid . . . They were picking on him."

Olivia's eyebrow went up knowingly. "I thought you said it was a little girl." She watched his facial expression turn regretful at the realization of his blunder.

"Uh . . . yeah," he said nervously. "That's what I meant."

Olivia nodded assuming that he was protecting someone by keeping up the lie about what had really happened. Something told her that this current foster home situation was truly no better than the last two he'd been to. Something about Noah made her feel inclined to get involved, but what could she do? Sure, he'd been a lot more open and honest with her today than during their last encounters, but she still didn't know who his foster mother was or how to contact her in order to find out exactly what was going on in that household. An idea came to mind, but she didn't dare voice it to Noah. She didn't want him to be any more skittish about speaking with her than he already was. Instead, she sat silently, watching him enjoy his snack and wishing that she could wave a wand and magically erase all of the hurt that was plainly etched on his young face.

The sound of the front door closing made Olivia hurry through the apartment and into the living room before Kasyn could make it any farther. He threw his briefcase on the sofa and began to pull his blazer off. The look on his face indicated that he was tired. She knew that all he probably wanted to do was have a drink and kick his feet up before having dinner—a dinner that she hadn't yet prepared due to entertaining her company.

"Hey, honey," she said with a little nervousness in her tone.

"Hey. You think you made enough cookies?" he joked, thinking about the platter of cookies that he'd seen resting on the counter in the kitchen when he first walked in. "You have an ETA on dinner?"

Olivia gave a slight smile thinking of how she'd known exactly what his mind would be fixated on. "Ummm, I thought of doing the skillet chicken and potatoes, but I think it may be a better idea for us to go out," she lied, turning her head to look up the hall behind her. She hadn't given any thought at all to dinner after answering the door a couple of hours ago.

He grumbled and shook his head. "Livi, I'm not up for it. After the day I've had and the long ride here . . . I just can't." He turned around and headed back into the kitchen. He went into the refrigerator and pulled out a Heineken.

As he removed the top with the bottle opener attached to the refrigerator door with a magnet, his eyes fell upon the plate of cookie crumbs on the table and the half-empty glass of milk both resting in front of the place setting facing him. Across from that seat, the chair whose back was turned to him was pulled away from the table. It appeared as if two people had been seated at the table. Kasyn took a swig from his beer bottle and looked over at Olivia who was wringing her hands together and continuously looking over her shoulder.

"Do we have company?" he asked her.

"Huh?" Olivia asked, looking at him, trying to figure out how to handle the situation she was currently in the middle of.

Kasyn nodded his head in the direction of the table where it was obvious that two people had been fraternizing.

Olivia looked over and quickly walked over to the table, pushing in her chair and retrieving the dishes in order to straighten up. "Ummmm. Yeah, that's what I wanted to tell you. I kinda had an unexpected visitor today."

Kasyn leaned against the counter and nursed his beer. "Yeah? Shanice?" he asked, grasping at straws.

Olivia placed the saucer and glass in the sink. She shook her head. "No. Um . . . My new little friend decided to pay me a visit. So, ummm . . . we sat and talked . . . and had cookies."

Kasyn's eyebrow went up. "New little friend?" he repeated.

"Mmm-hmm."

He set his beer down and glared at the usually rational woman that he expected to spend the rest of his life with. "I know you're not talking about that delinquent troublemaker."

Olivia was offended. Her hands flew to her hips, and her neck rolled as she gave off the stereotypical black woman attitude that she often tried to avoid feeding into. "How dare you pass judgment on someone you don't even know! A child, no less."

"A child that's out in the streets selling drugs, Livi," Kasyn shot back.

"He wasn't selling it! It was forced on him."

"Right. And you're gullible enough to believe that? Come on, Liv! We talked about this. The kid is a scam artist . . . a hoodlum."

Olivia shook her head. "That isn't a fair assessment to make."

"No? But it's a real assessment. Hell, I'm only going based off of what you've told me. So tell me what I'm missing . . . tell me what it is, because facts are facts, Liv. He came to you with crack . . . *crack,* Liv! He behaved aggressively, right?"

"But you don't know him."

"*You* don't know him. How do you manage to let a little street punk cloud your judgment?" Kasyn shook his head. "You should consider yourself blessed that he and his little buddies haven't hemmed you up in here and raped you or something."

"Now you're calling the child a rapist?"

"I'm just saying . . . He's a drug dealer from what my gut tells me. There's no telling what the hell else this child is into!" he yelled.

"Shhhh!" Olivia urged him. "Can you lower your voice? You sound ridiculous."

Kasyn was astonished. "*I* sound ridiculous?" he questioned, pointing to himself in the chest. "I sound ridiculous but *you're* the one sitting up here having milk and cookies with some pusher."

"He's a child!" Olivia argued, growing more and more impatient with her fiancé's lack of compassion. She shook her head and turned to look toward the entrance to the eat-in kitchen.

Kasyn followed her glance. The wheels of his mind turned quickly, and he stepped forward to the middle of the kitchen. "Why do you keep looking back? What? What, is he still here?"

Olivia looked at him without responding.

Kasyn didn't need to hear a word. "Damn it, Liv! What's wrong with you? This is unreal. I can't get my dinner, and you can't focus on finishing your little book because you're so caught up in this . . . this junior thug."

Olivia was speechless. Her eyes grew wide, and her mouth fell open in response to the words that had just left Kasyn's mouth. So much about his statements made her uncomfortable and flustered that she had no clue which part to address first.

"You have his criminal ass walking around here freely. There's no telling what the hell he's stolen back there while you're up here with your fresh baked cookies. This shit isn't an episode of *The Cosby Show,* Liv. This isn't a give him a cute little antidote and a plate of cookies and you'll fix his life type of situation. This isn't some far-fetched urban story line. This is real life, and the reality is that you're opening yourself up to a whole host of potential problems." He stared at her briefly before huffing and moving to walk past her. "This is ludicrous. I'm going to throw his ass out."

Olivia stepped into his path and outstretched her arms to grab him by his forearms. "No! No, don't do that! Don't bother him. Please. You don't know him."

He glared at her. "I'm trying to help you because obviously this kid has some kind of emotional hold on you. You're not thinking clearly."

She looked into his eyes and tried to plead with him to understand. "If you just give me a chance to explain . . . if you . . . If you talked to him, then you'd see that it isn't what you think. He isn't how you think he is. There's so much more there . . . so much more going on with him. I know I can help him, Syn. I know I can."

"Yeah? And who is going to help *you* if you let this punk keep taking your kindness for weakness, only to eventually get you caught up? Is that what you want? Are you prepared for that? Huh? Don't you realize that if you get caught with this child and he has major drugs on him, you're going to jail? And that's the less damning of

the possibilities you face by not opening up your damn
eyes to the truth. What are you going to do if you go back
there, and he's boosted your money you're hiding in that
vase on your dresser, huh? How are you going to feel
then?"

The shuffle of feet on the tile of the kitchen floor made
them both turn to face Noah who was standing there
now taking in their scuffle. His eyes were slit, his facial
expression was hardened, and his body language noted
that he was guarded. Olivia's heart fluttered thinking of
all the things the child must have heard before entering
the kitchen. She dropped her hands from Kasyn's forearms and turned her body to completely face Noah.

"Are you okay?" she asked weakly. "Do you . . .
ummmm . . . do you want more . . . more cookies?"

Noah shook his head aggressively. "Naw, I'm good.
I'm gonna go. Didn't mean to bother you. Thanks for the
cookies and for letting me use your bathroom." His eyes
cut past Olivia and stared straight into Kasyn's angry
glare. His tiny nostrils flared as he watched the man size
him up. Knowing it was time to bounce, Noah headed
for the door. Before turning the lock and letting himself
out, he looked over his shoulder and again made eye
contact with the man he'd never met but instantly didn't
like. "And don't worry. I didn't steal any of y'all's tissue,
toothpaste, or medicines outta your bathroom." Before
either of the adults could respond, he opened the door
and exited, feeling the need to get far away so that he
could release the angry tears he was holding on to.

The door closed softly behind him, and Olivia stood
there staring at the black steel door. She could only
imagine the feelings invading Noah's heart and mind.
She could see it in his eyes. He was devastated and
hurt that someone who didn't know him at all would
speak so horribly about him. Olivia felt bad that she
was powerless in silencing Kasyn and redirecting his

perception of the young child who had obviously grown on her. Thinking about the things Kasyn had said infuriated her. Immediately, she found herself remembering involuntarily . . .

"Can you hurry up?" her father pressed her.

Kennedy held the glass to the ice maker outlet on the front of the freezer and felt dismayed that the contraption was sputtering but not spitting out any cubes. She couldn't understand it. She opened the freezer and peered into the ice tray. To her surprise, there was no ice to be found. The lever had been left raised, and she wondered by whom. Because of that, ice was not being created.

"Great," she said to herself as she slammed the freezer door shut. She knew that this wasn't going to be good.

She filled the glass with water with the only three cubes she'd managed to retrieve that were slowly melting into the liquid. Sighing and bracing herself for the backlash, she carried the glass out to the living room where her father sat in the middle of their oversized couch holding court with some of his friends from the neighborhood. Mr. Brown from across the street sat stoically in the armchair near the window smiling at her as he usually did, and Lori-Ann from down the street was sitting on the love seat stuffing her face with some of the nuts that she'd grabbed out of the bowl on the coffee table.

Kennedy handed her father the glass of water as he continued to speak to his friends.

"And if he thought I was going to pay him that much for that truck with all those miles on it, that nigga's crazy," he told them.

"Whatcha tell 'em, John?" Lori-Ann asked, amused. "I know you told him where to go and how to get there. John don't be playing no games do he, Man Brown?"

Mr. Brown shook his head as to acknowledge his assumption that he too felt John was about to tell them the juiciest part of his story yet. "Mmmm-Mmmm. That's your people for you."

"Shit, I told that . . ."John looked down at his glass as his lips began to kiss the rim. "What the hell? Didn't I ask you for ice?"

Kennedy hesitated at the threshold of the kitchen. She turned around to see the annoyed expression on her father's face. "I put some in there," she said weakly.

He held the glass up for everyone to see. "Two," he commented, staring at the glass. "No, three. Three damn cubes. What am I supposed to do with that? When somebody asks you for ice, it doesn't mean put three damn cubes in there. Shit."

"That's all there was," she tried to explain.

John looked over at Man Brown. "Ain't that a shame? Can't do nothing right. I asked her to do something simple, and she can't even get that right." He held his glass in Kennedy's direction without looking over at her. "Take it back. I don't even want the damn water no more."

Slowly, she walked over and retrieved the glass, ashamed to look at the faces of the other two adults who neither said nor did anything to stand up for her. As she turned to leave the room with the glass in hand, her father's lip turned up in disgust. Kennedy hurried into the kitchen to pour the water out and finish washing the dishes for the day.

"I swear that girl's slow," she heard her father say. "Her mama talked so much about how smart she was when she was living with her, but she ain't nothing but *average, if that. Damn report card barely sees anything above a C."*

"Whatttt?" Lori-Ann egged him on. "I know you ain't going for that, John."

"Them schools up there in Georgia ain't shit compared to our schools down here," he told her. "So she could barely do shit and get away with it and they call her ass a genius up there. You can't do that shit down here. Florida's school systems don't play. But shit, if she can't grasp the concept of putting ice in a glass, then what you expect?"

"You try to get her some help?" Man Brown asked. "A tutor or something?"

"Ain't nobody paying no money for her stupidity!" John answered "Shoot, if anything, I should be getting some money for her."

Lori-Ann burst into laughter. "What you mean, like a check? John, you crazy!"

Kennedy's father chuckled. "I'm serious as hell. Come Monday, I'ma take her ass down to the county health department and get her evaluated so we can go-ahead and start getting a disability check for her ass. I'm telling you, it don't make no sense for nobody to be that damn slow. Can't do shit right. And her ass had the nerve to tell somebody she was going to college after high school."

"What college did she have in mind?" Man Brown asked.

"Don't even matter," John told him. "Ain't nobody accepting no dummies into their school. Shit, the best she could probably do is go into the army and manage not to get her ass killed."

Again, Lori-Ann doubled over in laughter. "Not the army, John! You a mess!"

"You gon' put that girl in the military for real?" Man Brown asked.

"Sure as hell," John answered. *"I'm not paying not one penny for her to go to nobody's college and flunk out. Soon as she turns eighteen, I'm getting her with a recruiter and come the day after graduation, she's getting the hell outta here."*

"Mmmm-mmmm," Man Brown said, leaning back in his chair.

"I'm sure as hell gon' miss them disability checks, though," John commented. *"I ain't gon' miss having no dumb-ass kid hanging around that I gotta explain every li'l thing to. Shit, makes no sense."*

Kennedy's eyes stung from the tears that were built up in them. She turned off the water and placed the last clean dish in the drainer. Perhaps they thought that she couldn't hear them over the running water, or maybe, knowing her dad, they just didn't care. Either way, it bruised her confidence to hear her own parent tearing her apart and making her out to be nothing more than a mere idiot. She dried her hands on the dish towel hanging from the handle of the oven, wiped her eyes with the back of her hands, and walked quickly out of the kitchen with her head down so that none of them could see the hurt on her face.

Their voices fell silent as she breezed through the living room and raced up the hall to her bedroom. Before closing the door, she couldn't help but catch her father's next words.

"Dumb ass probably gon' wind up pregnant on welfare before we even get her in the recruiter's office . . . about all she'll probably succeed in is being some thug's ho," he said with venom dripping from each word.

***

The fury built up within her and her chest heaved with anger. She had half the mind to run out and jump in her car to see if she could find Noah out in the streets and apologize. Knowing that he was probably somewhere feeling about two inches tall simply didn't sit well with her. The child had enough issues, enough people that weren't paying close enough attention to his well-being, to have to deal with being trashed by the lover of the one adult he seemed to be drawn to for whatever the reason.

"Well, good riddance," Kasyn said, turning around and retrieving his beer. He took a swig and shook his head, not believing the crazy day he was continuing to have.

Olivia spun around quickly and stared at him. She walked to him with her index finger pointing toward him like a scolding schoolteacher. "You are just about the most insensitive person I've ever known. How dare you make that child feel like gutter trash? He came here because he trusts me, Kasyn. *Me!* He trusts me, and he feels comfortable here. Everyone deserves a place to go where they feel comfortable."

"Then he should take his ass home," Kasyn countered. "What is with you?"

"What is with *you?* The child is troubled! Whatever happened to the saying that it takes a village to raise a child? Is it so wrong for me to want to be part of this child's village? Is that so difficult for you to understand?"

"These days you have to exercise a whole hell of a lot more caution with the children in the village . . . especially *this* village that you insist upon living in." Kasyn shook his head. "Look, I don't wanna do this. I don't want to argue with you. I've had a long day, I'm tired, and I just want some dinner. Now, is that *too* much to ask for?"

Olivia shook her head and shrugged. "No. No, it isn't." She turned around to leave the kitchen. "There's plenty of stuff in the freezer. I'm sure you can find something to throw together for your meal."

With that she hurried through the apartment and into the bathroom to release her frustration without being subjected to his scrutinizing stares or flippant comebacks. She closed and locked the bathroom door and let the tears stream down her face. She'd become quite emotional lately, and it was beginning to feel draining. As she reached out to grab a few sheets of tissue from the roll, she hesitated when her eyes fell upon the red droplets on the crisp white tile of her floor.

"What the hell?" she let out.

Her brain rapidly went through the possibilities. She wasn't on her cycle, and even if she had been, she was never nasty enough to have an accident and not clean up after herself. She looked at her hands and arms, and then touched her nose to make sure she wasn't experiencing a nosebleed. There was no hint of blood anywhere on her body. She didn't remember having any kind of incident earlier in the day. The only person that had used the bathroom other than her was Noah.

"Noah," she whispered, staring down at the small spots situated in front of her toilet. Investigative by nature, she tried to fathom how he could have managed to hurt himself resulting in bleeding. He hadn't said anything about any injuries before going to the restroom. The only thing she could conclude was that the dripping occurred just before or just after he'd used the bathroom. "How the hell . . . ." Her brain was moving rapidly. Two thoughts came to mind, but each suggested that something was seriously wrong with the boy. There was no way that blood should have been escaping his body from the areas that came to mind. Olivia covered her mouth in fright. Something was definitely wrong.

Chapter 6

Olivia took a chance. All she had was a hunch to go on so she did it. She visited the elementary school that was closest to her neighborhood, assuming that it would, in fact, be Noah's school. Her rationale was that his school had to be in some kind of proximity to her home since he couldn't be traveling very far from his own residence to her complex so often. Entering the school wasn't difficult. Although they allegedly had security procedures in place, all she'd done was pressed a button and informed the receptionist at the front desk that she was there to visit the school's guidance counselor. After signing in, she was directed across the hall to another office where she waited patiently in the cramped space for someone to acknowledge her.

"Olivia Collins?" a tall yet stout woman called for her as she stood at the threshold of her matchbox office with her glasses falling down the bridge of her nose.

Olivia rose and gave the woman a smile as she approached her. "Hi, yes . . . That's me."

The woman turned and entered her office leaving the door open behind her in suggestion that Olivia should follow her. "I'm Mrs. Perkins. What can I do for you, ma'am?"

"I wanted to speak to you about a child."

"And who is your child?" the woman asked matter-of-factly.

"Well, he isn't exactly my child," Olivia stated, taking a seat in the chair directly across from Mrs. Perkins's desk. "He's a boy that I've encountered in my neighborhood . . . Noah . . . ummm, I don't have his last name. But he's a young child. Eight years old, very frail and thin."

"Ahhhh! Noah Maxiel," Mrs. Perkins said, nodding her head. "Yes, he's usually truant."

Olivia wasn't surprised. "I wanted to talk to you about him because I'm concerned that something serious is going on with him. I've seen him in my neighborhood a couple of times and talked with him. I'm fairly certain that there's something bothering him . . . that he's dealing with something much greater than he lets on. I mean, have you noticed anything about him yourself?"

Mrs. Perkins laced her fingers together and looked over her glasses at Olivia sternly. "Noah isn't your son, correct?"

Olivia could feel the pending dismissal in the other woman's tone and stare. "No, he isn't," she responded meekly.

"I'm certain that it is a violation of confidentially for me to discuss one of our students with a complete stranger."

"I'm not a stranger to Noah."

"Mmm-hmm. The same child of whom you didn't even know his last name. Look, uh . . . Ms. Collins, there are over 799 students enrolled here at Lakeview. Nearly 400 of them fall under my caseload, so to speak. It's hard enough for me to keep up with them all and their academic needs, behavioral issues, and personal challenges. I certainly can't be focused on the ones who rarely show up at school to begin with."

Olivia was disheartened. "Yet, you knew exactly who I was referring to. And shouldn't those frequently absent or truant kids be the ones that you are most concerned about?"

Mrs. Perkins cocked her head to the side, and attitude laced her tone. "I do as much as I can for as many of these children as I can. Going above and beyond to muddle around in the lives of young people who aren't enthused or whose parents aren't enthused enough to so much as send them to school isn't necessarily in my job description. There are many kids who have issues outside of the school, but as a school guidance counselor, I can only do so much, and that's only when the child and the family want whatever help I could possibly offer."

"So the child has to come to you and say 'Hey, help me. Something's wrong'? That doesn't seem right. It makes more sense that if you recognize a red flag, you act on it."

"Your input is appreciated but unsolicited. If you have an issue with the way the county has this set up in the schools, I'd suggest that you contact the board of education."

"How much do you even know about your students?" Olivia asked, feeling her blood pressure rise in the wake of the other woman's apparent disdain for her presence and questioning. "I mean, you keep mentioning the child's parents, but are you unaware that Noah's a foster child? Wouldn't that automatically make him one of the kids that you'd pay closer attention to, being as though some real social, behavioral, and maybe even educational problems may have a greater chance of occurring with him?"

"And are you his foster mother?" Mrs. Perkins asked, already knowing the answer to her question.

"No, I'm not."

"So again, I'm not at liberty to discuss Noah with you. Now, if you feel like something's going on within his foster home, you'd be better off contacting DFCS with your accusations or calling the police."

Olivia was now livid. She slid to the edge of her seat and spoke through gritted teeth. "Aren't you a mandatory reporter? I'm coming to *you!* Aren't you obligated to do *something?*"

"I've given you the best possible advice that I have. Now, had I noticed anything about the child, who again is usually truant, then it would be my responsibility to assess whether there is some probable issue."

"So you're telling me you haven't seen the bruises on this child? You haven't noticed how malnourished he appears? The sadness in his eyes?"

"Many of our students come from underprivileged households. They don't always get the nourishment they need, but we are sure to provide our students with breakfast and lunch daily. One would have to be present in order to benefit from that."

Olivia rose from her seat. It was clear that she wasn't going to get any help from this woman. "I am telling you wholeheartedly that my gut knows that something is wrong with Noah. I would think that as a school employee that you'd have some compassion about the children you serve."

Mrs. Perkins now rose from her seat and removed her glasses. "And if you were so concerned and so convicted in your beliefs that something is so out of sorts, why on earth have you waited to come here versus calling the police and doing something about it yourself? I don't really take too kindly to strangers—or anyone—walking into my office and scrutinizing the way I manage my workload. I've seen kids like Noah come and go through these school doors over the years. They're all the same . . . mad at the world because of the hand they've been dealt. I can assure you that if Noah raised his head, buckled down, and came to school prepared to learn and do better, opened himself up to receiving friends . . . he'd have a much better scholastic experience."

"Yeah?" Olivia said, with anger burning within her chest. "And what happens if he's killed while in the care of his foster family . . . this underprivileged household you speak of? What happens then when he's unable to achieve this 'better scholastic experience' you speak of while everyone's busy ignoring the fact that something deeper, something beyond what happens in your school-house, is happening to this child?"

Mrs. Perkins was unmoved. "You don't have to be so dramatic, Ms. Collins."

"I think your nonchalant, uncaring nature is dramatic enough," Olivia shot back, turning to leave the room. "Glad to know that you're putting that master's degree to good use as you help to fail these children." She exited the office without listening to the rebuttal that Mrs. Perkins attempted to throw at her.

"I'm coming down to your job tomorrow," Olivia advised Shanice. They'd met for drinks after work at Dugan's on Flat Shoals Parkway. After the afternoon that Olivia had endured she needed something to help ease her mind. She'd just told Shanice all about her conversation with the guidance counselor at Noah's school. Her frustration was written all over her face and in her body language as she plotted her next move.

Shanice took a sip of her Bahama Mama and raised an eyebrow. "Why? Are you suddenly inspired to get your job back?"

"Hell no. I'm going to visit Noah's case manager on the second floor."

"What? Why?"

"I don't have any other option. Something's going on, and I need to get to the bottom of it. I was really hoping that the guidance counselor would be of some assistance, but that witch only cares about securing her paycheck. Those kids and their well-being don't mean boo to her."

"Is that really a fair assessment to make?" Shanice questioned. "I mean, everyone keeps telling you that this kid is nothing but trouble."

"You don't know him."

"And that seems to be your tagline, but, honey . . . come on. *You* don't know him. For whatever reason, you won't see this situation for what it is. You won't see this kid for what *he* is . . . a bad seed. It's as simple as that."

Olivia shook her head and began to regret her decision of inviting her friend out for drinks. She should have used the time to reflect instead of having to listen to continued negativity. "It's not that simple," she mumbled, her mind clouded with thoughts and memories that were beginning to pull her mood from anger to depression.

"It's not?" Shanice challenged her. "Tell me then, Liv . . . Tell me why you're so wrapped up in this kid despite what you already know, despite what everyone is telling you."

Olivia sighed and tried to shake the feelings that were coming over her. She looked into her friend's eyes with a tender expression. "You love Kylie, don't you?"

Kylie was Shanice's five-year-old daughter, and Olivia knew that she meant the world to her friend. Kylie was Shanice's only child, and if Kylie so much as coughed, Shanice was ready to go to war with the germs that had the audacity to infect her daughter's body.

"No doubt," Shanice answered. "But she's my daughter. She's of me, Liv, and she's not a junior menace to society."

"But what if something was happening to her that you didn't know anything about? What if she didn't feel comfortable telling you or her dad what was happening to her? I mean, it could be something going on at school or someone in the community bothering her . . . even a family member bothering her. What if she was a little older maybe and had a problem that she didn't feel you'd understand, and it was tormenting her to no end, but she had no outlet? You know . . . nowhere to go, no one to turn to."

Shanice fell silent as she contemplated the scenario that Olivia was painting for her.

"What if something was truly affecting your baby emotionally and physically, and the only person who knew was a stranger who just had a gut feeling? Would you not want that person to act on their hunch and have your daughter's best interest at heart? Would you not want them to do something that could potentially change her life? Save her even?" The tears built up in her eyes, and Olivia dropped her head. "The thought of a child dying for help . . . screaming on the inside for help is a hard pill to swallow. Feeling that this . . . This helpless being has no advocate, no one to pull them out of whatever hell they've been forced into and give the security and peace that every kid should have," she went on haltingly, hesitating every few words as she struggled to articulate her emotions without blurting out her complete truth and giving in to the daunting past that still managed to bruise her heart after all this time. "That feeling is heartbreaking, Shanice. It's a smothering feeling, and I can't . . ." she paused to swallow back the lump forming in her throat. "I can't breathe thinking about the possibilities."

Shanice took her friend's hand and squeezed it firmly. She had no idea where these emotions were coming from, but it was clear to her that Olivia was completely emotionally invested in this child.

"I don't want to be that person that feels like something is wrong yet says nothing," Olivia stated, looking up with red eyes and tears spilling over. "I don't want to be the one that waits until something fatal happens to say that I knew it all along." She shook her head, praying that Shanice finally understood where she was coming from and wishing like hell that she could divulge so much more of her truth. "I don't want to be that person that ignores her," she whispered.

Shanice's eyebrow rose yet again. "I thought it was boy," she said confused.

"Huh?"

"It's Noah, right? He's a boy. You said you didn't want to ignore *her*."

Olivia bit her lower lip, shook her head, and reached for her drink. "No, no . . . my bad, yes . . . Noah's a boy. Slip of the tongue." She didn't meet her friend's concerned stare as she gulped down her cocktail. She'd need about two more to get through the night and help bury the hurt that had risen to the surface.

Chapter 7

"So, you call yourself having a boyfriend, huh?" he asked, storming through her partially closed bedroom door with red blazing in his eyes and venom dripping from his tone.

Her heart thudded through her thin chest plate, and her mind was in a whirlwind as she tried to figure out how the hell he'd gotten that information. She'd been careful to erase Bones's home number from the call log on the phone each time that he called her or she called him. She made certain that he only called her during the three hours she was generally home alone after school before her parents returned from work. She'd never told anyone about him aside from Carmen, and she knew that her sister and best friend would never betray her trust. Still, somehow, he was privy to her secret, and she had no defense to get out of whatever punishment he was about to undoubtedly issue out to her.

He crossed the short distance of the floor over to where she stood next to her bed folding towels and pushed her with great force against her right temple. The push was so mighty that it caused Kennedy to stagger backward and fall back onto the bed. She remained silent. Nothing she could say would get her out of this so silence was probably her best course of action.

"Who the fuck is the nigga?" her father demanded. "Who is the nigga that you were down the street kissing?"

Her eyes grew wide. Did he have spies all over the neighborhood or something? Bones, her sixteen-year-old boyfriend who lived in another county, had met her at her bus stop for the chance to get a hug and kiss after several weeks of nothing but phone conversations. She'd been adamant that he couldn't walk her all the way to her house for fear that her neighbors would see and mention the occurrence to her father at some point. Nonetheless, it was apparent that someone had witnessed her moment of intimacy anyway. Now, here she was less than thirty minutes after coming in the house and being scolded about her actions. The rumor mill had outdone itself by relaying the message of her antics to her father.

"Who the fuck is he?" he asked her again.

"N-n-body," she said weakly for lack of anything better to whimper.

"Nobody!" he repeated angrily before reaching out and backslapping her across the face.

The ring that he wore assaulted her lip, and she felt the sting the moment her lip split just before the blood began to trickle into her open mouth as she cried out in shock and pain. Fear rippled through her body, unsure of what he was about to do next or the extremity of whatever that next move would be.

"You wanna go around being a whore?" he asked her. "You wanna be the neighborhood skank?"

He shoved her down onto the queen-sized bed and pinned her to the mattress with his large frame towering over her thin body. She just knew that this was it. This was the moment when his devilish acts would be escalated to the highest level of degradation. There would be no turning back, and she knew with all certainty and every fiber of her being that she would surely kill herself the moment it was over and he was far away from her. No way would she be able to live the rest of her life with that devastating of a memory burning a hole in her head and in her heart. It could never happen. Her flesh needed to die because the moment her greatest fear became a reality, then her spirit-man would cease to exist anyway.

He held her arms down with his strong, calloused hands and sneered at her. "Did you fuck him? You little whore. Did you fuck him? Is that why your hair's all messed up?"

She shook her head no repeatedly. "I didn't do anything!" she cried out. "I didn't, I swear!"

"Liar! You're a liar and a whore, and no man's ever going to want you. Nobody wants a stupid, lying whore for a wife. Nobody's gon' love something like you. You're nothing, and you can't do shit right."

Kennedy could feel his hot breath on her face as he talked down to her with his eyes piercing through her troubled, frazzled soul. She turned her head to the side and felt the tears she'd been crying run quickly into her ear. Her eyes peered over to the open door where her niece, Jariah, Carmen's daughter, stood in the doorway witnessing a scene she was too young to understand. Kennedy wanted to scream out for the child to go get help or at the very least run away so that she wouldn't have to see whatever vile act her father was about to engage in.

"You're nothing like Carmen," he told her vehemently, gyrating against her disgustingly. "Carmen's gonna get married someday. She knows how to take care of a man. She can cook, she's smart, she's pretty, and she knows what to do . . ." His voice trailed off as if he was considering what he'd just said. "She knows what to do," he repeated.

She figured if she just lay there still and quiet it would be quick and he'd be off of her before she knew it. But the seconds felt like eternity as her body became numb under the weight of his body. He shifted his weight, removed his right hand from her arm, and reached down to touch her shirt as if to slip his hand underneath the fabric. Her plea for God to help her was muffled inside of her own head, and she wondered if the Savior could still hear it, if he really knew her heart.

As she felt his hand touch her bare skin, the sound of a door closing just outside of her window reached both of their ears. He hesitated and jerked his head in the direction of the sound. Milliseconds later, the chime attached to the front door sounded, and he quickly abandoned his position on top of her. In a few swift movements, he left the room and disappeared to the back of the house, nearly knocking Jariah over.

Kennedy closed her eyes and exhaled. Maybe God had just spared her in the form of her stepmother coming home from work a little earlier than usual. While that was fine for now, the truth was that she was sure the dreaded day would come when he would finally violate her in the worst way ever.

A knock sounded upon her open door and her stepmother stared at her quizzically. "You up here lying down like you're on vacation or something? Take the trash out. I know you saw it overflowing."

Kennedy rose from the bed, adjusted her clothing, and ran her hand across her mouth. How her stepmom had managed to miss the red dripping from her lips was beyond her, but Kennedy lowered her head and walked out of the room to complete her chore as if nothing happened. Her stepmother joined her father in his studio/den, and she was sure that he was giving her his version of what had transpired, completely leaving out the fact that he was just a fraction of a second away from raping her before his wife walked through the door. Kennedy pulled the trash nearly blinded by her tears. She mindlessly walked through the kitchen, into the living room, and out the front door to walk around the house and dispose of the garbage. She was unaware of her staggering gait as she slowly made her way back to the front of the house.

"Hey! Hey!"

Someone was calling out to her, but Kennedy was in such a trance that she didn't even hear them.

"Hey, young lady! What's going on there?"

Finally she stopped and turned to see Man Brown standing at the fence that encased his land and faced the front of her family's home. His huge smile was inviting.

"Come on over here," he encouraged, waving her over.

Kennedy wiped the tears from her eyes and crossed the street to approach the gate to see what her friendly neighbor wanted. She was really in no mood for one of his jokes and hoped that he only wanted her to relay a message to her father, which she didn't really want to do.

"What's going on, young lady?" Man Brown asked as he took in her appearance.

She shook her head. "Nothing much," she replied solemnly.

"Yeah? You look troubled. Something happen?"

She looked up into his eyes and wondered if maybe she could trust him. He seemed like a responsible enough adult, but would he believe her? Would he care enough to get her far, far away from the man who was putting her through hell?

"You walking around with your head down like you got the weight of the world on your shoulders," he commented. "You have to walk with your head up . . . with

some pride and not all slouched over like you're beat up by the world." He squinted his eyes and took a good look at her. "What happened to your face, child?"

"I had an accident," she lied, looking down once more. "Nothing major. I'm okay."

"Hmmm." He pondered over her statement. "Well, you go wash your face and hold your head up. Whatever it is, I'm sure you can tell your father, and he'll tell you . . . No man wants to see a woman looking frail and defeated."

At the mention of her father and Man Brown's belief that he actually would give a damn enough about her to give her solid advice, Kennedy knew that she couldn't confide in this man. He was her father's friend. He would never believe her allegations because he was too busy thinking the world of the man of whom they were against.

Kennedy sighed. "I'll see ya," she told the old neighbor before turning away from the fence and crossing the street once more.

Slowly she entered the house and went into the kitchen to ransack the little tray that her stepmother kept the medicines in on the top of the refrigerator. Her hands shook as she searched through random bottles trying to figure out which prescription or over-the-counter drug would take her where she needed to go. Settling upon a bottle of painkillers, Kennedy emptied the bottle into her hand, poured a glass of lemonade, and downed the medicine quickly. She wondered how long it would be before the drugs would knock her out, whether temporarily or, preferably, permanently.

She staggered to her room and dropped to the floor, ready to cry into the carpet about the unfairness of her life. But the shuffling of feet in the hallway let her know that trouble was coming. Her parents appeared in the doorway and began to berate her about frolick-

ing around the neighborhood with someone they were calling a "strange boy." Their voices began to sound monotone and blended as Kennedy felt her body becoming woozy and her stomach felt heavy. She wanted to puke but felt too physically exhausted to do so. Fearing that she'd vomit all over herself if she continued to try to sit upright, she lowered her body into a lying position on her back against the plush carpet. Something about punishment and stupidity resonated with her during the long speech her parents were giving her. Soon, they were all talked out, feeling that they'd berated her enough and damned her to months of being grounded that would certainly prove the point that they would not tolerate her "fastness."

The moment their figures vacated the threshold of her room, Kennedy gripped her stomach with both hands and closed her eyes. Her body was in agony. She felt sick, worse than she had felt emotionally just before taking the pills. She tried to block out the feeling and prayed silently that God would go-ahead and kill her right now. Death was coming. It had to. Anything was better than the life she was enduring now. She continued to lie perfectly still as day turned to night and no one bothered to check on her. She wondered how long it would take before her last breath was released and how long her family would allow her to lie there moments away from being extinct. She wondered if she'd taken enough and if what she was experiencing was normal during an overdose suicide. Still, she was ready to be done with it all. She was ready to end the miserable life she'd been duped with and hoped like hell that God would forgive her of her sins and mercifully allow her entry into his kingdom.

***

The ride to the second floor seemed to take forever and did not prepare Olivia for the fifteen-minute wait at the window to get someone to acknowledge her presence. When she'd finally been addressed and asked to speak with Vanisha Hardy she was advised to sit in the waiting room, which took another twenty minutes of her life. It was quiet as an abandoned building, and Olivia was starting to wonder if anyone was truly at work in the government building despite all of the cars parked in the gated employee parking lot. She needed to be home writing, but this was an important matter so she was willing to sit there all day if the situation called for it, but prayed that the delay wouldn't be that extreme.

Just as she glanced down to check the time on her cell, the brown door behind her opened and the familiar face of the case manager she'd run into at McDonald's looked back at her. Olivia saw slight recognition flicker in the woman's eyes as she stood and approached the open door.

"You're here to see Ms. Hardy?" the case manager asked.

Olivia nodded. "Yes. I'm Olivia Collins . . . we met a few days back . . . at McDonald's . . . You were with Noah . . . uh . . . Noah Maxiel."

The woman nodded, and her body language relaxed noticeably. "Ahhhh, yes. Noah. What is it that I can do for you, Ms. Collins? What has our little friend been up to now?"

Olivia's brows knitted, dismayed that the woman would automatically assume that she was coming down to complain about something the child had done. Was he really that mischievous? "Ummm, are we able to speak in private?"

"Sure, come on back." Ms. Hardy led the way through the maze of cubicles, mostly empty, and rounded the corner to get to the last one on the left. She pointed to a chair situated in the corner of the cubicle as she turned her swivel chair around and faced Olivia. "Please, have a seat."

Olivia grimaced at the tight space but sat down on the chair offered to her.

"So, tell me what's going on. Typically, if one of our foster children has done something in the community that is criminal we'd suggest that you contact the authorities directly, but—"

Olivia held up her hand and shook her head. "No, no. It's nothing like that at all. I'm not here to complain about Noah."

Ms. Hardy looked confused. "Okay, then I don't understand. What's going on?"

"That's just it. I'm not really sure what's going on, but I have the feeling that Noah's being abused in some kind of way. I mean, I've noticed bruising and bleeding . . . did you not notice his eye the other day? When I talk to him, I get the impression that he's uncomfortable where he lives."

Ms. Hardy shifted in her chair, and her movement caused Olivia to stop talking. "You stated that you aren't sure if something's happening or not."

"Right. I can only go by what I see, you know, how he looks, and, of course, the feeling that I get when I speak to him."

"We have a hotline that you can call whenever you suspect that something may be happening to a child or that they are in some sort of danger. Are you aware of that hotline?"

Olivia shook her head. "No, I'm not. But I figured since you're his case manager that I could discuss it with you. I mean, who would know better what type of environment Noah's in other than you, right?"

"The truth of the matter is that children get bumps, scrapes, and bruises all the time, Ms. Collins. We can't always go screaming or assuming that the child's being abused because he ends up with some kind of boo-boo."

The woman's condescending tone wasn't well received by Olivia. She was beginning to lose her patience with these social service providers and the way they seemed to be dismissing her concerns. "I'm sorry . . . Please correct me if I'm wrong, but aren't you Noah's case manager? Like, aren't you supposed to be concerned about him, boo-boos and all? I mean, my assumptions could be nothing, true, but I'm very certain that they're a whole lot of something. Isn't your job to make sure that the children on your caseload are all well taken care of?"

Ms. Hardy waved her arm in the direction of her filing cabinet in which all of the doors were opened to reveal the many brown file folders tightly squeezed together. "*This* is my caseload. Over eighty children in DeKalb County are assigned to me. That's over eighty families that I have to pay visits to monthly. I'm doing my absolute best to keep up, but the truth is, there really isn't enough time for me to keep a close eye on each and every one of them."

"Then why the opposition to me coming in here and telling you that you should probably pay a little more attention to this particular child?"

"Look, I've interviewed Noah's foster mother, and I've visited the residence. I didn't get any vibes that foul play was occurring in the environment and with that being true, he's considered to be safe."

"Safe? Did you or did you not see the bruising of the child's eye?" Olivia asked again.

"Typical child type of incident. He got into a scuffle at school."

Olivia nodded. It was likely, but there was far more to her gut feeling than just the bruise on Noah's face. "And his weight? His demeanor? Hell, his school truancy?"

"And how would you know anything about his atten-dance record?"

"I think the real question is, how would you *not?*"

"*Excuse* me?"

"You said you've visited the home and talked to the foster parent, but have you ever actually *spoken* to Noah? Do you ask him how he feels about his home? School? The neighborhood? You ever just ask him what he's feeling, period?"

"The child is always the intricate part of the foster care process. I mean, it's all about the well-being of the child and—"

"The well-being of the child, huh?" Olivia mimicked, sensing the bullshit that the case manager was handing her. "What about doctor's visits? When was the last time the child was seen by a physician? I mean, an actual full-body exam?"

Ms. Hardy began to stutter. "I . . . I . . . I am not sure but—"

"You're *not sure?* But his well-being is being well assured, huh? And whenever he did last go, did you happen to see a report? Was there anything suspicious reported to you about the child's body?"

"With over eighty children that I have to keep tabs on, I can't always look at every single report that crosses my desk or keep up with every single appointment these children have. It's simply impossible."

"Then it's quite possible that he isn't even being taken to his appointments, assuming that any have been made for him like ever, and even more possible that something has been wrong with the child that's been overlooked because everyone's too busy to pay attention."

Ms. Hardy rose from her seat, a sure sign that Olivia had pressed a nerve. "I think this conversation is over,

Ms. Collins. I'm not at liberty to discuss any of the children we have in custody with someone who is not a guardian, parent, or court-appointed advocate."

Olivia heard the statement but failed to address it. "Have you *looked* at him? I mean, *really* looked at him? Do you see how frail that child is? It's as if he hasn't eaten in forever and you want to tell me that this is what *normal* and *safe* looks like to you?"

Ms. Hardy took a deep breath as her nostrils flared with annoyance. It was bad enough that she had her supervisor and the program administrators breathing down her back about the management of her caseload, but to have this random woman off of the street to waltz in and try to tell her how to do her job was just too much. Foster care workers simply didn't get paid enough to be berated by their bosses due to not being able to make robot-type miracles happen and forced to work with ridiculously large caseloads due to the state's inability to hire more bodies, only to have some citizen walk in and point the finger of blame as if the workers weren't doing all they humanly could. "Again, I am not at liberty to discuss Noah or any other child in custody with you unless you're a guardian, parent, or court-appointed child advocate of which you are neither, correct?"

"Oh, you wanna go by protocol now?" Olivia challenged, standing up.

Ms. Hardy took a step back. "Please leave now. I don't think we have anything further to discuss."

"Now you wanna try to do your job and stick to the rules, huh?" Olivia was heated. "You wanna put some of that energy toward at least checking into my story? Show me how I can make a complaint or whatever since you obviously don't give a damn personally."

Ms. Hardy reached over to pick up the receiver of her office phone. Quickly, she pressed a series of buttons and waited only a second for someone to pick up as Olivia continued to rant in front of her. "Security, can you please come up to the second floor for me? Cubicle 33. Hurry." She hung up the phone and eyed the seemingly crazed woman in front of her.

". . . incompetent employees," Olivia was going on. "I mean, how hard is it for you to simply pay attention to a child? You can look at that boy and tell that something's wrong." She looked at the certificates push-pinned to the fabric of the cubicle walls and rolled her eyes. "You got your cute little degree in social work, but what happened? They didn't make you take a course on sensitivity? Common sense? Gut instincts? Humanity, damn it!" Her hands were shaking as her voice rose octave after octave, emotion getting the best of her and drawing her completely out of character. Olivia could practically feel the veins popping out of her neck as she continued to give the case manager a piece of her mind. "That's why y'all's asses stay in the news, because you never wanna do shit until it's too late! If you don't care about the children, why the hell did you take this job?"

A firm hand gripped her shoulder causing Olivia to snap her neck around quickly. Looking up, her eyes fell upon the stern face of a tall, chocolate security officer whose expression said that he wasn't in the mood. Olivia didn't care. He could have all the muscles and intimidating facial expressions in the world, but it wouldn't change how passionately pissed she was at that moment. She jerked her arm away from his tight hold and stared at the woman who cowered in the corner in front of her.

"I want to see your supervisor," Olivia demanded. "If you won't listen, maybe she will."

"This building has a zero tolerance policy," the security officer stated.

Olivia ignored him. "Your supervisor! Can you at least give me her card, name, and number—something?"

"*He* is in a meeting out of the building," Ms. Hardy advised.

Olivia was almost certain that the woman was lying in an effort to expediently get rid of her. "Then give me his information, or is that too taxing for you?" she snapped.

"That's it," the security guard said in his broken English. "Out you go." Once again, he placed his hands on her shoulders and tried to move her out of the cubicle.

"So *this* is how you do concerned citizens?" Olivia questioned as she was practically pushed through the office space and out into the waiting room. "*This* is the response I get for trying to help someone? You don't even wanna hear why the hell I'm so angry? Just gonna toss my ass out on the street, huh?"

"I'm taking you to the door, and you'll find your own way to the street," the guard replied as he led her to the elevator. "Keep acting up and I'll call DeKalb County to come take you on a ride."

Olivia was astonished by the way the man was treating her, as if she were some petty criminal. Here she was doing a noble thing, or trying to anyway, and he was behaving as if she was showing her ass for the sport of it. She couldn't help but to laugh at the ass backward way that this situation was playing out. She'd come for help for Noah and was being escorted out of the building as if she was some troublemaker. Immediately she was reminded of the way the case manager had automatically assumed that Noah had been up to no good. *Damn,* she thought, *do they feel that everyone is a bad seed up in here?* She couldn't understand the resistance and hostility she was witnessing within a government building designed to provide services to help rebuild individuals and families. It was all a bunch of bullshit if you asked her.

"This is wrong," she told the guard as they rode down to the first floor. "The way y'all are treating me, the way that woman wouldn't listen to me, and the shady shit I feel happens here with regards to these children being messed over. It's wrong."

"Mmm-hmm, just like your behavior," the officer countered as the doors of the elevator released them from their temporary confinement.

Olivia exited first. "You can say whatever you want to about me, mister, but you don't know me from a can of paint. But let me assure you of one thing," she said, pointing her index finger at him as he stood firmly in the center of the now crowded hallway. "You have to be careful who you mess over because neither you nor her have any idea who *I* am, and that's okay because I'm damn sure going to show you. That's right, I'm about to put some calls in to the governor's office . . . When I'm done making waves and lighting a fire under those heavy hitters' asses, I'm going to make sure that you and that incompetent, disrespectful, lazy, paper-pushing fraud of a case manager find ya'selves standing in somebody's unemployment line."

The officer stood with his arms crossed, completely unfazed, and said nothing as Olivia turned away and marched down the hall toward the exit. Other citizens visiting the building witnessed the exchange and watched in shock as she tore through the lobby and pushed through the two sets of glass doors. Her exit was dramatic and noteworthy, especially to the building maintenance supervisor who sat in her office surveying the scene on the monitor resting in her office. The pot had definitely been stirred up.

Chapter 8

"So I just call them and sign up for the next training session?" Olivia asked, cradling the phone with her shoulder to hold it to her ear as she typed a Web address into her browser's search box.

"Yes. I'm pretty sure there's a fee of some sort associated with it, but I'm not sure how much. That's something that you can either find out on the Web site or from them directly," explained Attorney Daysha Mullen.

Daysha was a family law attorney who'd owned her own practice for close to four years. When Olivia was a student in college she'd worked part time at the law firm in Decatur where Daysha was merely a junior partner trying to make her way up the legal ladder. She'd also been Olivia's direct supervisor. During the one year that they worked closely together, Olivia became very fond of Daysha and began to look to her as a mentor and friend versus simply being her boss. Even after she left the law firm to work at the DFCS office, Olivia made it a point to reach out to her old boss from time to time. Knowing someone in family law was especially helpful now that she had a serious concern.

"Okay, I'm at the Web site," Olivia stated, her eyes scrolling down the page. She clicked on the volunteer link to get a look at the break down to the process for becoming a court-appointed special advocate as she'd learned the term to be officially. "Hmmm, this course is time-consuming. Ten weeks' worth of training . . . I'm not sure if I have that kind of time."

"It's not exactly something you can rush right into, Livi," Daysha stated. "They have to make sure you are aware of all laws, guidelines, and do a background check on you because they're not letting just anyone work with these kids."

"But, I'm just trying to help this one kid."

There was a slight pause on the other end. "Why don't you tell me what's really going on? I thought it was kind of out of the blue that you'd call me up and ask about becoming a CASA. I didn't even know that you liked children."

"Just because I don't have any of my own doesn't mean that I don't like them."

"Granted, but again, why don't you just tell me what's going on?"

"There's a kid I know . . . kinda know. He's in some kind of trouble. I mean, I think he is . . . and no one is paying attention to him or listening to me when I try to voice my concerns. It's as if the whole world has already written this child off as an insignificant lost cause, and he's only eight. They aren't the least bit concerned about his welfare, the people that are supposed to be concerned, I mean. He's just another item on their to-do list, another file in their caseload." Olivia stopped talking the moment the words came out of her mouth. She could almost see and hear Noah as he sat on her porch and explained to her how he was just a number. She understood now, and the realization of the accuracy of the young boy's statement broke her already fragile heart. "He needs me," she whispered, returning her attention to the screen and scrolling farther down to see when the next orientation would be, praying that in ten weeks it wouldn't be too late to rescue Noah.

"This kid that you kinda know, whom you think might be in trouble . . . have you talked to his parents? Have you contacted the police if you suspect something has been done to him since you say DFCS isn't helping?"

"No, I'm leery about contacting the police, and I don't know his parents. I mean, he's in foster care, and I—"

"How do you know this kid?"

"I met him by accident, and I'm telling you, Daysha, my gut instinct is telling me that something is seriously wrong with this child. I know it."

"Hmmm . . . You sound really passionate about this."

So used to everyone blowing off her concerns, it nearly stunned Olivia to hear someone sound as if maybe they weren't thinking she was crazy. "I am, Daysha. I really am."

"Okay, so here's what I'll do. I'll call over to magistrate and speak to Judge Amos to see if we can get you a temporary assignment as this kid's advocate."

Olivia's heart stopped, and her eyes teared up. "Thank you," she said in nearly a whisper.

"But hear me out. I'm about to step out on a limb for you here, so I need you to be sure to have all of your information together and correct. No hunches, Livi. You need to have something solid. Tell me what it is that you want to do . . . What are you trying to do with or for this child?"

Before she answered the question she could hear the front door open and close. She knew that it was Kasyn and didn't bother to stop her conversation. "I think he needs to be removed from the foster care home that he's in and switched to a different case manager."

"Because? I need full disclosure, Livi."

Kasyn approached the room that Olivia used as her office and perched against the door frame with his arms crossed. Olivia glanced over at him and quickly returned her attention to the conversation at hand as she mini- mized the screens on her computer. "Uh . . . because I believe, I mean, I'm pretty sure that he's being neglected and abused."

"And what exactly gives you that impression?"

"His mannerisms, his appearance, and I don't think he's had a physical in God knows how long. I mean, if he had, I'm sure a physician would have notified the case manager about suspicions, and to my knowledge, nothing of the sort has happened."

"And you know that because?"

"I talked to the case manager."

Kasyn's eyebrow rose and his nostrils began to flare as he continued to listen to his fiancée confess her secrets to whomever she was on the phone with.

"And the caseworker said what?" Daysha asked.

"She practically admitted that she didn't have time to keep up with his appointments and that she hasn't received anything from a doctor stating that anything is or has been wrong with Noah."

"So then, what concrete thing makes you believe that the caseworker is wrong about the child's well-being, Livi?"

"I saw blood, Daysha." Olivia could feel Kasyn's eyes piercing into her flesh as he stared at her in disbelief. She purposely didn't look in his direction because she wasn't ready to deal with his scrutiny or contempt for her continued involvement in Noah's life. "He used my bathroom one day, and when he left, there was blood on the floor. He wasn't bleeding anywhere that was plainly noticeable so the only thing that I could reasonably fathom was—"

"I get it, I get it," Daysha said, cutting her off. "Let me place a call and see what I can do. For the child's sake, I hope that what you're doing helps him if your allegations turn out to be true."

"Thank you, Daysha," Olivia said earnestly into the phone. "You have no idea how much this means to me."

"Just be ready to prove your claims. You're going to have to dig deep on this, Livi, since it seems like you clearly will have no support from his case manager."

"I know. I can handle it. Let me know what happens, and thanks again."

"No problem. In the meantime, though, go-ahead and register for the CASA training just in case this option doesn't pan out for us."

Olivia nodded. "Will do. Talk to you soon." She pressed the END button on her cordless phone and set it on the desk before pulling up the CASA screen once more and beginning the online registration process. Still, she said nothing to Kasyn and partially wished that he would just disappear from the room and leave her to handle her business.

"So you're just not going to acknowledge the fact that you stood me up for our dinner date at Ru San's or the fact that despite my continued advice against it, you're still meddling around in this kid's life trying to make something be what it isn't?" Kasyn snapped.

Olivia remained silent as her fingers tapped away at the keys.

"Oh, you're deaf and mute now, huh?" Kasyn taunted her. "You're so busy, so engrossed in this baby thug that you can't get your fingers to move that fast to finish your goddamn manuscript. You can't focus on real shit, important shit, like your work, your fiancé, your own damn life."

It stung that he'd hit so below the belt, but Olivia knew she had to stay focused. She was tired of arguing with him about something that he didn't understand. Kasyn had it fixed in his mind that he knew exactly who and what Noah was, and he wasn't trying to hear or admit to the fact that he could quite possibly be wrong. He was right about her needing to finish her book, though, but how could she focus on that when a child's life was possibly hanging in the balance? She couldn't; her conscience wouldn't let her do it. She had a social and moral responsibility to Noah, and despite how her fiancé felt about it, she wouldn't feel right if she abandoned the child now.

"Really, Livi? You're gonna ignore me?" Kasyn was steaming. "That's where we are with this? You're going to sit there and ignore me as if I'm not even here?" He waited a few seconds before walking over to her and staring at her as she continued to peck away at the keyboard.

Olivia didn't flinch or look in his direction. *Go away,* she prayed silently. *Just go away and let me do this.* She was nearly done with the registration form and was trying with all of her might to concentrate despite the fact that he was practically breathing down her neck at this point.

"Olivia," he stated, trying his best to be patient. "We've already missed dinner *again* . . . Are you going to let the night carry on like *this?*"

She said nothing.

"Olivia," he called her name again. "Livi!" Completely frustrated with her lack of attention and communication, he walked around her desk and yanked the power cord out of the power strip, causing her screen to instantly go black before she could hit the send button.

"Kasyn!" she screamed out, livid that he would result to such childish measures as a way of getting attention. "I was working on something important."

"It wasn't your book, so I think you'll be fine," he responded.

"I can't believe you right now."

"You can't believe me?" he fumed. "You can't believe *me?*" He looked at her in disbelief as he tossed the cord of her computer to the floor. "*You're* the one abandoning your own life for the sake of this . . . this kid. Running around town harassing people."

"Harassing people? You have no idea what you're talking about."

"Do *you,* Livi? Do you? You're grasping at straws trying to make something be something that it isn't . . . trying to implant yourself in this child's life like you're destined to be his hero or something. You're saving him, Livi? Saving him from *what?* The lifestyle that he was thrown into and the decisions that he's made for himself? You can't save someone that doesn't want to be saved."

Olivia rose from her seat and gritted her teeth as she met Kasyn's angry stare. "You have no idea what the hell you're talking about! I haven't harassed anyone! I am trying to help this child who's experiencing something you'd never understand."

"Oh, and *you* do?"

"Yes, I do damn it, and I don't care what you say, I'm not going let you force me into silence. Maybe you don't care, but *I* do!"

"Why do you care so much about this damn kid? Is it because you want to have a kid of your own?" he asked. "Hell, if that's the case, then you should spend more time with your fiancé . . . maybe feed me every once in a while, and then fuck me a time or two, and maybe you'd end up with a kid of *your own* to be concerned with."

"That's some crass shit to say!"

"But it's some real shit, Livi! Damn it! I'm tired of this."

"And you think I'm not? What I'm doing here matters to me. I need you to respect that. And trust, the last thing on my mind is getting knocked up with your kid for you to turn into a crybaby about me caring more about the child than tending to your needs!"

Kasyn was speechless. "I drive a long way constantly to be with you, Livi, and you're telling me that whatever is going on with this kid is more important to you than spending quality time with me? That you're not going to stop what you're doing to refocus yourself?"

"I am focused," she seethed in reply, "on what's more important."

He nodded his understanding and walked past her to exit the room. As far as he was concerned the conversation was over. Olivia watched his retreating figure and bit her bottom lip. She hadn't meant to be so harsh, but he'd thrown a couple of hard-hitting punches himself, and she knew there was no way that either of them could come back from some of the things that had been said. Still, she had an obligation to Noah, and her spirit wouldn't rest until she knew that he was okay.

The Brillo pad was crumbling in his hands from the continued usage, but Noah knew that he had to keep scrubbing until he'd gotten the skillet completely clean. He couldn't replace the pad because there were no more. The household was running out of stuff again, and just as usual, Ms. Mae hadn't been to the store. There was very little food in the refrigerator, most of which Mikey had staked claim upon. Ms. Mae was working around the clock, and Noah hadn't seen her for the past two days. Because he was avoiding his peers, he hadn't been to school in just as many days, resulting in missing both breakfast and lunch each day. He'd been living off of dry cereal since there was no milk in the refrigerator. Now, all of the cereal was gone, and his stomach wasn't shy about loudly reminding him that he was hungry.

As he resorted to scratching at the debris in the pan with his ragged nails, Noah tried to ignore Mikey who'd just walked into the kitchen to toss his empty plate into the sink.

"Make sure you wash this too."

Noah nodded trying not to say anything that would rub Mikey the wrong way. His eyes fell upon the remainder of the steak that was resting on a plate on the stove covered with onions and the small bit of instant mashed potatoes still resting in the pot next to the steak which Noah had yet to try to clean.

"Mikey," he called out nervously.

"Whadda you want?" Mikey asked as he tossed his head back as he took a swig from his can of Bud Ice.

"Can I have the leftovers?" Noah looked at his foster brother with eyes of fright, not knowing how this request would resonate with him.

Mikey lowered the can and a sneer curled his lips. "You want what's left of my food?"

Noah nodded his head as he held the skillet in one hand and the worn-out Brillo pad in the other, shaking with nervousness.

Mikey chuckled. "You know better than to be asking me for shit, you li'l fag. That shit's mine. I don't care if it was a whole steak or just two crumbs. That shit's mine. It's some eggs and shit in there. Make yourself something else and stop sniffing 'round my shit, li'l nigga."

Noah swallowed back his disappointment. Mikey was right. He could make himself some eggs, but he feared that the moment he touched the last three eggs Mikey would have a fit since he wouldn't have any left for his breakfast in the morning. Noah wasn't sure if Mikey was trying to set him up to beat him later, but he knew he had to eat something, so eggs it would be.

"Fuck you be thinking about?" Mikey shot at him. "You'd think yo' ass would know by now not to fuck with me. Maybe you need something to straighten yo' ass out since you acting like you stupid and shit." He mushed Noah, causing the boy to sidestep. "Li'l pussy ass. Bet yo' ass would die out on the streets by ya'self. Betta be glad I let yo' ass stay around here. Quit asking for my shit and be grateful for what you got."

Was he serious? Noah wasn't sure what he was supposed to be grateful for exactly. Was it the act of sodomy, being beaten for so much as breathing, or the emptiness he felt continuously in his stomach? Still, he remained silent. He knew better than to offer any kind of rebuttal. Eventually, Mikey would grow tired of messing with him and just walk away.

"Punk ass," Mikey spat out. "What the fuck you got on?" He eyed Noah's dingy, ripped jeans and the oversized T-shirt that slightly hung over his left shoulder. "Going around looking like some li'l reject. Ain't nobody ever teach you how to look like something, nigga?"

No, Noah thought. *All you ever taught me was how to be quiet so I don't get beat and to stay awake at night just in case you try to hurt me.* Noah refused to look up at Mikey as he continued to spew disparaging statements his way. He was determined not to cry, which was a hard task. Mikey's words stung, but his verbal lashings were nothing compared to the physical blows he liked to cover Noah with. Biting down hard on his bottom lip, Noah did his best to keep it together.

"Don't make no sense, man," Mikey stated. "Ya' li'l bitch ass." He took another swig from his beer can and glanced over into the dirty dishwater as Noah continued to scratch and scrub at the skillet. "Better get that shit clean too, else I'ma whoop yo' ass. Taking you too damn long. That shit ain't rocket science."

There was a knock at the front door, and Mikey immediately abandoned his position. "Hurry the fuck up and get the hell on," he ordered over his shoulder. "Don't come through here fucking with me."

Noah understood what that meant. Whoever was at the door was Mikey's company, and he didn't want Noah anywhere near them. He needn't worry because Noah had no desire to be around Mikey or his shady-looking friends. All they did was drink, smoke weed, make fun of Noah, and talk about girls, yet Noah had yet to see any of them with a female.

From the kitchen he could hear Mikey and his homeboys laughing it up in the living room. After what seemed like forever, finally he was finished cleaning the skillet and the rest of the kitchen. He'd carefully placed the remainder of Mikey's steak in a container with the few scoops of potatoes that were left. He had half the mind to scarf it all down and suffer the consequences later, but after mulling over the possibilities of the consequence that Mikey might rely upon, Noah decided it was much safer to leave his foster brother's food untouched. Instead, he boiled one of the eggs, and after six minutes, he peeled it, dressed it with salt and pepper, and devoured it as if it was a top-of-the-line delicacy. Afterward, he cleaned his own mess and sauntered through the living room with the intention of being unseen as he made his way to his room for the evening.

As he glided behind the sofa to head up the hall, his eyes caught an image on the screen that Mikey and his two buddies were fixated on. A woman was kneeled down between some guy's legs as he stood in a bathroom stall. His penis was in her mouth, and she was bobbing her head up and down and making noises as if she was really enjoying his private part being lodged down her throat. There was something oddly grotesque yet intriguing about the entire scene to Noah. He watched as the woman's breasts bounced up and down with her movements.

"Hell yeah!" Benji, Mikey's homeboy sitting to his left, called out. "That bitch deep throating that thang like a pro."

"She ain't got shit on Superhead, though," Marcus, Mikey's other friend to his right, commented. "That bitch can take two at one time."

"Shut up," Mikey jumped in. "Ain't nobody mouth that wide that they can take two like that."

"Shittttt," Marcus replied. "I'm telling you, bruh. I saw that shit with my own eyes on some video, nigga. Look it up on YouTube or some shit. No lie."

Their eyes never left the video they were watching as the trio bantered about the art of giving head.

"Aye, that bitch Ashley down the street got some fye head, man," Benji stated. "Talkin' 'bout she be sucking a nigga's balls and everything. And she'll let you hit too."

"You ain't hit that," Mikey fired back.

"You'on know what I be doing," Benji said defensively. "Man, I done hit that twice this month alone."

"Yeah, right," Marcus commented. "In your dreams." He and Mikey laughed at their buddy.

"Aye, y'all niggas laughing, but I'on see y'all getting no pussy 'round this bitch. Stop hating," Benji told them. "Y'all just mad 'cause ole girl servin' me up and not y'all."

The woman on the television screen was now making exaggerated faces as if she was enjoying what she was doing more than anything in the world. Her eyes rolled in the back of her head, and her moans became longer and louder. The man she was servicing had to reach out and balance himself against the wall of the stall as he stared down at the woman and forced her head down with his free hand. The veins in his pale, bald head were bulging, and he looked as if he was about to literally explode as he moaned almost as loudly as the woman between his legs.

Noah didn't even realize that he'd stopped walking to stare at the images on the screen. The others had paid him no attention as he stood behind them gawking at the totally inappropriate movie they were watching. It wasn't until he involuntarily sniffled that the others realized he was in the room, and he took notice of the fact that he'd defied his own mission to hurriedly make it to his room.

"The hell are you doing?" Mikey asked, glaring at Noah. Though the remote was in his hand, he failed to pause or turn off the DVD despite the fact that he'd come to know Noah, a minor child, was watching it.

"I-I-I—"

"Stuttering-ass li'l nigga," Marcus commented. "Get yo' ass on to the back!"

Noah was glad to be dismissed without consequence and started to bolt from the room. But before he could disappear up the hall, Mikey rose from his spot on the sofa and hollered for him.

"Nah, bring ya' ass back here!" Mikey demanded.

Noah closed his eyes and briefly considered his options. He could try to lock himself in his bedroom and hide, try to run past the trio and out of the house to avoid whatever humiliation was coming his way, or simply suck it up and reenter the living room to endure whatever Mikey had in mind. He knew that he'd never get past all of them and figured that Mikey would just beat the door down if he tried to lock himself away. With no other recourse, Noah slowly returned to the living room and stood behind the sofa, looking up at Mikey.

"You like being a nosy li'l fuck," Mikey commented. He looked over at the television screen where the female was now licking the head of the man's dick. "What you know about this shit, youngster?"

"He probably know 'bout as much as you do," Benji joked. "Since neither one of y'all getting no ass."

Mikey shot his friend an angry glance but ignored his statement. "Get ya' ass 'round here," he told Noah before returning to his seated position.

Nervously, Noah rounded the sofa and stood between Marcus and Mikey, being sure to keep his eyes away from the television screen.

"You want the rest of that steak in there?" Mikey asked him.

Was it a trick question? Noah had demolished the one little medium egg he'd boiled and his stomach was still eager to be filled with more substance. He could almost taste the sweetness of the sautéed onions and feel the bite from the steak sauce as he stood before Mikey trying to understand just where his line of questioning was headed.

"Answer me, man!" Mikey yelled.

All Noah could do was nod.

Mikey smiled, took a swig from yet another beer can he'd pulled from the six-pack resting on the ottoman in front of him, and nodded toward the television. "Since you been back there studying the flick and shit, show us what you learned."

"The fuck?" Marcus was shocked.

Noah's eyes grew wide as he contemplated the meaning of the order Mikey had just handed down to him. Was he *really* telling him to do what he thought he was telling him to do?

"If you can do what that chick on the movie's doing, then you can have the steak," Mikey told Noah, ignoring Marcus's outburst. "Otherwise, be hungry, nigga."

"Aye, man, that's some gay shit," Marcus stated.

"Yeah, man," Benji cosigned. "That shit ain't even cool. Hell you going through?"

Mikey shrugged. "He a li'l fag anyway. Like a li'l girl. A pussy is a pussy."

"You trippin'," Marcus commented.

Mikey stood up once again, untied his sweatpants, and slightly dropped them to expose his slightly erected dick. "Come on, li'l bitch. Can you do it like the ho on the TV?" He laughed as he wiggled his body to get his penis to jump.

"Drunk ass," Benji said, reaching for one of Mikey's beers and focusing his attention back to the television.

Noah considered running out of the room, but his stomach was trying to convince him that he could do this. He didn't know when Ms. Mae was coming home or when or what he would eat after tonight. That steak had his mouth salivating. It was a compromising situation, and Noah felt stuck. Mikey was laughing at him, and the other boys were wondering if he'd really have the balls to do such a damning thing. All Noah could think about was surviving.

"What you gon' do, li'l nigga?" Mikey asked jokingly, feeling lightheaded from the beers he'd been consuming.

Noah began to blink hard as he took one step closer to Mikey. Be humiliated and eat or save himself and starve? That was his current dilemma. He hated the position he was being placed in and wished that he never had to make these types of decisions. He was pretty sure that no other eight-year-old had to decide on stuff like this. He teared up as he lowered himself to his knees.

"Noooo, nigga!" Marcus called out. "This li'l nigga 'bout to do this shit for real."

Noah closed his eyes to block out the sight of the others staring at him and tried with all his might to ignore the sound of them laughing and hollering as well as the pleasurable noises coming from the woman on the screen. His stomach bubbled, and his heart raced. He couldn't believe what his young life was starting to amount to. Just as he moved his head closer to Mikey's body, he felt a warmness creep up his throat in sync with the feeling of being shoved in the face.

"Get the fuck out of here, you fag!" Mikey cried out, laughing as he spewed his verbal venom. He looked over at Benji and laughed. "See, told you he was like a li'l bitch. Nigga'll do any damn thing."

The bile that had risen to rest in his mouth was expelled in that moment, some landing right on Mikey's shoe and all over the carpet. Noah leaned over, still on his knees, letting out the egg he'd recently consumed and what felt like an endless amount of stomach acid. The taste was horrible, but it was nothing compared to the salty taste of blood that assaulted his tongue the moment Mikey punched him in the mouth, followed by a swift quick to his frail rib cage which sent him tumbling over onto his right side.

"You nasty li'l fuck," Mikey screamed as he repeatedly kicked Noah in the same spot. "Got that shit on my fuckin' shoes. Fuck's wrong with you, man?"

Benji and Marcus rose from the sofa and tried to pull Mikey away from Noah who was wincing in pain on the stained, soiled carpet. His arm was submerged in his vomit as he curled up from the stinging that rippled through his insides as Mikey showed him no mercy.

"Aye, man, chill out," Benji insisted, pulling on Mikey's arm. "Leave the li'l nigga alone."

"Yeah, man," Marcus agreed. "I think he gets it, man. Ease up."

Mikey snatched his arms away from his buddies and gritted. "Yeah, all right. What the fuck ever." He reached for his beer and plopped back down in his spot on the sofa where he promptly kicked off his sneakers. "Get the fuck on before I kill yo' ass," he said, snarling down at Noah. "Quit all that bitch-ass crying and clean that stinking shit up. And clean my goddamn shoes!"

The other two boys nervously returned to their seats watching Noah to see if he could even so much as move.

He waited several seconds before braving the pain and peeling himself from the carpet. His side ached worse than any pain he'd ever experienced, but he knew that if he didn't remove himself from the living room he'd be as good as dead. Still crying and cradling his side, Noah rose from the floor pulling Mikey's shoes into this free arm and slowly exited the living room. Behind him he could hear the trio laughing over how crazy Mikey was and the stupid shit he did. Noah didn't find any of it funny. He'd almost been coerced into something that made him cringe in retrospect, and now he was noticeably injured as a result of it. He couldn't win.

Once in his room he dropped Mikey's shoes, having no intentions of cleaning them or himself. He needed to go. He needed to escape this hellhole before Mikey and his friends got any more bright ideas. With the way his side had him doubled over in pain there was no way that he could stay there waiting for Ms. Mae to decide to come home regardless of whether or not he was locked in his room. Looking around his room in a panic he could only think of one place he could go where no one would call juvie on him. Once that was determined, he knew that he could only get out of the house one way. His eyes fell upon the window in his room. It was nighttime, but he was sure that he'd be okay. Anything was better than staying there and allowing Mikey to finish him off. Stricken with pain, smelling like vomit, and with blood dripping from his mouth, Noah struggled to lift the window and hoist himself up and through the tiny opening. Minutes later, he was on a troubled hike to the one place he knew he'd be safe.

Kasyn decided not to stay the night. Olivia wasn't surprised, nor did she care much. Her mind was completely occupied as she tried to focus on her book while temporarily putting her concerns about Noah on the back burner. As she lay across the couch in the living room poring over the pages she'd recently handwritten, a frantic knock resounded at the kitchen door. Olivia sat straight up and looked at the time flashing on her cable box. It was nine in the evening, and she wasn't expecting anyone. For a moment she thought that maybe it was Kasyn, and then promptly dismissed the idea since he had a key and could let himself in. The way the knocks came consistently and hurriedly, she knew that whoever it was on the other side was anxious.

As she hopped up from the sofa and made her way into the kitchen, she wondered if perhaps it was the police. The thought caused her steps to quicken. She looked through the peephole, but it was too dark to see anything. Apparently the porch light had gone out.

"Who is it?" she called out.

"Noah!"

The sound of his voice alarmed her, and Olivia wasted no time in turning the locks and opening the door. "Noah!" she exclaimed. "What are you doing out at this time of night?"

"Can I come in?" he asked meekly.

She stood back and nodded. As he passed her the distinct odor of vomit filled her nose and made her eyes grow wide. She closed the door and turned to get a good look at the young child she'd come to be quite fond of and concerned about. "What happened to you?" she gasped as his little face looked up at her.

He winced and tried to shrug off the severity of what was obviously going on with him. "I got jumped is all."

"Jumped? Coming here?"

"Uh . . . yeah . . . I was on my way here, and . . . uh . . . these guys came outta nowhere, and they pushed me down, and they punched me and kicked me."

"Oh my God," Olivia whispered, angling Noah's face upward by grabbing hold of his chin. She walked away to grab a couple of napkins and handed them to Noah. "Does it hurt anywhere?"

He dabbled at his mouth to try to clean off the blood. "Not really," he lied.

"Noah, please. This is serious. Please . . . Don't lie to me."

He lowered his eyes. "My side hurts a little bit."

Olivia nodded and grabbed her keys and clutch purse off of the counter. "Uh-huh, come on," she told him.

"Where are we going?"

"To the hospital."

He shook his head. "Nah, I'm okay. I don't need to go there. Besides, kids get jumped all the time. It's no biggie." He figured she'd just give him an aspirin and hopefully some food before agreeing to let him crash on her couch, at least until morning. So far, she'd been so cool that he hadn't considered the fact that she might get the authorities involved.

Olivia walked over to him. She noticed that he was cradling his left side and leaning over slightly. On a whim, she reached out and poked him in his side.

"Owwwww," he howled, tears filling his eyes once again as he leaned forward nearly falling to the ground.

"That's what I thought," Olivia commented. "It's very much a biggie, and you are going to the hospital." She placed her arm around his shoulders and lovingly ushered him out of the door.

The ride to the hospital was silent. The wait in the emergency room's waiting area was equally as quiet as Olivia struggled to answer the questions presented on the registration form. She didn't really know much about Noah, and he wasn't really forthcoming with any information to help her complete the form. She knew that he didn't want to be there, but once again, her gut told her that something was wrong, and this time, she was sure he was suffering from some physical trauma.

Within half an hour they were called back into an observation room where Noah continued to be silent. Olivia was becoming noticeably frustrated with his unwillingness to cooperate.

"I just need to get your temperature, suga," the nurse explained to Noah in her southern drawl as she begged him for the third time to open his mouth.

"Noah, please. It's a painless thing," Olivia stated. "Let her do her job, please." She gave him a tender look.

Noah sighed and finally opened his mouth.

The nurse stuck the digital thermometer under his tongue and grabbed her tablet before looking over at Olivia. "So what brings y'all in today?"

"Well, he said he was jumped, so I'd really like for him to have a full exam," Olivia replied. "I'm concerned that he may have some serious bruising or something on his left side there. But, I . . . uh . . . I really think it's best for him to be completely, *completely* examined." She moved her head in succession with her words and stared at the nurse to see if she understood her meaning.

The nurse frowned a little. "Hmmm, you think maybe something more than just a little tousling happened?"

Olivia nodded.

The thermometer beeped, and the nurse removed it from Noah's mouth. She recorded his temperature, and then smiled at him. "I'm just going to take your blood pressure now, okay, while your mom and I continue to talk," she explained as she slid the gray child-size cuff over his thin arm.

"Ummm, I'm not his mother," Olivia admitted. She figured it was best to be honest now before things went any further.

"Oh? Are you the aunt?"

Olivia shook her head and pursed her lips wondering how well this would go over.

"Sister? Cousin? Babysitter?"

"Kinda like a neighbor or . . . uh . . . friend."

"Okay, we need parental consent in order to care for him. Was he in your care at the time of the incident?"

"Not exactly. He was on his way to me. I mean, that's what he told me."

"Are you able to contact his mother?"

"Not exactly," Olivia stated again. "He's in foster care and I . . . uh . . . I don't think it's wise for me to contact his foster mother."

The nurse shot her a look. She started to say something but then caught sight of Noah in her peripheral and thought better of it. She removed the blood pressure cuff, recorded the findings, and smiled at Olivia. "I'm going to have the doctor come right in with you guys, okay?"

Olivia gave a polite smile. "Okay. Thank you."

The nurse left the room and as soon as the door sealed shut Olivia looked over at Noah. She could tell by the way he toyed with the bottom of his worn-out shirt that he was nervous. The truth of the matter was that she was scared too. Her fear was that they would deny him care simply because she was of no relation to him. That would only set the child back and now, knowing that he had some type of physical injury that could be proved within seconds, there was no way that she could send him right on back to the home where he was obviously unsafe.

Before she could open her mouth to try to offer some type of verbal comfort to the child, the room door opened and in walked a tall, Caucasian male in a white coat with blond hair and the bluest eyes Olivia had ever seen. Accompanying him was a short, stout woman with a neat bob hairstyle that simply had to be a wig.

"Good evening," the man greeted them as he reached out to shake Olivia's hand. "I'm Doctor Phillips and this is Ms. Culpepper, the hospital social worker."

"I'm Olivia Collins." Her eyes darted over to Ms. Culpepper, and then back to Doctor Phillips. "Social worker?" Olivia questioned just after shaking the doctor's hand.

"Yes, the nursing staff informed me that we have a unique situation here, and in instances such as these, it is hospital protocol for us to have the social worker present," Doctor Phillips explained.

"Okay." Olivia looked at Ms. Culpepper who still had yet to say anything. She wondered what the woman was thinking and if this visit was in vain. "So, are you going to examine him?" Olivia asked the doctor.

"First things first," Doctor Phillips began. He looked over at Noah. "How you doing, buddy?"

Noah shrugged.

"You came in today because something hurts, huh? Can you tell me about that?" the doctor inquired.

"I got jumped," Noah mumbled.

"By some kids? Your friends, maybe? Classmates?"

Noah shook his head. "Just some jerks from the neighborhood."

Olivia bit the inside of her mouth. He was lying, and she knew it. Just like when she'd questioned him about his family and the bruise on his face, he was lying. He was protecting someone and now definitely wasn't the time to be hush mouthed.

"Noah, is it?" Ms. Culpepper finally spoke up.

Noah nodded.

"Where exactly were you when you were jumped? Were you at home? Were you outside?"

"Outside," the child whispered.

Olivia wasn't buying it. He wouldn't even give the social worker eye contact.

"And how do you know Ms. Collins?"

"I know her from the neighborhood."

"So she's a neighbor?"

"Kinda."

"And you feel comfortable with her?"

Noah nodded.

"How did you end up with Ms. Collins?"

He shrugged. "After he beat me up I just went to her house."

Olivia sat up straight in her chair at the tiny inconsistency in his story. She hoped like hell that the other two adults caught it.

"He who?" Ms. Culpepper asked.

"Huh?" Noah looked up at her confused.

"You said after *he* beat you, you went to Ms. Collins's. Who is the he that you're referring to?"

"T-t-t-the guy that . . . t-t-that jumped me."

"I thought you said that it was some peers from the neighborhood, Noah," Ms. Culpepper said gingerly as she shifted her weight just a little.

"Obviously he's protecting someone," Olivia blurted out. "Someone's hurting this child, and I have been trying to get someone to hear me out, and now it's come to this."

"Maybe it's best if we speak to Noah without you in the room," Ms. Culpepper stated.

Olivia was stunned. "*Excuse* me? I'm trying to tell you that something is seriously wrong here. Look at this child. Look at him! And you wanna throw *me* out for trying to bring it to someone's attention?"

"I'm asking you to step outside because technically you are not the child's guardian and therefore have no right to sit in on his private health or social matters. Legally, you have no ties to this child, Ms. Collins."

Olivia stood up and shook her head. "I don't need a piece of paper or some bloodline lineage to care about someone. Do *you?*"

Ms. Culpepper sighed. "I have a job to do," she stated. She pointed to the doctor. "Doctor Phillips has a job to do. We can't do our jobs unless you cooperate with our hospital and state's protocols and laws. Please, leave the room. You can wait out in the waiting room if it makes you feel better."

Doctor Phillips looked over at Noah. "He claims he has no pain. Just looks like he's suffered a busted lip, but we can get one of the nurses to clean that up and give him some children's Tylenol to reduce the inflammation."

Olivia shook her head as she headed for the door. "This is preposterous. No one's listening. We all know this farce about being jumped is a bunch of bull."

"Ms. Collins, please," Ms. Culpepper said exasperatedly.

"Please *what?* Please make your job easier by shutting the hell up and letting it go? Why don't you actually focus on doing your job of protecting versus trying to get me to shut up and disappear?" She looked over at the doctor. "And you wanna put a Band-Aid on something that I know is much more serious than a little scratch or bruising." She walked over to Noah. She hated to do it, but she had to prove to them that her allegations were more than just a fairy tale. She poked Noah in his side once more, and the child let out an earsplitting scream. "You still wanna put a Band-Aid on the problem, Doctor Phillips?"

As Noah cried and turned red with agony, Doctor Phillips washed his hands and walked over to the child. "Noah, I just want to take a quick look, okay? I won't touch anything except for your shirt, okay?"

Noah was in too much distress to argue with the doctor.

Slowly, Doctor Phillips lifted Noah's baggy T-shirt to reveal his thin skeletal body. The boy's bones were nearly poking through his skin. Every adult in the room gasped upon the sight of the large purple bruised indent in Noah's side. Olivia covered her mouth with her hand and felt hot tears drip onto the back of it. Her emotions shifted from shock, to anger, to empathy, right back to sincere determination. There was no way that she was going to let anyone sweep this under the rug. Physical proof of foul play was right before their eyes.

Noah looked at the faces of all of the grown-ups and knew that it wasn't good. He was afraid of what would happen next and the only person he felt comfortable with and trusted was being asked to leave the room. He looked to Olivia, and then past her to Ms. Culpepper. "Can she stay please?" he asked.

Doctor Phillips took another look at the bruising, and then looked over at the social worker. "I have to send him up for x-rays."

"No, I won't go!" Noah cried out.

"Son, we've got to see what kind of internal damage has been done to your body."

"I'm not going nowhere unless she goes with me." He was serious.

Doctor Phillips turned to Ms. Culpepper yet again. "I really needa get him up to imaging now."

Ms. Culpepper nodded. "Go-ahead." She looked at Olivia. "Stay with him. They're going to need him to be calm, and it appears that he's comfortable with you. But by law, I have to contact the authorities and his guardian. We can't treat him and release him to you."

Olivia reached into her purse and pulled out the card she'd been carrying around for a while. "Here. This is his social worker's information. If anyone needs to be called it's her."

"Well, now," Doctor Phillips said to Noah, trying to sound upbeat, "I'm going to put in a quick call to radiology and one of the techs will come wheel you right on up, okay? We'll take a couple of pictures of your rib cage and your back just to make sure everything's okay."

"Is it gonna hurt?" Noah asked with a tremble in his voice.

The doctor shook his head. "No way. This part's a piece of cake." He winked at Noah and headed out of the room after throwing the women a concerned look.

"You stay with Noah, and I'll call Ms. Hardy," Ms. Culpepper advised Olivia.

Olivia gave her a stern look. "You do that."

Ms. Culpepper exited the room, and Olivia stepped to the door where she watched the woman disappear up the hall. Doctor Phillips was standing at the nearby nurses' station giving instructions to the nurse that had triaged Noah.

Olivia looked over her shoulder at the young boy. "I'll be right back, okay? I promise I'm not going far."

Noah nodded, though his eyes pleaded with her not to leave his side even for a second.

She gave him a reassuring smile and rushed out of the room and over to Doctor Phillips before he could walk off. "Doctor Phillips," she called out.

"Yes?"

"After the x-rays, will you look at him? I mean actually examine him beyond just looking at his side?"

"Is there a concern outside of the injury he's sustained from tonight's incident?"

"That's just it," Olivia said. "I don't think what happened tonight was some isolated incident, and I don't think he was jumped. I'm pretty sure he was abused at home . . . at his foster home. And I'd appreciate it if a rape kit could be done."

The doctor was flabbergasted. "What kind of proof do you have of that allegation?"

"Intuition," she replied. "Plus, I believe he was bleeding from his private areas."

Doctor Phillips's brow rose. "And how would you know that?"

Olivia didn't like the insinuation behind the look and tone he was giving her. "Because he was dripping blood while in my bathroom."

"Rape kits are usually done when victims come in via ambulance or police escort following an assault. Or when the patient requests it themselves or—"

"He doesn't even want to tell you the truth about who beat the shit out of him tonight," Olivia pointed out. "You *really* think he's going to openly admit to you that someone's been sexually abusing him?"

"I was going to say or when the guardian of a minor requests it."

Olivia took a deep breath. This entire ordeal was beginning to take a toll on her. "So, I have to be his guardian in order to tell you that I'm pretty sure he's being abused? Now, if his guardian is the one abusing him, how exactly does that work out?"

Doctor Phillips hesitated for a moment as he considered his options. It was clear to him that the woman had a strong, vested interest in the child. In a way he admired the courage she had to be a voice for the child, but on the other hand, he didn't want to cross any lines that would be a HIPAA or hospital regulations violation. Still, he had a duty to care for the ill, especially children, and he was becoming more and more convinced that the irate woman before him was on to something.

"Okay," he consented. "We'll perform a rape kit, but I will have to make a full report to provide to his social worker."

Olivia smiled graciously. "Not a problem. Thank you. Thank you so much." She clasped her hands, feeling the slightest bit triumphant before hurrying off to return to Noah's side.

Two hours later, after waiting just outside of the door
until permitted to return to Noah's side, the child had
been given x-rays and a CT scan, a full physical exam
including the requested rape kit, and had his busted lip
sewn up with three quick stitches. Now, he was laid out
on the hospital bed, knocked out from all the activity,
pain, and medication. Olivia sat in a chair by his side
with her head resting on the edge of the bed. She too was
exhausted but had no intentions of leaving until they'd
gotten answers.

A tapping at the door woke Olivia out of her restless
slumber, and she quickly looked over to Noah who was
still asleep. The door opened, and Olivia sat straight up
as a nurse entered the room.

"Ms. Collins?" the nurse asked, making sure that she
was in the right room.

Olivia nodded. "Yes?"

"I was asked to come and escort you down to the social
worker's office."

Olivia looked over at Noah. "No," she said. "I don't feel
comfortable leaving him."

"They really need to talk to you and if it's any comfort
to you, I'll come right back and sit in here with him just in
case he wakes up."

"It's that important?"

"I'm afraid so."

Olivia sighed. "Fine, but if he wakes up, please let him
know where I am and that I'll be right back as soon as I'm
done."

The nurse smiled. "Sure thing. Follow me."

Olivia followed the young woman through what felt
like a maze to get to their destination. The moment she
entered the office she was greeted by the somber faces of
Ms. Culpepper and Ms. Hardy. She knew that a verbal
sparring was likely to take place judging by the blatant

look of disdain etched across Ms. Hardy's face. *She's probably mad that she had to stop watching her shows tonight and come do some real work,* Olivia thought as she walked into the center of the room.

"Ms. Collins, I'm sure you're acquainted with Ms. Hardy," Ms. Culpepper stated by way of a halfhearted introduction.

"Quite," Olivia responded.

"I was just informing Ms. Culpepper here of how uncouth and belligerently you behaved when you were at my office," Ms. Hardy said. "And the way you had to be escorted out of the building by security due to your unprofessional demeanor."

"Unprofessional?" Olivia repeated with a smile. "A word I'm sure you're very familiar with."

"Ladies, there's clearly no love lost between the two of you, but we're all here tonight for a much-bigger issue," Ms. Culpepper stated. "There's a child's well-being at stake here."

"From what you said, he was out of the home when he shouldn't have been heading somewhere he shouldn't have been going and got accosted," Ms. Hardy recapped. "That doesn't necessarily implicate that his well-being is in danger. The problem that arises for me is why the child was trying to make his way to Ms. Collins's home in the first place. Exactly what type of a relationship do you have with this child that doesn't even live in your neighborhood?"

Olivia wanted to slap the woman out of the chair that she was perched on the edge of. "Are you implying that I am in some way having an inappropriate relationship with a minor?'"

"You said it, I didn't," came the woman's reply.

"Classic! Instead of admitting that I called it when I told you that something wasn't right with Noah, you want to try to turn things around and place the blame on me! You are certifiable."

"We're getting nowhere like this," Ms. Culpepper cut in. "This is completely counterproductive." The room was silent for a moment as the other two women fumed. "Now," Ms. Culpepper said calmly, slowly averting her eyes to Olivia who was still standing, "if you'd like to take a seat we can talk about this like rational adults."

"If it's all the same to you I'll remain standing," Olivia replied.

"Very well. The question of why Noah was leaving his home at such a late hour is a very logical inquiry, Ms. Collins. Surely you understand why Ms. Hardy, or anyone for that matter, would raise the question."

Olivia nodded. "Mmm-hmm. I see the point. However, since I'm pretty clear on what's real, him coming to me makes perfect sense. Apparently, after he got his ass whooped at home by whomever is in the house with him, he felt safe running away and coming to me, an adult that actually listens to him."

"And he told you that?" Ms. Culpepper asked.

Olivia's confidence wavered slightly. "Well, n-n-no. But he didn't have to. I can tell something's wrong with him judging by things he's said in the past and just little things I've noticed about him."

"Unfortunately, the burden of proof rests with you, Ms. Collins," Ms. Culpepper explained. "And if the child never said anything to you about being abused at home, and you never saw him being abused with your own eyes, you leave us with very little to go on in order to believe that that's what's going on here."

"But you saw that child's body," Olivia replied.

"I also heard him say that he was jumped by peers."

"Yeah, but you also heard him switch his story up to say it was just one guy," Olivia countered. "Kids lie. It's a survival technique. And this time, it's obvious that Noah's lying because he's afraid. He's protecting someone. His guardian maybe."

"Ms. Mae Johnson's background is squeaky clean," Ms. Hardy stated. "She's been a foster care parent for nearly fifteen years now and never once has a child claimed that she laid a hand on them. Noah's never said a word to me about anything mischievous happening while in Ms. Johnson's care."

"Well, who else is in the home, and did *that* person have a background check done?"

Ms. Hardy was clearly not expecting the question and hesitated before answering. "Her son, Michael, is in and out of the home, but to the state's knowledge, he doesn't live there. But he is her only biological son and is there often."

"Did you or did you not perform a background check on him?" Olivia questioned.

"Not that I owe you any answers or explanations but—"

Before Ms. Hardy could answer the question, the door opened and in walked Doctor Phillips with a grim look on his face. All three women stared at him in silence, waiting for him to deliver the results of Noah's tests.

"Is this the caseworker?" Doctor Phillips asked Ms. Culpepper as he nodded in Ms. Hardy's direction.

Ms. Culpepper nodded. "Yes. Ms. Hardy meet Dr. Raymond Phillips, the physician on staff tonight. He examined Noah upon admission."

"Pleased to meet you," Ms. Hardy stated blandly.

Doctor Phillips stood next to Olivia and gave her a reassuring smile, but his eyes told her that trouble was lurking. "Well, the CT scan reveals that Noah's suffered a fractured rib bone. Actually he has two fractures, one right below the other. With him being so young and resilient, I wouldn't worry too much. These types of internal injuries heal themselves, so no procedure is necessary. We'll put a brace around him to help with the healing process and limit his movements like turning and bending. The most important thing is keeping up with his pain management. I'm going to give him a light dose prescription for oxycodone to help with the pain." The doctor took a deep breath and looked down at the papers in his hand.

"Is there something else?" Ms. Culpepper asked, feeling the mystery in the air.

Olivia looked at the doctor expectantly. She knew what he was going to say before he even said it. His body language and the immense look of hurt in his eyes and sadness lingering in his expression told it all. It took everything within Olivia not to fall to the floor from the heartbreaking feeling that was tearing her chest apart.

"Yes," Doctor Phillips said heavily. "We did a full exam and rape kit on Noah."

"A rape kit?" Ms. Hardy questioned. "What on earth for? You all said that Noah admitted to being jumped in the neighborhood. How did that call for a rape kit?" She looked over at Olivia and squinted her eyes. "You," she said nastily. "What kind of mess have you put in these people's heads?"

Olivia ignored the woman's question.

"There was significant scarring and tearing around Noah's rectum," Doctor Phillips stated. "Which implies that some kind of object has been forced inside of him at some point. It's relatively fresh, and we've applied ointment to aid the healing. A prescription for that will be given as well. In instances such as these, we'd notify the police."

Ms. Hardy shifted. "Have you?"

Doctor Phillips handed her the full medical report he'd assembled for her files. "My job is to report to Ms.

Culpepper, and it is she who makes the call." He looked to the hospital social worker. "Ball's in your court. You have my findings. In my medical opinion, this boy's been sodomized." He sighed deeply. "I have patients so . . ."

"Thank you," Ms. Culpepper said, her heart heavy with the truth they were all left to deal with.

Doctor Phillips nodded before turning to leave. He squeezed Olivia's shoulder with his left hand before exiting the office.

"I'm sure there's some kind of explanation for what's happened," Ms. Hardy stated.

"Aside from the obvious?" Olivia snapped.

"He's always had trouble at school, and now with these boys jumping him . . . Maybe one of them assaulted him."

Olivia was astonished. "There was no jumping, Ms. Hardy. Why is that so difficult for you to believe?"

"We can only work with what Noah has reported."

"I can't believe you." Olivia looked to Ms. Culpepper. "Are you going to call the police or not?"

"I'd be expected to contact the police or social services," Ms. Culpepper answered. "Since his worker is already here and has been armed with the medical report, I'm putting it in the hands of the proper authority."

"Proper authority? So now what?"

"Now *my* office will investigate, Ms. Collins," Ms. Hardy snapped. "Now will you please allow me to do my job *without* your help?"

"Are you *kidding* me? If it wasn't for me insisting that the hospital do a rape kit or me bringing him to the hospital to begin with, you wouldn't even believe the allegations!"

"We can play 'what-if' all day," Ms. Hardy stated. "Unfortunately, nobody has time for that." She rose from her seat. "If you'll excuse me, I have a child to tend to and place in temporary custody until we can get this matter handled."

Olivia shook her head and headed for the door.

"Where are you going?" Ms. Hardy called out. "Because if you think you're going to Noah you can forget it. I don't need you getting in the way of this investigation. Thank you for what you've done so far. Thank you for bringing him to get medical attention, but I'll thank you even more to leave it to the professionals now. You're not his guardian, and I'd hate to have to get a restraining order against you."

Olivia turned and faced the woman. "Are you serious? I'm *not* the enemy here, and I'm certainly not the one that dropped the ball on this one leaving this child susceptible to being abused. What you're feeling right now is called guilt, Ms. Hardy. You may think it's a sense of responsibility for keeping Noah safe and trying to follow procedures, but that's a bunch of bullshit. You're feeling guilty that your neglect put Noah in this situation, and you're taking it out on me. But guess what? You can kiss my ass because I have no intentions of letting this go, not by a long shot."

With that, she exited the office and made her way down to Noah's room to get an update from the nurse. She planned to leave her number with the nurse so that she could be advised about Noah's condition upon leaving the hospital as well as obtain a copy of the medical report that the doctor had given Ms. Hardy. She'd gotten Noah this far, and she certainly wasn't about to bow out on him now.

Chapter 9

Her hands were clenched tightly shut as she sat in the cushioned chair in the rather small judge's chamber at the county's magistrate court office. Beside her sat her former supervisor and good friend, Daysha Mullen, looking confident and studious in her charcoal-gray pants suit. Across from them, seated behind his desk with his glasses perched upon his nose but his face close to the documents in his hand, sat the man who could get Olivia one step closer to saving Noah, Judge Melvin Amos. Daysha had done a lot of fancy talking and politicking to get this meeting, and once she'd given Olivia the time and date with only forty-eight hours' notice, Olivia wasted no time in preparing. She quickly made a trip back down to DeKalb Medical in search of the nurse who'd been so kind to her. Instead, she'd run into Doctor Phillips who didn't take much convincing to turn over a copy of the medical report he'd given to Ms. Hardy, as well as the printed images of Noah's fractured ribs.

She was hoping that this documentation, as well as her story, would be sufficient enough to sway the judge's decision. The meeting opened up with Daysha introducing Olivia to Judge Amos and giving her the floor to plead her case. With that out of the way, all Olivia could do was sit there staring at the man, willing him to have mercy on Noah's soul.

"This isn't a typical request," Judge Amos stated, still gazing over the paperwork before him. "And how do you know this child again?"

"Ummm, he wandered into my complex one evening while trying to escape whatever was going on at home, I assume," Olivia replied.

"You assume?" He looked up at her with a sour expression.

"Yes. When I asked him what he was doing out there, he was a little evasive about giving me an answer so . . . based off of the other things I've told you about his health, his appearance, his injuries, and his behavior, I can only deduce that he was trying to get as far away from his foster home as possible."

"What is it that you would like to ultimately see happen here?" the judge asked.

Olivia looked over at Daysha, unsure of how to respond to the question. Daysha nodded her head slightly, indicating that Olivia should be completely honest with the judge.

"I want him removed from that home," Olivia stated firmly.

"You do realize that there's a chance you could be completely wrong about this."

Olivia pointed to the medical report in the judge's hand. "The doctor has already gone on record to say that it's medically clear that the child has had some penetration to his rectal area, and I'm more than positive an eight-year-old wouldn't impale himself in that manner or consent to anyone else doing it. Sure, there's a fraction of a chance that I could be wrong about his foster parent, sir, but my heart is telling me that my assumptions are pure truth."

"Very well," the judge replied. "I'm going to sign this order to place you as Noah Maxiel's advocate for the sum of sixty days. During that time, if you wish to carry on, you must complete the proper CASA training. I will allow you to file a motion for us to hear you out about the removal of Noah from the home since you're convinced that DFCS hasn't or isn't properly investigating or monitoring the child's placement. You will receive confirmation of said hearing date via first class mail." As he spoke, he picked up a pen and placed his signature along a document that had been resting on his desk for the duration of their meeting. He looked up at Olivia, extended the paper across his desk to her, and nodded. "Make good use of this opportunity, Ms. Collins. It could very well change the course of this young man's life."

Olivia exhaled as she rose to retrieve the paper. This was all she needed. Now, she had the right to request a copy of Noah's file from Ms. Hardy, and she'd be able to visit Noah's home for herself to evaluate exactly what his living conditions were like. No one knew that she was doing this aside from Daysha. It would be a surprise to everyone once she popped up and started asking questions and making random visits. She knew that Ms. Hardy would have a fit, feeling as if Olivia had stepped on her toes; however, Olivia didn't care. She had one concern and one concern only as she walked out of the judge's chamber clutching the sealed document to her chest: preserving Noah's rights.

Chapter 10

"Kennedy!"

She cringed upon hearing him call her name. What could he possibly want now? She'd done the laundry, washed the dishes, and was trying her very best to remain inconspicuous so that he wouldn't bother her. She was sitting on the floor in her room with her back against the bed reading a book in an attempt to lose herself in the story line. Unfortunately, her plan didn't work out because here he was trying to get her to come into the living room with him. It didn't help matters that no one else was home but her. She wished that she could have gone to the store with Carmen, but her father had rushed her out, giving her strict instructions to hurry there and back. Kennedy was trying hard not to count the minutes until Carmen's return as she turned the pages of her book. She knew that her stepmother wouldn't be off of work until later in the evening, so hoping for her to come through the door and stand watch over her was pointless.

"Kennedy! Get in here."

She considered ignoring him. It was possible that he only wanted a glass of water, a snack, or maybe even had a legitimate, innocent question. But it was also possible that he had something devious in mind. In fact, since they were alone, it was much more likely. Slowly, she laid her book down on the floor and pulled herself up. She hesitated at the door, praying that she wouldn't have to run out of the house screaming for help. Then again, maybe that's exactly what she needed to have the courage to do: scream for help. But the question was, would anybody listen and actually help?

"Damn it, Kennedy!" her father yelled.

The raised octave of his voice caused her to jump, and she scurried out the door and up the hall where she found him sitting in the comfy oversized armchair situated on the right side of the living room up against the wall. Her gait slowed down as she entered the room, being sure to stop far enough away from him so that he couldn't reach out and touch her. A half-empty cognac glass filled with now-watered-down Hennessy dangled from his hand as his arm lingered over the edge of the arm of the chair. His body was slumped down in the chair, and a heavy expression had him sitting with his head held down.

He motioned with the glass over toward the sofa. "Sit down," he said in a stressed tone that she wasn't used to hearing from him. "I need to talk to you."

As she moved past him to take a seat on the sofa, Kennedy mentally went through any possible thing that she could have done to require a sit-down discussion. She came up with nothing. She was doing well in school, never was allowed outside so there was no neighborhood drama, and she hadn't been talking to Bones since that incident when her father had bust her lip. She feared what other bodily harm he'd inflict upon her so she'd promptly ended the relationship with Bones, much to his dismay.

Sitting on the sofa, Kennedy pulled one of the large pillows into her lap and held on to it for dear life. It gave her some kind of comfort, and it also covered up her thighs since she was wearing a pair of cutoff blue jean shorts. They weren't revealing, but with her father, *it didn't really matter much what she was wearing. If he felt like being inappropriate he was going to do it regardless.*

"Do you remember our little incident?" her father asked, sipping from his glass.

"Our incident?" she questioned, honestly not catching his meaning.

"Our incident," he repeated. "Our misunderstanding. You know, where you thought I was trying to do something to you, but I simply misunderstood your signals."

"My signals?" Kennedy was astonished. Was he really trying to say that his behavior was her fault? "What kind of signals?"

"You're always running around here hugging on me and climbing up in my lap . . . acting like you wanted some attention. Then when I tried to show you some, you acted all funny about it."

Kennedy was speechless. Her jaw dropped as she listened to his asinine explanation for how things went down. She wondered if her other friends experienced the same kind of devastation when they were around their dads. She'd seen plenty of girls hug their dads and seem genuinely excited to be in their presence with no indication that anything sinister was happening to them behind closed doors. Were their dads touching them at night too? If so, did they like it? It just couldn't be normal. Despite whatever he said to her, Kennedy just couldn't believe that it was a usual occurrence for a father to do to his daughter what he should have only being doing to his wife.

He was her dad. Didn't he get that? He was supposed to protect her from the bad guys and the boys who would try to take advantage of her. He wasn't supposed to turn out to be the one she should be leery of. When she hugged him, it was because she genuinely loved him.

After all, he was her father, her provider, her guardian, her teacher, and her male role model . . . or at least he was supposed to be. Whenever she sat in his lap, it was because she reveled in the bliss of being his princess, his baby girl, his pride and joy. Had she ever imagined that he saw it any differently she would have certainly kept her distance. But other girls' fathers embraced them, carried them, and held them in their laps. Why couldn't she be like all the other girls? Why couldn't her father adore her in that protective, parental kind of way? What made the other girls so special that their fathers didn't find it necessary to abuse, humiliate, and debase them? Why was she so unfavored as to be placed in this situation? What had she done to deserve this life?

Her body temperature rose as she continued to sit and stare at him in disbelief. She began to rock back and forth, trying to force herself to remain silent when all she really wanted to do was scream out all her "whys" at him. Her right foot shook nervously, and her eyes stung from the tears that were building. Still, he continued on.

"So I just wanted to make sure that you understood that it was all a misunderstanding," *he told her, taking yet another sip of his watered-down liquor.*

"A misunderstanding?" *she repeated.*

"Right. That's all it was. No harm, no foul, and it'll never happen again because I get it now."

It'll never happen again? she asked herself. Who was he fooling? Okay, so maybe he wouldn't force himself on her or slip his hands in places where they didn't belong, but what about his lewd comments, his inappropriate rubs and pats, the way he peeked under her skirts and nightshirts, the way he looked down her shirts when no one was watching? Would he stop doing those things now too? Was this some backward way of him apologizing for traumatizing her? If so, he was failing miserably. Kennedy was feeling more uncomfortable than ever. They'd never discussed his wrongness since the first incident, and sitting here now with him glossing over the factual points of their strained relationship, Kennedy wanted to just melt into the fabric of the sofa and vanish from the conversation. It was too much for her. Being in the house with him was too much for her. Living was becoming too much for her.

Silence lingered between them as Kennedy tried to keep herself from breaking down, and her dad gathered the nerve to make his next point. The tension in the room was thick with each person's agenda weighing heavily on their minds. Kennedy glanced at the large golden clock that hung on the wall across from her. Carmen should be back at any moment now, and hopefully, that would be the end of this uncomfortable discussion she'd been dragged into. But it could be worse; rather than talking about the things he'd done, he could be reenacting them or taking his sexual abuse to a whole other level. Kennedy silently counted her blessings and prayed that her body would remain safe for however much longer it took for Carmen's champagne Nissan Sentra to pull into the driveway.

"Someone may come to your school asking you questions," her father stated out of nowhere.

"Who?" Kennedy inquired.

"Someone from the state . . . from family services. I'm not sure that it's going to happen, I'm just saying . . . they might. They might wanna ask you questions."

"Questions about what?"

"What we just talked about," he snapped. "What I just said to you. Shit! About the incident."

Yeah, Kennedy thought. The misunderstanding. *She rolled her eyes and fought back the urge to vomit.*

"So if that happens," he went on, "I need to be sure that you aren't going to say anything crazy."

Crazy? she wondered, feeling certain that his definition of crazy was actually her telling the truth. "What is it that you want me to say?" she asked, staring him dead in the face as she waited for him to instruct her to lie.

"We're cool, right?" he asked, softening his tone and leaning toward her as he motioned his hand in the space between them. "We're on the same page now, right? You understand that it was nothing, right?"

All Kennedy could do was nod.

"Then ain't no reason to go talking about it anymore with anyone," he said. "So if someone asks you any questions . . . If anyone asks you if I touched you or some mess like that, then you just tell them no. Simple as that."

Kennedy looked away from him and quickly wiped away the first tear that escaped her left eye. He made it sound so unimportant, as if what he'd done to her hadn't changed the entire course of her life and her personality. He said it himself, the situation was simple in his eyes only, to her, it wasn't. To her, it was anything but simple and just bordered upon detrimental and overly disturbing.

"So, you understand?" he asked her. "Can you do that for me?"

Kennedy couldn't meet his eyes. He really thought that he could ruin her life and expect her to just disregard and write off the pain nonchalantly. She nodded, unable to form the words to confirm what he wanted to hear from her.

"You do know what'll happen if you decide to say anything crazy, right?" he asked.

Kennedy wondered why he kept referring to the truth as crazy. Maybe he wasn't as demented as she thought he was. Maybe he truly did understand that what he'd done to her was completely not normal, horrific, unbelievable, and outlandish. Maybe guilt was eating his ass alive, and now, here he was, trying to cover his tracks and get her to ease the heaviness that had settled upon his conscience. That was assuming that her monster of a father actually had a conscience.

Kennedy shrugged in response to his question and quickly peered out of the window. Still no sign of Carmen. She wondered what the hell was taking the older girl so long.

"They'll take you and your little brother, your sister, and possibly your niece and put y'all all in foster care," he told her with an eerie tone. "You don't want that to happen, do you? You don't want them to put the kids in some home where you'd never see them again, and God knows what would happen to them."

Kennedy thought about it. She was petrified of being in her own home with her own parent. She couldn't fathom how she would feel being forced to live with strangers who had no ties to her and could possibly pose a greater threat than she was already accustomed to. The thought of her brother and sister or even her niece, Carmen's daughter, having to endure any kind of trauma at the hands of a stranger, or even her father, bothered Kennedy. Since her failed attempt to kill herself with the pain pills, she felt that the only purpose she was intended to serve was to watch over the younger kids and make certain that the same molestation didn't happen to them. So far, she felt she was watching over them well enough, because, to her knowledge, they were all unharmed. But her father's words had her fearful of the possibility of not being able to protect them.

"Kennedy," he called her name pleadingly.

Kennedy turned and took notice of the pitiful expression he was giving her. She knew what he wanted to hear, and she knew what she needed to do. "I won't say anything," she said softly, watching as relief washed over him. "It was a misunderstanding."

He nodded his head feeling certain that all was now right in his world. "Okay," he told her. "That's it." He was dismissing her now that he'd managed to get her to agree to cover his ass.

Kennedy rose from the sofa just as headlights caught her eye through the picture window of the living room. Carmen was back finally. Kennedy didn't linger to watch her sister come in. Instead, she returned to her room to the same position she'd been seated in previously on the floor. She picked up her book and stared down at the open pages before her. Someone was coming. Finally, someone was coming who would be interested in hearing her story and getting her away from the turmoil that brewed within the confines of the place she called home. At last, someone was coming to rescue her, and she had every intention of allowing them to do so despite the lie she'd told her father. She loved her siblings, but she was tired of slowly dying daily while living under the roof of the devil. It was time for her to be set free.

Chapter 11

All of the houses on his block were relatively small and seemingly unkempt. The home located at the address that she'd obtained from Noah's DFCS Foster Care file was no different from the others. The yard was unmanaged, the paint on the shutters and front door was peeling, and the siding was badly in need of pressure washing. But, just because it looked like a hot mess on the outside didn't mean that it would be the same on the inside. Olivia tried to remain objective, although she already had a sour opinion of Ms. Mae Johnson, Noah's foster mother, and the way she cared for the child.

It was ten in the morning on a Monday. She knew that Noah would be in school and didn't want him to have to be present for the first showdown between herself and his foster mother. It had taken nearly a week for Ms. Hardy to hand over the requested copy of Noah's file and for the official hearing notice to be sent to her following the motion Daysha helped her file to have Noah removed from Ms. Mae's care. It astonished her to learn that DFCS hadn't had the foresight to go-ahead and place the child elsewhere following the information received via Doctor Phillips's medical report. How they could feel that Noah was safe in an environment where he was obviously not being properly supervised judging by the injuries to his body was beyond Olivia's understanding. Talking to Ms. Hardy was like pulling teeth. Now, more than ever, the woman was icy and uncooperative, leaving Olivia to fend for herself with regards to acting in Noah's best interest. Her next request would be to move the child off of the woman's caseload, but honestly, she felt sorry for all the other neglected children in the system that didn't have a court-appointed advocate looking out for them and making sure that these workers were doing their jobs to ensure their safety.

Olivia got out of her car and walked past Ms. Mae's outdated sedan. She trotted up the short walkway to the porch and knocked with vigor on the tattered front door. Moments later, the door swung open and standing before her was a heavyset, older woman with her hair pulled back in a bun and a very irritated look on her face.

"Can I help you?" Ms. Mae asked. "Whatever you selling, we'on want it."

"I'm not selling anything," Olivia assured her.

"Humph. Well, if you one of them Jehovah's Witnesses you can just thump ya' Bible right on back down the damn driveway to ya' car 'cause I'm already saved and don't need you telling me nothing 'bout yo' views on the Lord."

Olivia chuckled to herself. A part of her seriously doubted that the woman had a relationship with the Savior given the fact that she couldn't even be bothered to properly care for one of the Lord's precious children.

"No, you have it wrong," Olivia told her. "I'm Olivia Collins, Noah's advocate."

The woman's entire demeanor changed from basic annoyance to blatant disdain and indifference. "Oh, *you* that woman going 'round stirring up trouble where there is none."

"I beg to differ."

"Oh, I just bet you do. What you want anyhow?" the woman asked, looking behind her to see the time flashing on the clock situated on top of her television in the living room. "It's still morning time. Noah's at school."

"Is he?" Olivia challenged, fully aware of Noah's tendency to skip school from time to time. "And you're sure about that?"

Ms. Mae crossed her arms. "Well, if you think I'm lying like ya' tone says you do, then you can drive ya'self on down there and find out."

"Maybe I will."

"You do that." Ms. Mae moved to close the door.

Olivia held her hand out and pushed against the door. "Wait! Although I'd love to make sure that Noah's safe and sound in his class, I came here to speak with you."

"What I got to say to you?"

"Well, as his advocate, it's my job to make sure that his home environment is up to par and adequate for a child."

"You mean to say you just want to be nosy and see what we got going on up through here 'cause this ain't yo' job. You don't get paid for this. You went out yo' way to place yourself right on over in our family business for whatever the reason. But you wanna be nosy, Ms. Goody Two-shoes, then come on in!" Ms. Mae stepped back to allow Olivia to enter.

Olivia crossed the threshold and the scent of mothballs and cinnamon accosted her nostrils. The house was cluttered but not necessarily dirty. She took notice of the raggedy green sofa in the living room and the old-model television situated across from it.

"Anything in particular you want to look at?" Ms. Mae asked.

"Can we go into the kitchen?" Olivia asked, trying hard to be polite when what she really wanted to do was jump the woman every time the memory of Noah's bruised body came to mind.

Ms. Mae waved her hand in the direction of the kitchen, tooted her lips up with attitude, and stood back to watch Olivia walk on by. She trailed right behind the woman, eager to see what she would do next. As Olivia took the liberty of looking in the refrigerator and the pantry, Ms.

Mae felt grateful that she'd had the foresight to go grocery shopping the day before, fully stocking the house. She too had gotten the notice about Noah being appointed an advocate and Ms. Hardy had told her all about Ms. Collins accusing her of abusing the child. During an impromptu home visit, Ms. Hardy had encouraged her to make sure that she was on her p's and q's because "this Collins bitch is out for blood for whatever the reason." Ms. Hardy had also questioned her about Mikey's presence in the home since he wasn't listed on her application as a resident, nor was he on her lease for the house. She'd stuck to her lie about Mikey coming and going periodically, but just to be on the safe side, she'd urged her son to stay away from the house for a while until the allegations and bullshit died down. Based on Ms. Hardy's statement, Ms. Mae had a feeling that Olivia Collins would show her face at her house sooner or later. Now here she was, taking note of every little thing in order to build a case against her. If there was one thing Ms. Mae didn't do, it was let somebody mess with her money. If this woman found any just cause to have Noah removed, then that was a check Ms. Mae could kiss good-bye. She didn't need those kind of issues in her life.

"You got all you need?" Ms. Mae taunted Olivia as the woman closed the last cabinet door and spun around.

Olivia gave a sarcastic smile. "Just about, thanks. I wanted to ask you a question, if you don't mind."

"Well, you already been invading my space like you got a damn warrant, so you might as well say whatever it is you got to say."

"What happened to Noah?"

"Pardon me?"

"I mean, looking at you, I'm not really getting the vibe that you would have the indecency to place a hand on the child . . . to molest him. But I'm not fooled at all enough to believe that you knew nothing about it."

"First of all, ain't nobody molesting nobody up in here. DFCS talked to Noah, and he told them that he was jumped by somebody on his way to yo' house, a place he ain't have no business on his way to. Kids be picking on him 'cause he different . . . Them kids did that to him. They can be cruel out in the streets, but in here, in this house, that child's safe as he can get."

Olivia wasn't buying it. "And when he was on his way to my place that night, how is it that you didn't know he was out of the house?"

"Child snuck out the window. Noah ain't no perfect child, Ms. Collins."

"No child is, but he was obviously running from something. And you didn't notice anything about him that evening? I mean, before he snuck off, that is?"

"Naw," Ms. Mae answered with a lack of confidence.

"Or were you even here? Rumor is that you work a lot."

"Ain't no crime against being a hard worker and providing for yo' own, and Noah's just that. He's like a real son to me."

Olivia gave another one of her fake smiles. "Awww. That's so endearing. Tell me, Ms. Johnson, where's your *real* son? Michael, is that his name?"

Ms. Mae shrugged. "Mikey don't come 'round here that often. Ain't seen him in a minute now."

"Mmm-hmm." Olivia was done listening to the woman lie to her face. She may have fooled Ms. Hardy and DeKalb County DFCS, but Olivia was no idiot. She could see right through the cover-up. She knew all about putting up a front and saying exactly what someone needed to hear to think that everything was okay. "I guess I'll head on now. Thank you for allowing me into your home. I'm sure we'll be seeing plenty of each other in the future."

Ms. Mae grimaced. "Humph. I'm sure."

Olivia retraced her steps and let herself out of the woman's modest home. Ms. Mae didn't even bother to follow her to the door. Instead, she clutched her chest and pondered over the possibilities. Something about Olivia Collins's persistence didn't sit well with Ms. Mae, and she was honestly worried about what the future held.

Life was more stressful now than ever before. His every move was being monitored by everyone these days it seemed. One would think that the adults hounding him had his best interest at heart, but Noah knew the truth. They all just wanted to cover their own butts and make sure that nothing he did or said got anyone else into trouble with their bosses or the police. The school guidance counselor, Mrs. Perkins, made it a point to poke her head into his classroom each morning for the last two weeks just to ensure that he was there. Ms. Mae dropped him off at school personally each morning, cursing all the way there because he was disrupting her sleep or making her late for her shift at Target. Ms. Hardy had questioned him until he was exhausted about the incident causing his fractured ribs. She'd also questioned him about whether anyone had been touching him inappropriately, but Ms. Mae had already made it clear to him what he needed to say in the event of that type of questioning.

Noah knew that he couldn't hide the fact that someone had done it to him. Doctor Phillips had given him a long lecture on the importance of telling an adult when someone has hurt him following the physical exam he'd had that night at the hospital. The doctor told him that he could tell that someone had hurt him and that Noah could trust him enough to tell him who it was so that he could help him. At the time, Noah was more embarrassed than anything to have someone know with certainty that he'd been used the way he had been. While in the privacy of that exam room, Noah had remained silent, electing not to disclose the truth to Doctor Phillips for fear that the man wouldn't believe him.

His fear was different now. Given the rants, lectures, and cursing out that Ms. Mae often issued to him behind closed doors these days, he knew that the old woman knew the truth. He hadn't said a word to her about the beating or Mikey's antics, but from her words and tone, Noah could tell that she knew. It was the reason why she told him that he'd better be sure to tell the social worker that the kids from the neighborhood had hurt him versus bringing trouble to her home. She threatened him, telling him that life would only get worse for him if he was to tell anyone what she called "lies" about their household. She knew they weren't lies. She was just afraid of what would happen should the truth ever really get out. Noah was afraid of what either she or Mikey would do to him if he uttered one word that contradicted his previous statement about being jumped. He was stuck, and the only way he could see himself being free from it all was through death. Unfortunately for him, he was just a kid and figured he had a long time before he'd finally die and leave this hateful, untrustworthy earth.

Ms. Mae was in her room, struggling to pull on her shoes to take Noah to school. It had become her single most dreaded task in her effort to pretend like all was well. Noah was fully dressed and had developed a slight sense of comfort now. He figured that as long as he remained silent and played the role of the good, quiet kid sticking to the lie Ms. Mae was forcing him to tell, then he'd be okay. Mikey hadn't been around in a minute, and Noah had actually had a full night's sleep for the past couple of nights. His body was still healing, and he was starting to relax, thinking that maybe things would settle down and be okay so long as he never told a soul the truth behind the misery he was living with.

Noah opened the refrigerator door and pulled out the milk jug. He knew he'd get breakfast at school, but was thirsty now so he didn't see the harm in having a quick drink. He turned his back to the doorway to get a cup from the cabinet and poured himself some milk. Still standing in the same position, he turned the cup up to his mouth and savored the fresh flavor of the diary product. For the longest he was used to outdated, sour milk being left in the refrigerator. Now, the kitchen was stocked plentifully with all fresh foods. Just another perk of Ms. Mae being afraid to be caught off of her game.

"Who the hell told you that you could drink my milk?"

Noah turned around and instantly spat out the milk he'd just sipped, messing up his Goodwill hand-me-down Polo shirt. He dropped the cup in his hand, spilling milk all across the linoleum. The sound of the man's voice struck a fear in him like no other wave of fright that he'd ever experienced. Every moment of pain, every memory of tears, every instance of disgust and horror returned to Noah's heart, brain, and body as he stood before the person that had caused the majority of the turmoil in his life. He began to shake and was angry with himself for being so lax and being stupid enough to believe that he could ever be safe while still living in this house.

Mikey sneered at him. "You think you done did some-thing, huh?" he asked Noah, feeling empowered by the intimidation he was causing. "You running around mak-ing folk think you getting abused and shit. Got my mama all scared for me to be in my own house. I'on know what kinda shit you telling these folk, boy, but you betta watch ya' mouth. Ain't nobody going to jail off yo' crybaby ass and yo' imagination."

His imagination? Noah blinked disbelievingly. Had Mikey convinced himself that all the things he'd done to Noah never really happened? Never in a million years would Noah have conjured up such a gruesome story via his imagination. No kid wanted to imagine half of the horrible things that he'd experienced. If he could, he too would like to pretend as if it had never happened, but it simply wasn't something that his brain would allow him to do.

"Fo' you go around telling folk all kinds of mess you better think about what's gon' happen to you," Mikey warned Noah as he stepped closer to the child. "You think them kids be messing with you now, what you think they gon' say when word gets out that you a faggot?"

Noah balled up his fists, prepared to defend himself should Mikey get any closer.

Mikey noticed his demeanor and laughed. "Oh, you wolfing up? You think you got balls now, younge'on? Hell you gon' do with them fists? You ain't man enough to use 'em, bitch ass." He sneered at him with a look in his eyes that Noah knew all too well.

"Don't you touch me," Noah heard himself squeak out. Rarely ever had he voiced his wish to not be bothered since he knew that none of his pleading or begging ever worked when Mikey or Ms. Mae was dead set on doing whatever to him.

"Hell you say?" Mikey asked, walking completely up on the boy and pinning him against the counter.

"I'm not a faggot!" Noah stated in that same whiny voice. "Don't you touch me!"

"Or else what?" Mikey challenged. He jacked Noah up by the front of his shirt and gritted at him. "I hate yo' li'l ass. Don't you know I'd whoop the shit out of your disrespectful ass?"

"Mikey, let that boy go!" Ms. Mae snapped, entering the kitchen. She was surprised to see Mikey in the house, especially after she'd asked him to lie low for a while. It angered her when he didn't listen. He had a habit of doing that, especially when she was trying to tell him stuff for his own good. "We got enough problems, you hear?"

The phone rang, and everyone's eyes darted over to the old-school extension hanging on the wall. It was 7:20 in the morning. Who could possibly be calling at that time?

Ms. Mae reached for the receiver at the tail end of the second ring.

"Hello?" she offered a questioning salutation.

"Good morning, Ms. Johnson. It's Olivia Collins. I was calling to see if Noah had gone off to school yet."

Ms. Mae rolled her eyes at the sound of the woman's voice. She was really beginning to be a pain in the ass with the way she popped up or called whenever, not to mention the court notice that had come in the mail summoning her to appear in one week regarding a possible change in Noah's placement. "We was just on our way out the door," she advised the advocate. "He's gon' have to call you this afternoon."

"If it's all the same to you, I'd like to have a quick word with him right now, please."

Ms. Mae looked over at Noah who was still being hemmed up by a menacing Mikey. Now wasn't the time for the child to communicate with the woman, but Ms. Mae knew that if she denied the advocate's wish she'd have to answer for it later. She sighed deeply into the phone. "Fine," she hissed. She covered the mic on the phone and glared at Mikey. "Let that boy go! This damn woman pick up on the fact that you're here and you gon' fuck up this job for me!"

Mikey snarled at his mother and looked down at Noah. "Ain't gon' be no problem, Ma. Is it?" he asked Noah, still holding firm to the child's shirt.

Noah shook his head.

Mikey let go of him with a violent shove, and then pushed him in his mother's direction as she held the phone out to Noah. Noah took the extension and looked from Mikey to Ms. Mae, realizing that they weren't going to give him any privacy. Ms. Mae narrowed her eyes, ready to focus in on his conversation. Mikey crossed his arms and stood right in front of Noah, daring him to say one disparaging word.

"Hello," Noah spoke weakly, trying not to let his tears spill over.

"Hi, Noah. It's Olivia. You all ready for school?"

"Yeah."

"Well, I don't want to make you late. You were on my mind, and I just wanted to let you know that I'm coming over this afternoon to take you out for a bit. While you're at school, think about where you'd like to go eat, okay?"

"Okay . . . sure." The thought of escaping Ms. Mae's house even for a little while was a relief. Even though he'd never be able to disclose even to Olivia what he was going through, just being with her and away from his reality gave him temporary comfort.

Olivia hesitated as she focused on Noah's tone. "Everything okay?"

"Mmm-hmm."

"Ms. Mae waiting to drop you to school?"

"Mmm-hmm."

"Is she right there?"

"Mmm-hmm."

"Hmmm. You feel uncomfortable, Noah? Do you need me to meet you at the school?"

"N-n-no. I'm fine."

She didn't believe it. "You don't sound fine. Did something happen? Have you been hurt?"

"No." It wasn't a lie. No one had done him any physical harm . . . this morning as of yet. All the hurt he was experiencing was purely emotional at that moment.

"Noah, is anyone there other than you and Ms. Mae?"

Noah's eyes darted over to Mikey who was giving him a deadly stare. He knew that it was time to wrap up this call before his trembling voice denoted his fear through the phone line. "N-n-no. I really gotta go now. I'm gonna be late for school."

"I'll see you this afternoon, Noah. I promise, okay?"

"Okay. Bye." He quickly hung up the phone and made a beeline for the door.

"Where you going, boy?" Ms. Mae asked.

Noah stopped in his tracks. "To change my shirt for school."

"No time. You shouldn't have messed ya'self in the first place and carried on so long on the phone. Get ya' bag and get in the car. I needa get back here and catch me a nap before work. I swear, you got my schedule all messed up with ya' foolishness. Go on now!"

Noah didn't like the idea of going to school smelling like sour milk, but he was used to the ridicule that he typically experienced anyway. So much for thinking that maybe things would get better as long as he followed the script he'd been handed. Noah grabbed his tattered book bag off of the dinette chair in the kitchen and trailed toward the front door to head outside to wait for Ms. Mae.

Upon hearing the front door shut, Ms. Mae turned to face her only son. "You just dead set on messing up this money for me, right?"

Mikey waved his mother off and peered into the refrigerator. "Man, go on with all that."

"You don't hardly do nothing around this place. Don't contribute worth shit to none of these bills, but you wanna come in here and try to mess up this easy money. All I asked you to do was to do something with ya'self until I got this handled."

"You expect me to stay out in the streets like a bum or some shit? A nigga wanna be in his own home, his own bed, man."

"You watch yo' tone with me. It's yo' fault we in this mess."

He slammed the refrigerator door shut and glared at his mother who was considerably shorter than him. "*My* fault? *You* the one always running these kids up in here."

"It's a job, something you don't know nothing 'bout."

"Then you should do yo' job and watch 'em instead of expecting me to babysit these li'l niggas all the time."

Ms. Mae huffed. "You can't be here right now, Mikey. I'm trying to keep this money coming in and keep yo' ass outta jail."

"What I'm going to jail for?" Mikey asked nonchalantly as if he had no clue what she was referring to.

Ms. Mae shook her head and turned up her lips. "Who you thinking you talking to, boy? You think I don't know you? You think I don't know what you been doing to that boy?"

Mikey looked away and opened up a cabinet pulling out a box of cereal. "I'on know what you talkin' 'bout, Ma. Ain't nobody did nothing to that boy. He get wrong, his ass get punished just like any other kid."

"Yeah? Well yo' kinda punishment gon' land yo' ass in jail if you don't stop it."

Mikey shot his mother a knowing look. "Seems to me like it ain't just my kinda punishment. Learnt it from somewhere . . ."

Ms. Mae caught his meaning and was temporarily speechless. The unspoken truth of his comeback lingered in the stale air of the kitchen. It was a Pandora's box that Ms. Mae didn't wanna open—now or ever. Some things were just better left in the past and undiscussed. To her, this was one of them despite what the residual hurt and recurring memories were obviously doing to her only biological son. She took a deep breath before reaching for her purse on the counter. "Eat yo' breakfast and clean that mess up off the floor," she told him. "You gotta be outta here before afternoon comes."

Before he could respond, she turned and left the room, and then the house. Mikey stood still for a moment, fuming over the thoughts battling with one another within his head. He bit his bottom lip hard as his cheeks puffed out in frustration. His fists were planted firmly on the counter as he held his head down, trying to overcome the surge of raging emotion that was filling his body. The silenced, damaged, inner kid that lingered in his spirit wanted to cry. The broken, angered, destructive man he'd become wanted to break something. He was in conflict with himself, the worse kind of position for any person to find himself in. His complex wrath forced him to step back and abruptly turn around to punch a hole straight through the wooden cabinet door over the counter. He hollered out as he assaulted the door and shook his bruised knuckles after the fact. He stared at the hole, which reminded him an awful lot of the one that had been long ago pierced into his heart.

McDonald's was Noah's favorite restaurant. The only time he ever really got to go was when he had one-on-ones with his case manager. Now that Olivia was his advocate, he planned to always ask that she take him there so he could devour a Big Mac. Besides, he enjoyed being with Olivia much more than Ms. Hardy. Sitting at a table in the dining area of the fast-food joint, Noah dipped his fries into his ketchup and shoved them into his mouth, savoring the salty flavor. Olivia smiled at him, happy to see him appearing to have half of the zest of a normal child his age.

"How's school?" she asked him.

Noah shrugged. "Okay, I guess."

"Kids still bothering you?"

"Yeah . . . they say stuff . . . try to push me around some, but I just ignore them."

"What about the kids or the boy you said jumped you that night you were coming to my house? Any trouble from them?"

Noah's eyes never left his burger as he took a bite and shook his head.

Olivia stared at the child feeling her heart break. His inability to make eye contact, his body language, and his lack of verbal response told her what she already knew. She leaned over the table and looked at Noah intently. "Do you understand what it means when I tell you that I'm your advocate now?" she asked him.

He glanced up at her and shrugged again. "That it's okay for me to hang out with you and Ms. Hardy won't get pissed no more?"

"It's more than about just hanging out. It means that we can hang out and you can tell me anything. My job is to make sure that whatever you tell me is acted upon . . . If you need something, you get it. I'm here to make sure that no one ever hurts you again." She paused. "Especially if it's someone you live with. I have to make sure that you're safe at home, Noah, and the only way that I can do that is if you're always, always, always truthful with me. Can you do that for me? Be truthful always?"

Noah stared at her for a moment before nodding his consent and reaching for his fries once more.

"I'm going to ask you some questions that I need you to be honest about, okay?"

He nodded again.

"You weren't jumped by any boys outside that night, were you?"

For a moment he did and said nothing. Then, he slightly shook his head. It was answer enough for Olivia.

"Do you like living with Ms. Johnson?"

He shrugged.

"Did Ms. Mae hurt you, Noah? The way the doctor confirmed that you'd been hurt in your private area . . . Did Ms. Mae do that to you."

"No." His answer was soft but firm.

Olivia believed him, but his response only halfway confirmed her exact belief. "Does her son, Michael, live with you guys too?"

"Not really," Noah replied in an iffy tone.

"Not really?"

"He's not supposed to . . ."

Olivia knew that much to be true. But still, she had a hunch. "So he's not supposed to be living there, but he's there a lot?" She paused to allow him a chance to respond, and when he didn't, she tried again. "Maybe he used to be there a lot?"

Noah nodded.

She had to ask him. This was a defining question and would make all the difference in court the following week. "Noah?"

The child looked up at her.

"Did Michael do that to you? Was he the one that beat you? Did he hurt you like the doctor said you'd been hurt?"

Noah's eyes teared up, and the truth was right there in his expression, yet he remained silent.

Olivia reached over and grabbed his hands lovingly. "You can trust me. I'm here to make sure that no one ever hurts you again, Noah. Let me help you. That's what I'm here for. It's what I'm supposed to do." She fought back her own pleading tears. "If Michael did any of that to you, you can tell me."

Noah considered it. For an eight-year-old, he was a pretty perceptive kid. Adults looked at him and either saw him as a lost cause or a stupid puppet of a kid. Other kids simply viewed him as lowly and pathetic. Some of it may have been true, but the one thing he wasn't was stupid. He'd come to learn how to read adults and discern between who he could trust and what he should and shouldn't say or do in order to survive. Ms. Mae and Mikey had made their threats very clear and had instilled enough fear in Noah to force him to remain silent. He trusted Olivia, and he liked being around her. With Olivia, he didn't fear being hurt, and for the longest, he was really sure that if no one else in the world cared about him, she seemed to. But now, he was beginning to question that belief.

"Because it's your job?" he asked her meekly.

Olivia was confused. "Come again?"

"If he did do it, I can tell you because it's your job to find out stuff like that? To ask me questions?"

"It's my job to make sure you're safe," she replied.

"So you get paid to care about me?"

Olivia blinked profusely as she tried to quickly figure out how to redirect Noah's mode of thinking. Somehow, they'd gotten their wires crossed, and he was obviously viewing her position in his life as a negative thing instead of the positive situation that it was. "No, it isn't like that," she offered weakly.

"Ms. Mae gets paid to take care of me," Noah said. "I'm not really sure she should."

"Get paid or take care of you?" Olivia asked.

"Either. I don't really think people should be paid to care for kids . . . You can't pay somebody to love you. That's not real."

"No . . . no, it's not. But I—"

"Ms. Mae said that you're taking us all to court trying to take me away from her and that if they take me, I'll end up somewhere where people will be mean to me and hurt me all the time. She said that Mikey would get mad if I said what he did to me and that he'd probably hurt me worse than ever."

"But if we get you out of there he can't touch you anymore, Noah. If you let me help you, then you won't ever have to worry about Michael again," Olivia said, feeling grateful for the slip of admittance on Noah's part. "He can't get to you if we take you out of Ms. Johnson's home."

Tears rolled steadily down the child's cheeks, falling onto his abandoned, half-eaten hamburger. "So it's your job to move me from there to somewhere worse?"

Olivia shook her head. "Who is to say it will be worse? Just because that's what they told you? You can't believe everything they say to you, Noah. There's something wrong with Ms. Johnson and her son, and I'm going to make sure that you get far away from them and their influence."

Noah lowered his head, overwhelmed with fear and sadness.

"When I say it's my job to help you, I mean that it's my responsibility," Olivia tried to explain. "It's what my role as your advocate entails. I don't get paid to do this, sweetie. I don't get any money for it at all. I'm doing this because I care about you, Noah. I'm doing this because I get it . . . I believe you. And I don't want to see you hurting anymore."

They sat in silence for a moment as Noah cried his tears of confusion and fear. Olivia rose from her seat, walked around to Noah, and placed her arms around his tiny body. "It's going to be okay," she promised him. "You can trust me. As long as you tell me the truth I promise you that I'm going to make sure that everything's okay. I just need you to always, always be truthful. Okay?"

Noah nodded, pressing his head against her chest and breathing in the aroma of her light musk perfume. He reveled in the firmness of her embrace and felt himself melt into her arms. He couldn't remember the last time he'd been hugged. There was an unfamiliar yet temporarily pleasant sense of security there within her hold. For the first time in a long time, someone was touching him in a way that didn't make him feel uncomfortable, used, hurt, or ashamed. He wanted to believe that the end result she promised would be as positive as she tried to make it out to be, but even with the reassuring, loving hug she summed it up with, Noah was still afraid of what lay within the future.

Chapter 12

No one came. He'd been so concerned about social services coming to her school to question her that it made Kennedy feel as if it was truly going to happen. She went to school continuously on alert waiting for the moment when she'd get called up to the principal's office to meet with someone from the state. For weeks she kept up that enthusiasm believing that each day could possibly be the day she'd be saved. But, after a few weeks, that hope began to dwindle until finally, she just abandoned the idea altogether. She had no idea why he'd been so guarded, but whatever he'd been preparing for obviously wasn't going to happen. Once again, she became the depressed, tormented soul that she'd grown accustomed to being, sleeping lightly every night just in case she had to fight off her father.

Writing became her outlet. Since she was convinced that no one wanted to hear her truth or listen to her private thoughts, fears, and needs, she figured hiding them between the pages of a notebook would be sufficient. She couldn't just let it all sit within her. She had to get it out some kind of way. It first started out as fragmented thoughts scribbled mindlessly on the pages, but then it became more lyrical as complete thoughts transformed into verses. Before long, her bright orange notebook became filled with poems that mirrored her life.

"What you writing, girl?" LaTasha, her friend and classmate, asked her.

Consumed with frustration following a night of her father's drunken slurs and passes, Kennedy was scribbling away. Her eyes never left the page. She didn't even hear the question come out of her friend's mouth.

LaTasha eyed her suspiciously before leaning over her desk to take a peek at what she was writing. As she finished each line, LaTasha's eyes grew wider and wider. They were in journalism class and were supposed to be working on helping their teacher, Ms. Holt, get things together for the upcoming printing of the school's monthly newspaper. But, clearly, Kennedy's heart and mind were elsewhere, and now, LaTasha was engrossed in the emotions being laid out in writing.

"What y'all doing?" Donald, another classmate, asked as he noticed the girls huddled over Kennedy's notebook.

"Man, she over here writing some deep stuff," LaTasha stated.

Donald stared at the emotionally focused Kennedy as she flipped the page and continued with her poetic expressions. He noticed her tears flowing freely and dropping onto the pages, smearing the blue ink of the lines on the notebook paper. "What's it about?"

LaTasha couldn't really give voice to the heavy thoughts she was reading as Kennedy began to write quicker and more feverishly. She looked up at her friend. "What happened, Ken?"

Kennedy didn't respond. She just kept writing until her crying turned into uncontrollable loud sobs as snot dripped from her nose and the tears blinded her eyes from the sting of their saltiness. She dropped her pen and gave in to the tidal wave of emotions that shook her body. LaTasha was stunned. She wrapped her arms around her friend and squeezed her tightly.

"Who did it, Ken?" LaTasha whispered into her ear. "Talk to me."

Donald snatched the notebook up and several other classmates gathered around as they all read Kennedy's words with intrigue. Some understood the metaphors and similes, others just thought that it was a beautifully written poem that was pretty deep for their age.

LaTasha was one of the few that got it explicitly. She squeezed her friend lovingly as she pleaded with her for information. "Don't hold this in, Kennedy. You can talk to me . . . I understand. It's happened to me too."

Her words stunned Kennedy. This was the second time she'd been told by another girl that they'd been in the same hellish position as her. She pulled back and looked into her friend's eyes. "Did you tell?" she whispered.

LaTasha shook her head.

Any hope that Kennedy may have felt plummeted into the pit of her stomach, jump-starting her emotional bout all over again. Was that the way it was? Were they all being sexually abused and expected or forced to say nothing? Was it more of a norm than she thought it was? Her body shook more violently, and her tears came harder and faster. She was no longer crying for herself. She was crying for all the girls everywhere who knew the pain and dysfunction that she lived with daily. She cried for their inability to break the cycle and find an end to the madness. She cried over the fact that no adult seemed to have the foresight do something to save any of them. She cried because no one seemed to notice the change, the effect that this type of trauma had on any of them enough to say "Hey, something's wrong!" She cried because she feared that this was what life was supposed to be like for women . . . used by whomever for whatever sexual perversions any man had. She cried relentlessly because it was clear that help was not coming.

***

Her weeping grew louder and more passionate by the minute and before long, she was practically kicking and screaming in her sleep. Kasyn flicked on the lamp and shook her with all of his might. Although their relationship was strained, at best, these days, he was still trying to hold on to what they had. They didn't talk much, and when they did, the conversation always seemed guarded, like they were each trying their best not to step on the other's toes. Still, she was his fiancée, and even though they weren't seeing eye to eye, he just couldn't stay away from her for too long. Now, here she was having another one of her nightmares and keeping him up after he'd driven down just to spend the night with her since he'd missed her over the last couple of days.

"Olivia! Wake up. Come on, wake up! Livi! Wake up!" He caught an elbow to his eye as she flailed her arms out of astonishment while being jolted away. "Damn it!" he hollered, unhanding her and touching his now tender eyelid.

Olivia sat up in a daze. Her chest rose and fell heavily, and she felt the tears covering her face. Her shirt clung to her body due to the sweat that trickled down her back. She felt panicked. Just like every other time she'd awaken from a nightmare, it took a few moments for her to realize that she was safe within the confines of her bedroom. But this time, unlike the others, she didn't feel that instant sense of security. Instead, she clutched her chest, unable to rid herself of the overcoming emotion of fright and devastation. She sensed that something was terribly wrong. She dreaded that something she couldn't change was just past the horizon and the fear kept her tears rolling.

"I have to save him," Olivia whispered inaudibly.

"Wake up, Livi," Kasyn insisted once more. "Come on, snap out of it. You're up now. It was just a dream."

Olivia shook her head but didn't look in his direction as she stared straight-ahead at the shadows on her bedroom wall while envisioning the worst tailored by her own memories. "I have to save him," she mumbled once more.

Kasyn leaned over, blinking his eye against the sting from her blow. "What's that? What are you talking about?"

"I have to do something . . . I have to save him." She moved to get out of the bed.

Kasyn grabbed her forcefully by her forearm. "Wait a second! Save who?" He frowned. "Please tell me this is not about that kid."

Olivia finally looked him in his eyes, her own red from the tears. "I have to help him," she said in a tone that was so heart-wrenching that Kasyn was stunned.

"This obsession is driving you crazy, Livi. Do you see what it's doing to you? It's already put a wedge between us, and now he's haunting your dreams. What the hell already? Why can't you let this go and let the system do their job and deal with him?"

Olivia shook her head and tried to free her arm from his grasp. "You don't understand," she huffed. "You just don't get it."

"You're right, I don't. This kid is obviously a bad seed from the wrong side of the tracks who's caught a couple of bad breaks. You did a good deed with the hospital thing, which I still think was a risk, now let it go. Why is this so important to you? I mean, damn, baby! Your life is passing you by because you're all wrapped up in this child. But why?"

Pissed with his lack of sensitivity, she finally snatched away from his hold and rose from the bed. "I have to save him," she repeated. "It's my obligation. I have to do it."

"You're not a case manager, Livi. He's not your kid. So why the hell does it have to be *you* to save him?"

"Because nobody saved me!" she screamed back, turning to glare at him frantically with her hands in the air and her voice high and shrill. She was finally breaking. Her eyes protruded as she stared at the man who didn't really know her at all. "Nobody saved me! Nobody cared! *Nobody!*" She backed up quickly, blinded by her tears, and placed her back against the wall. Slowly she slid downward as her heart plummeted into her stomach. For the first time, she was giving voice to a truth that Kasyn didn't even know existed. Her body shook violently, and again, she was that girl rocking with raw emotion in the classroom trying to get out her feelings on a piece of paper that would later become as silent and ghostly as the voice she'd yet to find.

They were on the docket for 2:30 p.m. to go before Judge Amos. Seeing as though he'd granted her the temporary advocacy for Noah, Olivia felt certain that the judge would rule in her favor, overruling DFCS's decision to keep Noah with Ms. Johnson and forcing them to find a more suitable placement. The judge had already read over the medical report from Doctor Phillips, but now, Olivia had something even better, something much more damning and critical to her motion. Noah's statement. Now that he'd told her the truth, and she knew from his firsthand account that Ms. Johnson's son had been abusing him, the court had no choice but to deliberate in her favor. All she had to do was give Noah the floor in hopes that he trusted her enough to follow her advice and tell the judge exactly what had happened to him and by whose hands. To Olivia, this was an open-and-shut case, no guesswork needed at all as to what the right decision was concerning Noah's best interest.

Daysha was there with her simply for support. Even
Shanice had shown up because she was so intrigued
by Olivia's immense concern for and dedication to this
child. Kasyn wasn't there. Following her outburst a
couple of nights back, Olivia shut down so much that
communication with Kasyn simply wasn't possible. In
response, he took that as his cue to pack the majority of
his belongings and left without any word about when she
could expect him to return. At the time she hadn't cared.
She didn't even bother to try to call him to sort things
out. All she needed then was space. In the wake of that,
he couldn't even be bothered to put in an appearance in
order to grasp an understanding of why Noah's rights
were so important to Olivia.

Situated at the table, beside the brown oak one that
Olivia sat at nervously, was the legal representation for
DeKalb County DFCS and Noah's case manager, Ms.
Hardy. Their icy looks were of no consequence to Olivia.
She was there to act in the best interest of Noah. How they
felt about that meant nothing to her. As they waited for
the judge to finish consulting with the court reporter and
bailiff, a stir occurred in the back of the room. In walked
Ms. Mae who was holding tight to Noah's hand. Noah
was dressed in decent-fitting pants and a button-up shirt
that was not too big, faded, or tattered. This was the most
presentable Olivia had ever seen Noah. She attempted to
give him a reassuring smile, but the moment he made eye
contact with her, Noah quickly looked away. He and Ms.
Mae took a seat behind the DFCS workers and waited
silently for the hearing to begin.

"We're hearing county-appointed advocate Olivia
Collins on behalf of minor Noah Maxiel, ward of the state,
vs. DeKalb County's Department of Family and Children
Services represented by Lucretia Dunkin," the judge
stated, reading the paper in front of him. He looked up

in Olivia's direction. "Ms. Collins, you've petitioned the court to have Noah removed from his current foster care placement . . . the home of . . . uh . . . Ms. Mae Johnson, based on the premise of neglect and abuse. The court is in receipt of medical documentation from a Dr. Raymond Phillips noting evidence of slight malnutrition, two rib fractures, and apparent sexual abuse. You contend now, Ms. Collins, that these things are a direct reflection of the care being given to the child by the appointed foster care parent?"

Olivia hesitated before speaking. "Uh, partially, sir," she answered.

"Partially?" Judge Amos removed his glasses and frowned his brow. "Explain your position."

"Initially, I was concerned that Ms. Johnson could have been abusing Noah because I wasn't certain until recently that her son, Michael, has also been residing in the home although paperwork states that he is not supposed to be an inhabitant. Ummm, I do think that Ms. Johnson has dropped the ball on making certain that Noah is fed properly and daily, but I'm convinced that the physical and sexual abuse the child has endured has been inflicted by the son."

"And you know this because . . .?"

"Noah told me," she replied. "And if it's okay with you, sir, I'd like to give Noah an opportunity to speak up for himself . . . to . . . uh . . . to give a firsthand account so you hear his testimony, if you will, directly from him."

With her back to Daysha, Olivia missed the grimace upon the attorney's face. She did, however, turn to the right just in time to pick up on the slight smirk gracing Ms. Hardy's lips.

"Um, Your Honor, if I may?" Ms. Dunkin, DFCS's legal representative interjected.

"Proceed."

Olivia looked over to the woman intently waiting to hear what far-fetched rebuttal the woman could possibly have at this point in the hearing.

"Considering the nature of the incidents at hand, I believe that it is far too traumatizing to ask such a young person to take the stand and rehash the details for us," Ms. Dunkin stated. "It's certainly not in Noah's best interest to more or less put him on display and make the child feel as if his statement is being picked apart. Surely you can see how it'd be intimidating for a child his age to come before the court to pretty much bear his soul."

"I'm not asking him to bear his soul," Olivia objected. "But what better way to assess the truth rather than to get it straight from the horse's mouth? Straight from the source? I mean, no one can tell you better what happened to him other than him."

"Agreed," Ms. Dunkin replied, pointing her index finger toward Olivia just before reaching into a manila folder resting on the table before her. "Which is why we allowed Noah to write a statement, in his own words, in the presence of only his case manager so as not to have influence by Ms. Johnson or her son, who, coincidentally, visits his mother's home frequently. This statement is not coerced and is unbiased . . . a direct account and testament to the fact that Noah was assaulted by peers, although violently, and not by his foster mother or relatives within his current housing placement." She rose from her seat to hand the judge the original signed and date stamped statement before handing Olivia a photocopy of the document.

Olivia stared down at the childlike script and felt her body grow weak. In just a few short sentences, Noah had penned a statement negating everything they'd discussed and the accusation she'd just placed before the court. In his own words scribbled in black ink he told how some neighborhood thugs attacked and brutally abused him, even going so far as to say that an object that he was sure was a stick was lodged up his behind. Olivia found herself biting her lower lip to keep it from trembling. As an author, she knew what she was looking at: pure fiction.

Moments later, the judge cleared his throat and looked past the legal representative and case manager to get a good look at Noah. "This is the young man in question?"

Ms. Dunkin looked back at Noah and nodded her head. "Yes, Your Honor. This is Noah Maxiel."

"Young man, can you stand up for me?" Judge Amos requested.

Ms. Hardy turned and gave a raised brow expression to Noah as Ms. Mae urged him to stand up. The room remained perfectly quiet as no one knew what was going to be said or done next.

"Noah, did you write this letter?" the judge asked him.

Noah nodded without making eye contact with the judge.

"Look up and use your words," Ms. Hardy hissed.

Noah's sad eyes found the inquisitive stare of the judge seated high up upon his bench. "Yes . . . sir . . ."

Olivia saw the way his foot fidgeted. He was nervous. She knew that about him. In just the short amount of time that she'd gotten acquainted with Noah, she'd become acclimated with his behavior patterns and quirks. She knew that when he was uncomfortable, scared, and lacking trust, he couldn't be still. The others either didn't notice or simply didn't care. All they were concerned about were the empty words coming out of the child's mouth.

"And no one told you what to write?" the judge asked.

"N-n-no, sir."

"And this what you wrote . . . This is the truth as you know it?"

Noah nodded again.

The judge looked over to Ms. Mae, and then back at Noah. "Beside you is your foster mother, correct?"

Another head nod.

"Do you feel comfortable with her?" Judge Amos inquired. "Are you happy living where you are, son?"

"Yes," came Noah's weak reply.

The judge nodded. "Very well. Have a seat, son."

Noah's eyes darted over to Olivia who gave him a questioning look. Her heart was breaking as she peered into his soul seeing the tormented child that she was familiar with, silently begging him to retract his statement and be brave enough to air the truth.

"And a thorough investigation of the home and the guardian has been done by social services?" the judge asked, turning his attention back to Ms. Dunkin.

"Yes, sir. The case manager, Ms. Hardy, has done an extensive interview with the parent, surveyed the home, and the office has sent out an investigator to interview neighbors and the school's guidance counselor. All individuals contend that they've neither seen nor heard of anything happening within Ms. Johnson's home to insinuate that the boy is being abused or that the home environment is unsafe." Once again, she rounded the table to hand the judge several more papers. "All signed affidavits from all individuals interviewed."

"Can I . . . Can I say something?" Olivia asked, feeling things spiraling out of control and heading in a direction she wasn't prepared to deal with.

"Go-ahead," the judge replied although his attention was focused upon the papers he'd just been given.

"She said the school guidance counselor was interviewed, but I spoke with her myself, and she didn't have the least bit of concern for Noah. In fact, she stated that since he was frequently absent from school, she couldn't put much energy into keeping up with what was going on with him. I question, sir, how any statement from an individual who shows such lack of interest in the child could be seriously considered as evidence."

"Since the incident, Noah's attendance has been stellar," Ms. Dunkin shot back.

"Yeah? Well, we're talking about things that happened leading up to the incident," Olivia snapped. "Not this reactive behavior that's obviously in play due to the heat being on Ms. Johnson and her son."

The judge banged his gavel. "Order!" he called out. "Please make your point clear, Ms. Collins."

"My point, sir, is that any statement issued by Mrs. Perkins has to be fraudulent because prior to Noah's hospital visit, this woman had no clue what was going on in the child's life."

"The statement provided by Mrs. Perkins attests to the fact that she has never once received a verbal or written complaint from Noah denoting any kind of discomfort regarding living within Ms. Johnson's domicile," Ms. Dunkin stated matter-of-factly. "She contends that she has no record of any teacher voicing concern about Noah's physical, mental, or emotional well-being. That is not fraudulent. That would be a fact judging by Noah's school file being void of any incident reports, notes about discussions with the child on his home life, or written concerns." Ms. Dunkin stared at Olivia as if daring her to come back with the slightest utterance.

All Olivia could do was shake her head. She was drowning. They were burying her in a sea of bullshit and there was no life jacket in sight. She turned slightly to look over at Noah whose head hung low. *Maybe it wasn't a good idea for him to be here*, Olivia thought. This was turning more into DFCS trying to prove Olivia wrong versus actually doing what was best for the child. The entire thing disgusted Olivia. She looked up at the judge and crossed her fingers, hoping that she could get through to him despite the crap that Ms. Perkins was coming up with. She needed to appeal to his emotions. It was the only way that she'd have a shot at getting him to rule in her favor.

"Judge Amos," she called out. "Please, look at this child. We're sitting here going back and forth about what neighbors and others think about a home none of them have to live in. Noah's the one who has to live there. He's the one whose feelings and well-being we're supposed to all be concerned with, right? I mean, do you think he'd really be sitting there looking broken the way he does if nothing in the world was wrong? Ms. Dunkin is telling you how everyone else says that Ms. Johnson's environment is safe and that he seems to be okay where he is. Well, if we're viewing this . . . this written statement as gospel, then why aren't we questioning Noah's supervision? Why isn't anyone concerned with how he was able to get out of such a secured home in the middle of the evening which allegedly led to him being beaten and sodomized? Why aren't we asking people in the neighborhood if they saw or heard anything to confirm the story that's being told? Why hasn't an arrest warrant been issued for whomever allegedly assaulted him? Has anyone asked the child who his attackers were? If he could identify them? I mean, if we're going to buy this as truth," she stated holding up the paper filled with lies.

"Noah has been questioned by both social services and an investigator from DeKalb County Police Department upon his return home from his hospital visit. Each time, Noah stated that he didn't know the assailants and that no one else was around." Ms. Dunkin pulled out yet another sheet of paper and smirked at Olivia. "This would be the official police report."

Olivia was livid. "Let me see that!"

"Gladly." Ms. Dunkin handed her a copy as well as the judge.

"Impossible," Olivia stated. "When I received Noah's file from Ms. Hardy, this document was not present." Her eyes fell upon the date etched in print at the top of the page. She was furious. No one had once told her that this investigation had been done. Something within her was saying that perhaps it was as bogus as the written statement from Noah.

"In light of the evidence presented here today . . ." Judge Amos began.

Olivia's eyes grew wide as she stared at the family court judge before her. She could almost guess what was about to flow from his lips next.

". . . and comparing the information previously received by the court, I have to deduct that the unfortunate occurrence experienced by the young man is in no way indicative of the care he receives by Ms. Johnson."

"Are you serious?" Olivia blurted out, water filling her eyes.

Judge Amos's eyes shot over to Olivia as if to warn her to be quiet. "In parenting, we all make mistakes, and we can't always protect our children from the evils of the world. Could Ms. Johnson have exercised better supervision? Perhaps. But we can't put all of the blame on the foster parent in this instance. It is the professional opinion of social services and the familial opinion of the community who knows Ms. Johnson which contends that the current placement isn't any less sufficient for the development of young Noah than any other environment."

"No," Olivia said, shaking her head. "No no no. Please, don't do this. The evils of the world?" she questioned frantically. "It isn't the evils of the world that concerns me pertaining to Noah. It's the evil lurking within the walls of Ms. Johnson's home that scares me!"

Daysha reached over and placed her hand on Olivia's shoulder in an effort to calm her down. She could see the frustration building within the judge's face and didn't want her friend and former protégé to end up behind bars for being in contempt of court.

Judge Amos banged his gavel once more as he held his jaws clenched tightly. "Ms. Collins, I'm going to encourage you to exercise some self-control. This is a courtroom, not an open field, and you most certainly may not speak over me at any point in time."

"But Your Honor . . . I'm begging you here . . . Don't do this. If you send this child back with that woman, God only knows what'll happen next."

"Ms. Collins, you simply have not convinced me that danger presents itself within Noah's environment. The child himself has told us—"

"It's a lie!" Olivia screamed desperately. "It's a lie. I'm more than sure that they forced him to write that. One of them, either of them. I *know* what he told me."

"So you'd stand here before the court and the child whom you advocate for and call the child a liar to his face?" the judge challenged.

Olivia turned to face Noah. Appealing to the judge was no good. He needed to hear it from Noah. But how could she get him to step up before it was too late. "It's okay, Noah," she said. "It's okay."

"Order!" the judge declared.

"You have to tell them the truth. Tell them what you told me. Tell them!" She rose from her seat and took two steps in the child's direction, ready to fall to her knees at any moment and beg for his compliance. "You *have* to tell them," she said between passionate sobs. "It's the only way. It's the only way I can save you."

Noah's eyes met hers, and she saw him soften just a tad. They communicated nonverbally, and she sensed his strength building as she gave him the most reassuring expression she could through the emotion she was involuntarily expressing.

"Your Honor, she's practically badgering the child," Ms. Dunkin observed. "Surely this is unacceptable behavior for a CASA."

The sound of the gavel nearly breaking as it pounded the top of the bench was an oblivious noise to Olivia. She was too busy pleading with Noah to set himself free by letting his voice finally be heard right then and there. His lips parted slightly, and Olivia nodded profusely, convicted in her belief that this was the defining moment that would redirect the course of Noah's life. Triumph was just within her grasp, and she'd claim the victory in the name of all the abused children who'd never gotten the opportunity to be freed from the tormenting hell they suffered silently within. But then it all came crashing down the moment Ms. Mae took a firm hold of Noah's hand, and he broke the stare they'd been holding. It felt as if a vital organ had been mercilessly snatched from her body and the air pushed haphazardly from her lungs.

"No," she said, panting with disbelief and shaking her head. "No, no! No, Noah, don't do this."

"Order order order!"

Daysha was quick on her feet as she caught Olivia the moment her body wavered. "Stop it! You're making yourself sick, and you're gonna end up in jail." She placed her hand over her friend's mouth and held her tightly.

"I'm dismayed by the behavior displayed here today," Judge Amos stated. "While I appreciate the advocate's passion, I will not tolerate disrespect! Final ruling, Noah Maxiel's placement will remain as is unless further sufficient evidence is provided to the court verifying the need to reconsider." He banged his gavel. "Court dismissed. Counselor," he called out, addressing Daysha.

"Yes sir?"

"I suggest you have a word with your associate surrounding the proper decorum for the courtroom."

"Yes, sir," Daysha repeated, feeling Olivia's body grow limp.

Olivia's eyes were fixated on the way Ms. Mae quickly pulled Noah along and scurried out of the courtroom. Everything within Olivia knew that the judge had just made the single worse deliberation of his life. Watching Noah exit the courtroom with Ms. Mae was an overwhelming display of defeat. Her head felt woozy, and her vision became blurred. Everything around her was spinning, and the voices of her adversaries sounded like computerized noises.

Ms. Hardy voiced something to Ms. Dunkin, who immediately called out to the judge for his attention. "Your Honor!"

Judge Amos had just risen from his seat as he stopped to glare at the woman calling out to him. He was done listening to adults squabble with one another like children, ironically, over a child. "What is it, Ms. Dunkin?"

"May we make motion to have Ms. Collins replaced as Noah's advocate? Given what's happened here today, it doesn't really appear that she's . . . uh . . . stable . . . enough for this position."

"That's the decision of the court. Again, her passion is commendable. If you have any other just reason for such a motion, then I suggest you file it accordingly." With that, the judge exited toward his chambers.

Olivia was done. Her senses and self-awareness had left her as she crumbled in Daysha's arms. Shanice rushed to her aid, and together, the two women struggled to get her in a seated position in the chair she'd abandoned. But it was too late. By the time her bottom hit the seat, her body slipped downward as darkness took over.

The disappointment and grief over the possibilities that now surrounded Noah's existence were all too great for her. Slipping out of consciousness was the only way that she could temporarily escape from the fear and the pain that haunted her daily.

Chapter 13

She drifted mindlessly through the quiet of her apartment with a concerned Shanice trailing close behind her carrying the bottle of Belvedere that Olivia had insisted upon getting. From the kitchen, Olivia grabbed two glasses, opting not to fill them with ice as she sauntered on into the living room. She kicked off her heels in front of the sofa and stared into space, lost in her thoughts. Shanice took the glasses from her hands before they could drop to the carpeted floor. As her distraught friend dropped down onto the sofa, Shanice opened up the bottle of liquor and poured them both a shot. The afternoon had taken a turn for the worse, and Shanice had never seen Olivia so out of it and disconcerted. Following the episode at the courthouse, an ambulance had been called to escort Olivia to the hospital. Her blood pressure was through the roof, and Shanice had sat with her for nearly two hours in the exam room waiting for the medication they'd given her to work its magic by stabilizing Olivia's pressure. By the hour and a half mark, Shanice had been sure that the doctor was going to admit Olivia. No way would they discharge her with her stats being so unsettling. But soon, she received a normalized reading, and the nurse set her free with instructions to visit her general physician within three days.

Now, Olivia was silent. It worried Shanice to know that her friend was holding in her emotions. It was apparent to her just how passionate she was about helping this child. Not that she didn't applaud Olivia's humane endeavors where Noah was concerned, but she still couldn't understand exactly why it was that Olivia had allowed herself to get this emotionally attached to a child she had no legal or familial obligations to.

"Here," Shanice said, offering Olivia her shot.

Olivia took the glass and quickly threw back the warm alcohol. Immediately, she held the glass out to Shanice in a request for another.

Shanice obliged and watched as Olivia wasted no time, yet again, in draining her glass. She hadn't even waited for Shanice to get down her first one. This behavior was alarming coming from Olivia. When Olivia held her glass out to her once more, Shanice's eyebrow rose. "Maybe you should slow down a little and get some food in you."

Olivia rolled her eyes and reached for the bottle to pour up her own drink. This time, the cognac glass was filled halfway, exceeding the amount of a shot.

"Livi, I don't think—"

Olivia shook her head and held the glass near her lips though she did not yet drink. "I don't need that. I don't need any lectures from anybody." She gave Shanice a stern look, and then proceeded to sip from the mighty potion flowing from her glass.

Shanice sat back in the armchair she was situated in. "So *this* is your plan? To drink away your problems?"

"You don't know nothing about my problems," Olivia mumbled.

"Look, you tried, Livi. You went in there, and you gave it your best shot. That's about the most anyone could have done. There was nothing you could have done differently."

Olivia could think of several things she could have done differently, starting with recording her conversation with Noah that day at McDonald's. Maybe Ms. Dunkin was right. Maybe it was a little too intimidating and a bit much to expect Noah to stand up in the courtroom with Ms. Mae sitting right there and admit to the things that had been happening within her care. But, Olivia knew without a shadow of a doubt that between the foster mother, the legal representation for social services, and the case manager, that somehow, Noah had been forced to pen that bogus statement freeing Ms. Mae's son of any guilt. It just killed her that she had no way to prove it.

"It's a heartbreaking situation, Livi, but you gotta have faith that things will be okay," Shanice stated. "I mean, maybe the judge's call was right. Not to discredit any of your concerns, but . . . That's what these people get paid for, right? To make the best solid and sound decision possible based upon the facts."

Olivia couldn't believe her ears. She loved Shanice, but at that moment, she wanted to bang the woman's face into the coffee table. "Spoken like a true privileged individual."

"Excuse me?"

"You don't know anything about Noah," Olivia snapped. "You don't know shit about what it's like to live in fear and feel as if you can't say anything to anybody about it. You have no idea the personal conflict that child's battling with trying to do what he has to do in order to survive. Even lie out of fear for his life."

"What makes you so sure he's lying, Livi? Can I point out that until just a little while ago, you didn't know this child either? Maybe it's possible that anything he told you was fabricated."

"It wasn't. And it isn't so much what he's said, but what I know. What I sense."

"What you know, huh? So you've seen this woman's son abusing this child, Livi?"

"Don't sass me, Shanice."

"I'm just asking a question. You're so convinced in your belief, I'm just asking you why, especially after you saw today in court how everything you sensed was dispelled."

"You just don't know . . ."

Shanice moved to the edge of her seat and bugged her eyes. "What? I just don't know *what?* Why don't you tell me so that I can know? What can you tell me now that you didn't say in that courtroom today to help plead your case, Livi?"

Olivia remained silent as she nursed her drink. Tears dripped down into the clear liquor and Olivia neglected to wipe them away.

"I'm not trying to sound insensitive, but I think that maybe it's time for you to step away from this. It's becoming an obsession that's effecting your emotional and physical health. You could have died today, Livi, with the way your blood pressure shot up. That's not cute, boo." Shanice studied her friend for a moment before going on. "It's over now. Exhale and focus on something else. For whatever the reason, you've engrossed yourself in a story line with Noah that may or may not exist. It's time to focus on some reality."

"Reality?" Olivia questioned. "You want me to focus on reality?" She sat up and narrowed her eyes to zero in on the look that Shanice was giving her. "Okay. How about every two minutes in America someone's sexually abused? How about one in four girls and one in six boys will be sexually abused before they reach the age of eighteen?"

Shanice hesitated to respond to the sudden bout of statistics being thrown at her. "O-o-okay." She tilted her head to the side, slightly caught off guard by the turn of their conversation. "And while that's unfortunate, who's to say that—"

Olivia continued speaking, cutting Shanice off abruptly. "How about the fact that eight out of nine sexual abuse acts are committed by someone the person knows personally? A family friend, a neighbor, a sibling, a foster parent or babysitter . . . a goddamn parent!"

Shanice grimaced at the thought, but before she could respond, Olivia hit her with more damning information.

"How about because of that last little tidbit, only 12 percent of child sexual abuse crimes are reported to the authorities? Kids are afraid to speak out against the people they know . . . afraid to get them in trouble, afraid of what might happen to them if they tell." Olivia gripped her glass tightly with both hands as she perched upon the edge of her seat with her eyes bugged and unblinking, staring into the awed pupils of her friend who was apparently reeling from the dose of reality that Olivia was serving her. "How about someone you know more than likely has been sexually abused," she spat out, pointing a finger at her friend. "But this is not the type of shit we sit around the dinner table and discuss, now, is it?" Olivia rose to her feet, the tears never ending, and stared down at her now shocked friend. "How do I know what's going on with Noah? Because *I've* been there! Because *I* was Noah. Because *I'm* a fuckin' statistic, a part of that one in four girls. Now, how's *that* for some fuckin' reality?"

Olivia turned away and headed to her office leaving Shanice to sit with the harsh truth that had just been thrown at her. Feeling the effects of the Belvedere and having not eaten, Olivia flipped on the light and swayed over to her desk. Sitting down, her eyes zeroed in on the envelope propped up in front of her keyboard with her name on it. She set her glass down and ripped the envelope open. Inside was a single-page letter. She didn't have to skip down to the signature because she recognized his handwriting immediately. Her eyes adjusted to read the fine script, and her body went numb with each word she processed.

Dear Livi,

In the last couple of months I've come to realize that I don't really know you at all. The woman I fell in love with, the woman I proposed to, wasn't this woman who shuts me out, makes rash decisions, and throws her entire being into anything or anyone without some sound justification for it. I can't keep begging you to be in this relationship. I won't beg you to let me in, to help me understand what it is that's going on with you. It's clear to me from your outburst that you've got some deeply rooted psychological things going on that you never even wanted or cared to share with me. How can I help you if you won't let me in? How can you be married to someone you don't trust with your deepest, darkest secrets? Obviously, you didn't trust me enough to disclose this part of yourself, and the fact that you clearly haven't dealt with your repressed emotions and issues would certainly weigh heavily on our marriage if we chose to move forward. At this time, I don't think that's wise. I'm giving you your space to deal with whatever demons from your past are so great that you feel we can't battle them together. I wish you nothing but the best, and I hope that you'll understand my reasoning behind walking away instead of seeing it as me bailing on you. Right now, you need something that you've already determined I can't give to you, and quite frankly, I need something you haven't given to me: a woman who's all in and trusts me. If I may impart one piece of advice . . . You can't help Noah or anyone else until you've first helped yourself. Take care of yourself, Olivia.

Love and respect,
Kasyn

The paper slipped from her fingers, and Olivia reached for what was left of her drink. The glass was nearly empty, much like her soul felt at that moment.

He was alone. Surely it wasn't the ideal situation for a kid his age, but it was much better than being babysat by a child molester. Ms. Mae was working a double shift and had given him a stern warning against leaving the house while she was out for the evening. She didn't have to worry, though. Noah had no intentions of stepping foot outside of the door. With the house to himself, he felt oddly safe. He had plans of making a sandwich out of the meat loaf that was left over from dinner the night before, and then sitting in front of the television in the living room watching some of the shows his classmates often discussed at school. Typically, he was banned from watching television because Mikey was always hogging the set. But now that Mikey was basically missing in action, Noah had free reign and could do as he pleased, at least until Ms. Mae came home.

As he showered he began to think that maybe things wouldn't be so bad after all. Sure, he'd lied in court and possibly made Olivia mad at him, but he wasn't being harmed, and things were seemingly quiet in his life now. Maybe he'd done the right thing by doing exactly what Ms. Mae had forced him to do. He hadn't wanted to write the note full of lies about what happened to him, but Ms. Mae had made it clear what would happen to him should he implicate Mikey in any way. Scared that life in the system would do him in or that Mikey would find him and do something fatal, per the picture that Ms. Mae had painted for him, Noah felt it best to just scribble the story that she instructed him to share.

Turning off the shower, Noah wrapped himself in his worn-out terry cloth towel, grabbed up his dirty clothes from the floor, and happily opened the bathroom door to exit. Before he could step one foot out onto the carpet, he was bum-rushed from the right side as a figure caught him in a choke hold and grabbed his right arm to twist it behind his back, causing him to drop the clothes he'd been carrying. Noah screamed out in fright, thinking that someone had broken into the house while he was showering. As the powerful being pinned him facing forward to the wall, Noah felt his already loose towel drop to the ground. He was completely vulnerable and exposed and had no idea what was about to happen to him.

"Ya li'l bitch ass thought you was just gon' lay up in my mama's house pretending like you her real son or some shit?"

Mikey leaned into Noah as he spoke with his face close enough to Noah's, which was pressed sideways up against the plaster, so that the child could smell the liquor heavy on the man's breath. His speech was slightly slurred, and Noah knew without a doubt that Mikey was drunk. He also knew exactly how violent and belligerent Mikey could get when he was intoxicated. Feeling the way Mikey was pressed up against him, memories of the night his foster brother had allowed some stranger to violate him returned to the forefront of Noah's mind.

"You're hurting me," Noah squealed. "My arm, my arm!"

Mikey showed no mercy as he continued to twist the child's arm, bruising his delicate skin. He licked Noah's ear and laughed sinisterly in it. "Dumb ass. Thought you was gon' run me away from my own house? Ain't no bitch alive gon' scare me outta my own home. You can cancel that shit. You know who run this, don't you?"

Noah's arm felt as if it would snap at any moment, and he was petrified. He remembered the day that Mikey had snuck up on him causing him to spill milk all over the kitchen floor. Just like that day, today, Noah had felt a slight sense of peace and relief, yet, here came Mikey proving to him that such peace would never exist for him. He was beginning to regret his decision to stick to the story Ms. Mae had outlined for him. He silently wished through his loud, earsplitting screams that he'd listened to Olivia instead of putting himself in this position. Chill bumps now covered his little body as he shivered and trembled from the brisk air and the pain that Mikey was inflicting.

"Teach you to fuck with me," Mikey said. "What you gon' do now, huh? You gon' call ya' li'l friend to come save you? You think she gon' come down here and snatch ya' ass up right quick? She'on care 'bout you. Don't nobody care 'bout ya' ass. Ya' own family don't care 'bout ya—that's how ya' ass ended up here in the first place. Reject kid. You only good for one thing, and ya' ass can't even shut the fuck up and do that right."

Noah's throat was raw from screaming. It was clear that no one was going to come knocking down the door to save him. All of the people that Ms. Hardy and the investigators had allegedly interviewed in the neighborhood were obviously hard of hearing or had adopted that mind-set of minding their own business. Never mind the fact that it sounded as if Noah was on the verge of death. His body grew lethargic from the screaming, crying, and pointless struggling against Mikey's strong hold. The screams simmered down to a mere whimper by the time he began to feel lightheaded from the overwhelming pain that was consuming his body.

"What you gon' do?" Mikey taunted. "What you gon' do now?" He pressed his body closer to Noah's, and then sharply kneed the child in the arch of his back.

"Owwww!" Noah cried out, snot shooting from his nose and a new excruciating sting shooting up his back. His body was being tortured in so many ways that he couldn't focus on any one pain more than the other.

"Shut up!" Mikey demanded. "Don't nobody wanna hear all that whining like you a li'l-ass girl. Man up! Break loose and go call ya' li'l friend."

The faint sound of the door opening and closing at the front of the house was followed by the sound of heavy feet padding quickly down the hall.

"Mikey! Mikey, get ya' hands off that damn boy!" Ms. Mae called out, huffing as she approached the scene. "Goddamn it, Mikey!"

Mikey let Noah go, and the child quickly grabbed his towel and hurried up the hall to the safety of his room. Ms. Mae stood clutching her chest and staring angrily at her son who, in return, shot daggers with his eyes at the woman who'd given him life.

"You crazy or something?" Ms. Mae asked him.

"If so, I got it from my moms," he replied, chuckling hatefully at her.

"Listen here, now . . . I went to bat for you, cleaning up ya' mess and keeping ya' ass outta jail."

"You'on care about me!" he shot back. "All you care about is that piece of a check them white folk cut you for babysitting that bastard you'on even like. Don't be pretending like you trying out for mother of the year up in this piece."

Ms. Mae was taken aback. "No, you won't come up in my house talking to me like that."

"This is *my* house too!" Mikey shot back. "What, you forgot? You believing yo' own lies now? I'm done hiding out and creeping at other folks' place. That shit's over."

"You stay here you gon' have to keep ya' hands to ya'self."

"Fine one to talk," Mikey said moving to walk past his mother.

Ms. Mae reached out and grabbed her son's arm. "You can stick ya' chest out and huff and puff like the world owes you something, but we all got our own crosses to bear. Don't need you tryin'a lay yo' guilt on me or blame me for the shit you doing. Truth is, I done saved you, boy. You better remember who the parent is."

Mikey shoved his mother with enough force to send the elder woman stumbling to the ground. Her shrill cry meant nothing to him as he glared down at her in her state of vulnerability. She threw her arm up to brace herself when he bucked as if he was about to hit her. Never had Mikey been so angry and intoxicated that he had the balls to assault his mother. His aggression had escalated to a record high, and for the first time, Ms. Mae feared her son.

"I can't change the past, son, but I tried to save ya' future," she cried out. "Now you messin' it on up. Don't do it. Don't you do it."

"You tryna save me?" he asked her through gritted teeth. "And who the hell was 'pose to save me from *you* and that sorry-ass nigga you chose for my daddy?"

Ms. Mae closed her eyes as if blocking out the memories that sparked from the words he'd just spewed at her. "Hush up with that, boy! Live in the present! You keep this here up and you' gon' be sitting in jail just like ya' damn daddy."

"What difference it make to you? You ain't never want no kid anyway . . . remember?" He shook his head. "You so worried 'bout ya' check!" He shook his head at his mother in disgust. "I ain't got time for this. Finna go make me a sandwich."

Ms. Mae struggled to get herself up from the ground. Barely in a standing position, she called after him. "You not gon' try to stay here keeping up no mess, Mikey. They gon' be watchin' this place . . . watchin' me. You can't be doing this foolishness."

Mikey waved her off, never even turning back to look at her. "I'll do what the fuck I want. Ain't nobody never cared about me, I damn shoul' ain't caring 'bout nobody."

Ms. Mae was floored. She'd convinced Noah to keep his mouth closed about Mikey's indiscretions, but if it continued, she wasn't sure how much longer she could protect her son . . . or herself. She had half a mind to call Ms. Hardy and just have her remove the child altogether. She'd miss that income, but at least she wouldn't have to worry about facing criminal charges along with Mikey. Not only did she fear the outcome should social services find the slightest issue occurring in her home, but she also was afraid of the monster Mikey had become. His behavior was far more deviant than ever, and with the strength he'd used to shove her, there was no doubt in Ms. Mae's mind that Mikey could—and would—kill someone if given the opportunity. With her and Noah being stuck under the same roof with him, it was just a matter of which one of them Mikey would target next.

Chapter 14

It was after 7:00 p.m., and the last group session of the day had just let out. Olivia sat in her car watching the handful of women file out of the small building, bid one another farewell, and then hop into their respective vehicles. Once the parking lot was cleared, with only the little gray Ford Expedition that she knew belonged to the counselor presiding over the session that just ended and her own car, Olivia slid out into the brisk air of the evening and headed to the front of the building. She rang the bell, knowing that the door was locked, and waited to be let in. Within seconds she was greeted by a warm, familiar smile.

"I was hoping that you weren't going to cancel," Emily Roberts said gingerly as she stepped back to allow Olivia to enter the building.

Olivia smiled yet said nothing as she followed Emily through the reception area, down the hall, and to the very last office on the left. She settled down in the chair she'd so frequently occupied just a short while ago and looked around the room. Not much had changed since she'd first become acquainted with Emily and the center.

Emily took a seat in the chair next to Olivia and drew her legs up to tuck her feet underneath her as she got comfortable. "So, how've you been?"

Olivia shrugged. "Making it, I guess."

"I was surprised to hear from you, but very pleasantly so. I'd be lying, though, if I said I didn't notice the distress in your voice. What's going on in your life these days?"

"Well, I'm still writing."

"That's good."

"I'm still in my mom's apartment." Olivia looked over at Emily to gauge her expression. Back when she'd first told Emily about her decision to stay in her mom's place the counselor had made no bones about how unhealthy it could be for her to remain in the home of her deceased parent. "Well, you know I was engaged," she went on once Emily didn't utter a word. "I'm not anymore."

When she'd first started visiting the rape crisis center, she'd done so secretively as a result of the nightmares she'd started having after moving back home. At the time, Kasyn had been freaked out by the way she'd called out in the middle of the night when the dreams occurred. Scared that she would never be able to control the dreams or her emotions without running him off back then, Olivia had sought out the help of a professional. It was the first time in her life that she'd spoken to a professional about the darkest era of her life. Never once had she told Kasyn that she was seeing a therapist because then she'd have to explain to him why. Once it appeared that the dreams were under control judging by the infrequency of their occurrence, she immediately abandoned her weekly sessions. She'd done a great job of repressing her emotions and blocking out the memories ever since then. That was . . . until Noah entered her life.

"What happened?" Emily asked, referring to Olivia's failed engagement.

"He left me."

Emily remained silent for a moment. "Was that unexpected?"

Olivia considered the question. "I think I expected some resistance considering the things I've been doing lately, but not this . . . not a complete shutdown."

"And what exactly have you been doing lately? What's going on?"

"My dreams . . . They've come back," Olivia admitted. "The nightmares."

Emily noted. "Exact same?"

"For the most part. But I think my reactions have been more . . . intense."

"It's been awhile since you've experienced this, right?"

Olivia nodded.

"So something's happened to trigger the return." She studied Olivia's reaction. "I'm assuming that whatever happened is also the same thing that you expected your fiancé to have opposition to."

Olivia nodded again.

Emily waited patiently for Olivia to open up and disclose the information surrounding what was causing her recurring dreams. Olivia fiddled with the hem of her blouse, trying to find the words to begin to explain how she'd gotten to this point of helplessness and unrelenting turmoil.

"I met a child," she stated. "Noah. A cute little kid . . . a foster kid . . . From the first day I met him I knew that something wasn't right with him, you know? I sensed that something was wrong. I could see it in his eyes, in his face, in his movements, in his demeanor. I knew that sense of fear that just reeked from him." She swallowed hard. "And then things started happening . . . little things, and then big things."

"Such as?" Emily inquired.

"Him flinching when it seemed like I was going to touch him. Blood droplets in my bathroom after he'd used it. Him lying about bruises and scars. Lying about his family life. Him being forced to do things . . . illegal things. His ribs being fractured," she whispered the last remark.

Emily's facial expression saddened as she envisioned the sight of a young battered boy, and her emotions fell under the spell of Olivia's disconsolate tone. Though she felt Olivia's pain, she remained silent to allow her the floor to purge her emotions.

"Everyone kept telling me he was just a bad seed," Olivia said. "My friend, my fiancé . . . They both told me to leave the kid alone. That he was just a little street punk probably trying to set me up or pull the wool over my eyes, but I knew better. Since meeting him, the dreams have been practically haunting me. Even during the day, I'm regressing back to that time . . . when I see him, when I hear him . . . I'm that pitiful, scrawny little fourteen-year-old all over again." She sniffled as she fought back a sob. "I tried everything I could to get him out of that home where I know he's being abused in every kind of way. He even told me himself. But, when we got to court . . . when I tried to get him to tell the judge what he'd told me . . . he lied. He protected them. They forced him to lie to protect the woman and her predator of a son."

Emily reached for the box of Kleenex resting on the table between their seats. She offered it to Olivia while being sure to keep her tone low and even. "These kind of encounters can be retraumatizing. It sounds like perhaps that's what's happening to you. Were you ever able to get your support circle to understand your connection to Noah?"

Olivia blew her nose into a soft sheet of the tissue and shook her head.

"Ahh. So this is why he left?"

"I had a dream one night, and he just . . . He couldn't handle it anymore. He said that I was letting this thing with Noah drive me crazy."

"Did he ever know what the dreams were about?"

"No," Olivia whispered. "I never went in-depth. All he knew was that someone was hurting me in them . . . not exactly who or how . . . but, this last time when he asked me why I was so concerned with helping Noah, I told him that it was because no one had helped me."

"So, in a sense, you admitted your secret to him without giving him full disclosure. At that point, did you not feel comfortable letting him in?"

Olivia shook her head.

"What about afterward?" Emily asked.

"I didn't think he'd understand. I mean, I didn't want him to look at me differently. I didn't want him to view me as damaged."

Emily took Olivia's hand. "Honey, you have been scarred, but how can you expect to ever have a whole, complete relationship when you don't completely let anyone in? Everyone processes things differently, so there's really no way to tell how he would have handled the information had you actually talked to him. But you didn't even give him a chance, Olivia. Everyone's not out to hurt you. He's not your father. I'm gathering that he is someone who loves you and only wanted to take care of you and be there for you, and you wouldn't allow him to do that."

"Maybe you're right," Olivia conceded. "But in the same respect, why couldn't he have been more patient with me? He made me feel stupid and naive because of my dedication to helping Noah. He didn't understand why it was so important to me."

"Because you didn't help him to understand, Olivia. Everyone doesn't come from a world of abuse, so they don't get it, but it doesn't mean that it can't be explained to them."

"I just felt that he could have tried harder . . . been more patient."

"Maybe he just needs a little time. You never know what the future holds. But what about Noah? How did that situation end?"

Olivia sighed deeply. "Well, the judge ruled that he would stay in the care of the trifling foster mother. I worry for his safety . . . I fear for him every second of every day. I don't know what else to do to get anyone to believe me when I say that he's being abused."

"Where there's a will, there's a way. Sometimes we have to go hard and do some unconventional, albeit, dramatic, stuff in order to advocate for the voiceless. If you feel it in your heart that you're right, you can't stop trying. You have to keep going until someone listens. Be the voice you would have wanted someone to be for you."

Olivia took in Emily's words. She had no intention of giving up. There was no way her spirit could rest knowing that there was a chance that Noah could be hurt again. She just needed to figure out which moves to make now and pray that she worked it out before something devastating happened.

It was the day of their preplanned visit. Olivia hadn't seen Noah since the court hearing regarding his placement and was anxious to see how the child was holding up. When she arrived at Ms. Mae's house, Noah hadn't even given her an opportunity to put the car in park before he dashed out of the house and hopped into the passenger seat. No one saw him out, and no one watched from the window. Olivia found it strange but didn't question it.

"Hey, there," she greeted Noah, noticing that he wouldn't face her.

"Hey," he mumbled.

She wasn't used to his despondent behavior where she was concerned. Over time, he'd come to be fond of her, and she was used to him chattering away with her, not being so clammy. During the ride from Ms. Mae's to McDonald's, his favorite spot, Noah remained quiet. Olivia asked him a few questions about school, and he gave very brief, undetailed replies with nothing of substance. Olivia didn't push. She figured he was a little pensive following the way things had gone down in the courtroom. She wanted to apologize to him for him having to be placed in that situation to begin with, but didn't know whether it was best to address the subject or not.

Upon pulling into a parking spot, the duo exited the car and walked around to the back of the vehicle in order to cross the street to get to the restaurant's front door.

"Noah," Olivia called out to him before making any further strides away from the car.

He glanced over at her.

"I just want you to know that I'm really glad to see you, and I hope you enjoy our afternoon out." She cocked her head to the side and waited to see if he would respond. When the child said nothing, Olivia held her arms out to him in a gesture of goodwill. "Can I have a hug?" She wanted him to know that no matter what, she cared about him. Nothing said that better than a hug.

Slowly, Noah shuffled over and fell into Olivia's embrace. The minute she placed her arms around him and slightly squeezed around his arms, he winced. The sound was noticeable and alarmed Olivia. She pulled back and stared down into his face.

"Noah? Are you okay?"

He didn't say a word. What could he say? The last time he'd told her the truth they'd ended up in court, and he was forced to tell a lie. After that, he'd nearly had his arm pulled out of the socket. There was no way that he was going to mumble a word of what Mikey had done or the conversation he'd heard between Ms. Mae and Mikey that night. Noah had it fixed in his mind that the best thing for him to do was simply run away. First, he had to figure out where he'd get the money from to make it far away from Atlanta. The last thing he wanted was to be picked up by the police and returned to DFCS custody. He didn't know what kind of hell would await him there and had no intentions of finding out.

A lightbulb clicked in Olivia's mind and she grabbed Noah by the hand. Quickly, they hightailed it into McDonald's, bypassing the order counter and scurrying into the ladies' room situated at the back of the establishment. Once inside, Olivia locked the door and turned to face the young child. She lowered herself to become eye level with him and took a deep breath before speaking.

"Everything I ever do for you or say to you is for your own good, Noah," she told him. "I need you to believe that I would never ever intentionally place you in a compromising situation. I only want to help you. Do you believe that, Noah? Do you trust me?"

Noah lowered his head and nodded.

"You're in pain," she stated. "Something hurts. I could tell when I hugged you." She pulled her cell phone out and looked at him once more. "I wouldn't ask you to do this if it wasn't important, Noah, but we can't let anyone hurt you. I won't let anyone keep hurting you. I need to see your arms and chest, okay? Can you take your shirt off for me just enough for me to see? I promise you that I won't touch you, and I'll even step back if you want me to."

Noah hesitated. The last time he was in pain she'd taken him to the hospital. True enough, because of her he was able to get the medicine that he needed for the pain, but everything that happened after that had ultimately led to this very moment. Noah wasn't sure how much more he could take. If Ms. Mae or Mikey found out that Olivia knew about his arm, he didn't know what they'd do to him. He didn't want to risk being gravely punished yet again before he was able to take off on his own.

"I need you to trust me, Noah," Olivia pleaded. "Please . . . Let me help you."

He was conflicted. How could she help? She'd tried before, but he hadn't let her. He'd stood there in the courtroom and practically called her a liar to her face. But, there she was, willing to stick her neck out for him once again, and he wasn't sure that he wanted her to. How could she save him? How could she keep Mikey from ever touching him again? What kind of match did Olivia really think she'd be for Mikey when his own mother couldn't even tame the beast he'd become? But he was tired. Noah was exhausted from sleepless nights, worrying whether Mikey was lurking around every corner, and trying to protect himself. It was too much for a little kid, and it didn't seem fair that this was the life he'd been forced to live.

Tears trickled down as he weighed his options. He could refuse to show her the proof of her assumption and go on to enjoy his hamburger . . . only to return to the pits of hell, or he could be honest and give her what she wanted and risk whatever the outcome may be. *Maybe they're wrong,* Noah thought. *Maybe Ms. Mae and Mikey are just suckering me into believing that any other placement would be far worse than this one. After all, Mikey had said himself that all Ms. Mae cared about was the check that the county gave her for caring for me. A dollar amount,* he thought. Just another number which he was associated as.

Slowly, he began to peel his right arm from his sleeve. Olivia noticed the pained expression on his face as he struggled to do so. Once he'd freed both arms, he pulled the shirt over his head and turned to the side. Olivia gasped as she noticed the bruising covering Noah's arm.

She checked the rest of him and was satisfied to see that there were no other signs of abuse. With her camera phone she flicked a few photos while trying to keep her feelings in check.

"Okay, baby," she cooed. "Put your shirt back on." As he did so, her eyes never left his face, filled with defeat and shame. "I want to tell you something," Olivia said, feeling a moment of complete vulnerability. "When I was younger, I lived with my dad, my stepmom, two sisters, a brother, and my niece. When I was fourteen, my dad began to molest me. He would touch me in places that no one had any business touching me, doing things to me that made me feel dirty and ashamed. And no one knew. Well, my older sister did. But outside of her, no one else knew, and I didn't feel like I could tell anyone because my dad had told me that no one would believe me. He told me that I'd end up in foster care and that people would do horrible things to me. I was afraid of what would happen to me if I told. I was afraid of people not believing me or thinking that I was crazy for even voicing such a claim.

"When I look at you, Noah, I see a lot of me. I remember what it was like to be hurt, beaten, talked down to, and uncared for. I remember what it was like to feel like no one loved me . . . to be afraid every day. I don't want that for you. I don't want you to feel like that anymore. I swear, I'm going to do something to make sure that no one ever lays a hand on you again."

Noah wrapped his left arm around her and cried into her shoulder. "I'm sorry I lied," he stated. "I didn't want to. I didn't wanna make you mad or nothing, Olivia. I-I-I didn't—"

"Shhhh," she coaxed, hugging him tightly. "You don't owe me any explanations. You did what you felt like you had to do. That was my bad. But it's okay, because I'm going to fix this," she promised him. "I'm going to fix it."

***

With her new evidence of child abuse courtesy of the pictures she'd taken, Olivia decided that it was time to take a more dramatic stance. Instead of returning him to Ms. Mae's at the designated drop-off time, she took Noah home with her. There was no way in hell that she was about to return him to the home where he was obviously continuing to be abused. Once home, Olivia phoned Ms. Hardy and left a message for her to return the call promptly. She had every intention of holding on to Noah until the authorities viewed her pictures and revisited her accusations.

While Noah was enjoying a plate of freshly baked cookies, Olivia tinkered with the idea of going ahead and calling the police since she'd yet to hear from Ms. Hardy. Nearly an hour had passed since she'd left the case manager a message, and Olivia was beginning to get antsy. Before she could walk out of the kitchen in search of her cell phone a loud knock resounded at her back door. Alarmed, she hurried over and glanced out of the peephole. To her surprise, there stood the woman she'd been looking to hear from. How the woman had gotten her address was beyond her, but Olivia opened the door anyway, prepared to get straight to the matter at hand.

"I've been waiting for you," she stated the moment she flung the door open.

"Olivia Collins?" a male's voice boomed out. Immediately, a DeKalb County police officer stepped in front of Ms. Hardy with a scowl on his face.

Olivia was shocked. "Y-y-yes?"

"You're under arrest for the kidnapping of a minor," he stated. "Please turn around and place your hands behind your back."

"Excuse me?" Olivia exclaimed, nearly choking on her words.

"Where is he? I know he's in there!" came the shrill voice that Olivia knew belonged to Ms. Mae. The woman bounded the stairs and stood next to Ms. Hardy just behind the officer.

"What is the meaning of this?" Olivia asked, still facing the crowd that was glaring at her.

"You were supposed to return Noah to Ms. Johnson nearly two hours ago," Ms. Hardy stated. "Visitation is clearly established in the agreement you signed to become his advocate. Failure to adhere to the guidelines provided is punishable by law."

"Are you crazy? I called you over an hour ago to tell you where he was," Olivia countered. "You never called back."

"But *I'm* his guardian," Ms. Mae cut in. "You shoulda called me, but you shouldn't have taken it upon yourself to just up and take him off nowhere. Noah!" she called out. "Noah!"

Noah rose from the kitchen table having heard everything occurring on the other side of the door. His heart pounded, and he wondered just how much trouble he would be in once he got back to Ms. Mae's house. He considered bolting out of Olivia's front door but had no idea where he'd run to. Before he had an opportunity to make a decision, Ms. Hardy barged past Olivia and came face-to-face with the trembling child. As the officer began to read Olivia her rights, Ms. Mae entered the home and stared at Noah.

"Boy, now you know you shoulda called home," Ms. Mae stated. "Come on here. Had me scared to death worrying 'bout where you were. You know you not 'pose to be going to nobody's house. Not even this one. It ain't right."

"You can't do this," Olivia screamed out. "If you'll just . . . If you'll just let me explain."

"Tell it to the judge," Ms. Hardy stated. "You've taken far too many liberties, and this time, you've gone too far."

"You can't take him back there," Olivia said as she winced from the tightness of the handcuffs squeezing her wrists. "If you take him back there, there's no telling what's gonna happen to that child."

"Haven't you had enough of theses shenanigans?" Ms. Mae asked.

"Ma'am, you may want to remain silent," the officer stated, reminding her of her rights. "Let's go." He moved to pull her across the threshold.

"Wait! Wait! You can't do this. You're not going to let me get my purse? You can't just leave strangers in my house! Wait a minute!"

Ms. Hardy ushered Ms. Mae and Noah out of the apartment. "No worries, we're gone. And if I can help it, you'll *never* see this child again."

The officer pulled Olivia onto the porch, put the bottom lock on her door, and pushed it closed before guiding her down the stairwell. Olivia's head was spinning. She hadn't expected this turn of events and was confused about what to do next. Her eyes met Noah's as he rounded the stairwell to head to Ms. Hardy's awaiting vehicle.

"I'm going to fix this," she told him through her tears.

"Get in the car, Noah," Ms. Hardy instructed the child as he stood motionless, watching the police drag Olivia to the squad car.

"I'm going to fix this," Olivia repeated. "It's okay. It'll be okay. I promise. I'm going to fix it."

The officer pushed down on her head to help her into the backseat of the patrol vehicle. Noah continued to stare in disbelief, wondering if his only way out was on her way to jail, never to be seen or heard from again. His chest heaved with the tears and emotions that overcame him.

"Noah, get in the car!" Ms. Hardy snapped, angered by the way the child seemed to be soaking up Olivia's every word.

Reluctantly, he climbed into the backseat and stared out of the window at Olivia's reflection. His tiny heart broke into a million pieces and some feeling of certainty assured him that he would never see her again. Whatever opportunity he'd had to be released from the torture he was continuously subjected to had just passed with the simple closing of the squad car door beside him. He waved to her saying good-bye without being able to really say it.

Chapter 15

She was confused. The buzz of people going in and out of the building left her head spinning. Everyone was focused on their destination. There wasn't one friendly or inviting face around. Asking for help didn't really feel like an option. After sitting in a holding cell at the DeKalb County Jail for a total of three hours and forty-seven minutes, Olivia had seen the light. Ms. Hardy and Ms. Mae would apparently do anything to cover their own asses just so that they wouldn't have to admit their wrongs. They'd even resorted to having Olivia arrested. But not even a row of steel bars was going to keep her from doing what she had to do to keep her promise to Noah. Sure, they were going to try their best to get her removed as his advocate. The whole kidnapping thing would probably be a no-brainer to the judge or whosoever had the final say about that. But it was okay. After Daysha had come down to the jail to bail her out, she'd imparted a little bit of wisdom upon Olivia that spearheaded her next move. The people she was dealing with were clearly corrupt, and if they wanted to play hardball, then she was ready to step up to bat.

Armed with Noah's file, a copy of her motion to have him removed from Ms. Mae's home, his medical records from the night of his hospital visit, and prints of the photos she'd taken with her camera the day of her arrest, Olivia was ready to take her accusations a step higher. Standing in the Office of the Inspector General for the state of Georgia, Olivia was ready to file a complaint contending abuse of power against the department of Social Services. Hopefully, her voice would now be heard and something serious would be done by way of looking into the allegations against Ms. Mae and her son only after showing how the foster care division was exercising an abuse of power.

She entered an office suite and was encountered by a woman whose only salutation was a brief glance.

"Um, I'm here to meet with Jordan Pierce," Olivia told the woman. "Uh, Senior Deputy Inspector General Pierce."

"Do you have an appointment?" the receptionist asked.

"No, but I—"

"What is your visit pertaining to?"

"I want to file a complaint, and I—"

"Complaints can be filed by filling out a paper form, since you're already here," the woman said, cutting her off and pointing toward a stack of forms nearby. "Or you may fill out a complaint form online or report your claim via phone." She handed Olivia a card with the appropriate number for call-in reporting.

Olivia respectfully declined the card. "That isn't necessary. Please, if you could just tell him that Olivia Collins is here and that Daysha Mullen sent me."

The woman rolled her eyes and spoke with disdain. "Ma'am, the deputy inspector general's schedule is compact. If you'd like to schedule an appointment I'd be glad to do so."

Olivia was just about sick of everyone dismissing her as if her mission was of little importance. She was determined to stand her ground. "If you could please just call him, e-mail him, or whatever, and let him know that Olivia Collins is here as referred by Daysha Mullen, I'd greatly appreciate it," she said through clenched teeth.

"Really, it'll only take a second out of your otherwise very busy workday, and I'd hate to have to let Mr. Pierce know how unhelpful you were upon my next encounter with him."

The woman gave Olivia a questioning look, and then rose from her seat. "Very well. Please, wait here." She turned away and disappeared from Olivia's sight.

Olivia let out a quick breath and looked around the office. It was seemingly quiet, not like the buzz that she'd navigated through down in the lobby. *God, I'm leaning on you*, she silently prayed with her eyes half-closed and her back to the receptionist's desk. *I'm grasping at straws here, but I know there's got to be a light somewhere at the end of this dark tunnel. If you get me through this . . . If you can open just one door for me, I swear I'll never give up, and I'll die trying to save this child.*

"Ms. Collins," the receptionist called from behind her, jarring her out of prayer mode.

Olivia spun around. "Yes?"

"Deputy Inspector General Pierce will see you now."

A sigh of relief escaped her body, and Olivia gave a polite smile. "Lead the way," she stated. *Thank you, God*, she offered up praises.

Olivia followed the woman down the hall and around the corner to an impressive-sized office. The receptionist tapped on the partially opened door. "Sir, Ms. Olivia Collins is here."

Deputy Inspector General Pierce was a handsome, middle-aged man with a goatee that connected to his neatly trimmed sideburns and mustache. His brilliantly bald head glimmered in the light of his florescent bulbs. It was clear to Olivia why Daysha had once been in a very steamy personal relationship with the man, hence, the assurance Olivia had had that he would be willing to meet with her.

"Ms. Collins, please come in and have a seat," Pierce invited.

Olivia entered his office, shook his firm hand, and took a seat in the chair across from his desk. "Thank you for meeting with me. I won't take up much of your time, sir."

"No problem. I got a message earlier stating that I just might receive a visit from you."

Good ole Daysha was consistently looking out for her.

"So, what can I do for you?"

"Well, sir, I've been trying like hell to have a foster child removed from the placement his case manager has arranged for him due to the physical and sexual abuse that I can prove he's sustained while in the foster care parent's care."

"They have special investigators within social services to deal with that type of claim."

"Granted, but I'm pretty sure that upon our court hearing, social service officials trumped up some documentation and forced the child to provide a false statement to cover up their neglect, thus resulting in the judge ruling to keep the child in the custody of the foster parent in question. Since then, the child has turned up with physical evidence of abuse yet again. Certainly this is a cause for your office to get involved in because if the agency abused their power and has provided fraudulent information as a means of simply not doing their job . . . Think of how many children in state custody are suffering as a result."

Pierce's eyebrows knitted together in concern. "Can you prove that the information they provided to the court was falsified? Can you prove that the agency was aware of whatever abuse you mention?"

"I have the child's medical documentation, and I can attest to the child's proclamation that he was forced to pen a false statement."

"That's not a lot to go on. I need physical, black-and-white evidence that an abuse of power and fraudulent acts have occurred."

"Sir, if you just look into it. Interview the parties involved, follow up with the individuals that they claimed to have interviewed when the department did their alleged investigation, I'm certain that you'll find something to support my claim."

"Daysha trusts your instincts," he told her. "Because of that, I'm inclined to do the same. Fill out an official complaint form and we'll get the ball in motion. But once we do this, you had better hope that you're right, Ms. Collins, because heads will roll once this is determined as a valid complaint. And once the media catches wind of it, the Department of Family and Children Services will be under fire."

"Good," Olivia stated. "Maybe now these people will do their jobs and not just collect a paycheck."

The heat was on, and Olivia was now the grill master.

He was sitting in the living room trying to wolf down a bowl of cereal before Mikey returned. Here lately, Noah had been on guard trying to make sure that he didn't allow himself to be trapped alone at any time by his foster brother. Whenever he saw Mikey coming, he ran the other way. Ever since Olivia had been arrested, things around the house had been more miserable than before. Ms. Mae constantly berated him about trusting everybody and not doing what she said. She never passed up an opportunity to tell him how stupid he was for believing anything Olivia said, trying her best to convince him that it was Olivia who intended to harm him. She insisted upon calling his advocate a crazy criminal, using her fallout at the courthouse as her selling point for how insane the woman was. Noah didn't buy any of it. He knew the truth. He knew that Olivia cared about him, but he also knew that Ms. Mae and Ms. Hardy were dead set on making sure that Olivia never saw him again.

Staring out of the window, Noah nearly choked on a spoonful of Cheerios. A beat-up hooptie on enormous rims pulled into the driveway and out jumped Mikey from the passenger side followed by a man that Noah had never seen. With no intentions of sticking around to find out who the other guy was, Noah made a beeline for the kitchen where he tossed his bowl into the sink without so much as clearing out its contents, and then turned around to jet up the hall to his bedroom. But he wasn't quick enough.

"Aye, punk ass!" Mikey called out as he burst through the front door and caught sight of Noah's figure trying to retreat.

Noah froze for a second, threw a glance over his shoulder, and offered a weak greeting. "Oh, hey, Mikey." He began to walk swiftly.

"Stop!" Mikey hollered walking into the middle of the living room. "Bring ya' ass back here. I got somebody that wants to holla at you."

Noah was nervous. The last time Mikey brought home someone that wanted to "meet" him, it turned into a nightmare that Noah would have liked to forget but couldn't. He was in no way interested in getting to know any of Mikey's associates and began to tremble at the thought of just what this person actually wanted from him.

"Get ya' ass in here," Mikey demanded.

Noah slowly turned around and entered the living room. He didn't say a word as he looked from Mikey over to the heavyset, dark-skinned guy with the sagging jeans and brand-new snow-white sneakers on his feet. His hands were in his pockets as he stared back at the child.

"This here is my . . . uh . . . business associate, Bite," Mikey explained, sneering at Noah. "Awhile back, you took some shit that belonged to him and didn't make good on it. I been covering ya' ass ever since, but I figured it was time for yo' ass to grow the hell up and face the consequences of yo' actions like a man."

Noah's eyes grew wide. He knew what Mikey was referring to. He was talking about the crack that he'd stashed in the tree trunk near Olivia's house that time. The same crack that Mikey had tried to force him to sell. The same crack that he had snuck back into Mikey's room shortly after breaking it to him that he just couldn't do it. So, why was he standing there giving him a speech about not making good on the product that he'd returned? Bite hadn't lost anything since Noah returned the stash. But looking at the man's angry expression, Noah knew the truth. Mikey hadn't given the drugs back and hadn't attempted to sell it himself in order to get Bite's money. Whatever he'd done with the stuff was of no consequence, because now, Bite was there glaring at Noah and waiting for some form of an explanation.

"Uh . . . but . . . Mikey, I—" Noah stumbled.

"Nobody wanna hear your excuses," Mikey told him. "Don't talk to me. Holla at Bite. That was *his* shit. When you play a man's game you gotta handle a man's punishment."

"Punishment?" Noah was afraid. He wondered why Mikey had waited so long to bring Bite to the house to torture him. The incident had happened so long ago that compared to everything else that had happened, this particular thing was a distant memory to Noah. Not wanting to stick around to find out what was going to happen next, Noah began to walk backward, never taking his eyes off of the silent Bite. "I . . . uh . . . I don't wanna play a man's game. Please . . ."

Mikey reached under the back of his shirt and pulled a pistol from the waistband of his jeans. Quickly, he aimed the gun at Noah and narrowed his eyes as he spoke. "You might wanna be yo' ass some still before I get in yo' ass with *this* steel."

Noah was in shock. He was rooted to the spot with his hands out in front of him pleadingly and his eyes bugged out in fear and disbelief though he said nothing.

"Aye, man, what the fuck?" Bite finally spoke, hitting Mikey on the arm. "Put that shit away, man. You ain't tell me that he was a li'l-ass kid. Thought you had a li'l shorty working for you, man. A li'l teenager or something. Shit, somebody over ten. You trippin'."

Mikey didn't like being checked in front of Noah, especially by his street boss. His temper got the best of him, and he cocked his head to the side to look at Bite. "Ten, twenty, six . . . don't matter. This li'l nigga cost us money, and you gon' front like that shit ain't important?"

"Watch ya' tone and put the piece down fo' you let ya' mouth write a check that ya' ass can't cash, homeboy," Bite warned.

Mikey's rage was escalating. This wasn't going the way he'd intended. He wanted to scare the shit out of Noah by bringing Bite in to torture him about the money he'd lost for the dope Noah had been given. Never mind the fact that Noah had returned the dope and Mikey sniffed it with his crew versus pushing it to get the funds. Bite didn't need to know that. True, it had happened awhile back, but Bite had been asking for the money Mikey owed him, and Mikey had to tell him something. Putting the blame on Noah and letting Bite get in that ass was a win-win for Mikey; it took the heat off of him, and it also gave him a chance to show Noah's ass not to fuck with him. He had no idea that Bite would turn out to have a heart when it came to kids.

"This is 'bout money," Mikey told Bite. "This punk cost you money, Bite, and you 'bout to tell me you gon' let that shit ride?"

"You put the dope in the hands of a baby, man," Bite replied gritting his teeth. "And you think I'm gon' come up in here and rough up some li'l kid 'cause of yo' dumb-ass decision? You done lost it. But I ain't gon' tell you no more to put that shit down before it gets real up in here. You already into me for a few stacks. You sure you wanna piss me off some more?"

The situation was turning on Mikey, and the way he saw things, it was Noah's fault. He lowered his gun without thinking as he addressed Bite. "What you tryin' to say? That 'cause he a kid you gon' put that on me? Now *I* owe you? Man, cats in the street be flippin' that shit at all kinda ages. Age ain't nothing but a number. Business is business."

Seeing that the two of them were more interested in arguing with each other than dealing with him at the moment, Noah took the lowering of Mikey's gun as his cue to flee from the room. He backed up a couple of more steps before turning around and making a dash for it. Instinctively, Mikey adjusted his focus, raised his gun, and pulled the lever placing a bullet into the wall just as Noah's figure moved out of his vantage point.

"Bring yo' ass back here!" Mikey hollered. "Who told you to move?" He took off down the hall after Noah, determined to take his frustrations out on the boy.

"Nigga, you trippin'," Bite said grabbing for Mikey's arm as he flew by. But Mikey's anger had his adrenaline pumping, and he was moving way too quickly for Bite. Bite considered his options. With the gunshot, he knew that somebody in the neighborhood was likely to call the po-po, and he couldn't afford to be caught up in some bullshit. Deciding that he'd catch Mikey's ass in the streets later and remind him who the boss was, Bite fell into survival mode and hightailed it out of the front door, down the driveway, into his car, and away from the house as folks from the neighborhood began to peer around in wonderment.

Noah ran into Ms. Mae's room and locked the door. He took the chair that sat at her vanity and wedged it underneath the knob for extra security. His heart was pounding, and his hands trembled as he hurried over to Ms. Mae's bedside to pick up the phone. Ever since Olivia became his advocate, he'd secretly worked to remember her phone number just in case he needed to call her. Sure, he should have called the police, but he didn't have a lot of faith in any authority figures these days. On the other side of the door, Mikey banged relentlessly, first with his fist, and then with the butt of his gun. Noah was afraid that he'd soon shoot a hole through the door so he lowered himself to the ground, crouching beside Ms. Mae's bed as Olivia's line rang and rang.

"Hello?" she answered, recognizing the number as Ms. Mae's home line.

"O-O-Olivia," his voice quivered.

She was instantly on guard. She could hear the banging in the background and wondered what was going on. Given the sound of his voice, she was confident that he was in some kind of danger. "What's the matter, Noah? Who is that? What's going on?" Even before he could give a response, she grabbed her keys and purse and headed out of her door.

"Unlock the goddamn door!" Mikey yelled from the hallway just before kicking the door.

The chair shook, and Noah's eyes grew wide as he wondered how much longer he'd be safe inside of the room. He thought about escaping through the window, but ever since the last time he'd done so, Ms. Mae had nailed all of the windows shut, even her own. He was literally a prisoner in the house and had no ideas on how he could get out of this situation.

"Where are you, Noah? Tell me what's going on!" Olivia asked as she started her car and backed out of her parking spot.

"In Ms. Mae's room," Noah informed her. "He's gonna get me," he cried as Mikey continued to kick at the door. "He's gonna get me! He's gonna get me! Please . . . I-I-I can't get out."

"Is the door locked?"

"Yes . . . yes . . . but—"

"Stay in the room, Noah. Stay in the room. I'm on my way. Don't hang up, okay? I'm here. Hold on . . . Stay with me . . ." She struggled to look down at her screen in order to place a three-way call to 911.

"911, what's your emergency?" the operator answered the call.

Olivia connected the call and tried to speak over the increasingly loud banging sound in Noah's background coupled with the child's insistent crying. "Ummm . . . My name's Olivia Collins, and I'm the advocate for a foster child named Noah Maxiel. He's at home in danger. Someone, I believe his foster brother Michael, is attempting to attack him."

The operator could hear the commotion on the other end. "Are you at the incident site, ma'am?"

"No, no. I'm on my way there, but Noah's on the line."

"I need the address of the home where the incident's occurring."

Olivia rattled off Ms. Mae's address just before cursing the second red light she'd gotten stuck at.

"I'm gonna kill yo' punk ass!" Mikey screamed as he gave a mighty kick against the door causing the frame to crack. Seeing the result of his forceful assault against the door, he gave a succession of three more swift kicks and finally, the chair gave way as the door ripped from the frame held pitifully by the lock stuck within its groove.

Noah screamed into the receiver from his position on the floor as he watched the chair fall from the door. "Please! Please, help me!"

Hearing the chaos on the other end, the emergency operator felt her heart plummet. The child's cries for help were alarming. "A patrol car has already been dispatched to that location due to another call," she advised. "Noah, can you describe the person who's trying to get in?"

Noah couldn't answer. He was too busy shaking with fright and crying hysterically.

"I don't know what he looks like," Olivia chimed in, finally nearing Noah's neighborhood, "but like I said, his name is Michael, and he's been abusing Noah for God knows how long."

Mikey jerked the handle of the door and peered through the crack. "I'm gonna break yo' fuckin' neck, you piece of shit," he seethed.

Taking his gun he shot at the lock twice, causing Noah to drop the phone and scream before crawling underneath the bed. The door fell open, and Mikey rushed into the room, oblivious to the sound of the police sirens in the distance.

"Where the fuck are you?" Mikey called out. He looked in the closet and found nothing. He saw the receiver laying on the floor and instead of hanging it up, he lowered himself onto his knees beside the bed and saw Noah's stocking feet underneath the bed. "Bingo," he called out victoriously just before pulling the child from under the bed by his ankles.

"No! No!" Noah screamed. "I'm sorry! I'm sorry! Please don't!" Noah just knew that Mikey was going to turn that gun on him and blow him away. It was the only thing that was left for the crazed man to do.

"Noah? Noah?" the 911 operator called out. "He's no longer on the line," she observed as she listened to the child's screaming and the muffled sound of movement.

"Oh my God!" Olivia exclaimed, tearing up over the grim possibilities after having heard the gunshots herself.

Mikey tossed Noah onto the bed and climbed on top of him pinning the child to the quilted mattress. "You fuck up everything! From the moment you got here you ain't been nothing but a pain my ass. You worthless, good-for-nothing piece of shit." He pointed the gun at Noah, placing the end right against the child's nose while holding his throat tightly with his massive left hand. "I should shoot you! I should fuckin' shoot you and put you out of your miserable-ass existence. Nobody wants you around any-fuckin'-way."

Noah was no longer able to make a sound as Mikey's grip crushed his windpipe and severed his vocal cords. His eyes bulged out in pleading agony as his hands tried to pry Mikey's hand away unsuccessfully. Noah's face was turning blue, but Mikey didn't notice nor did he hear the banging at the front door.

"You can't do shit right!" Mikey spat out, still threatening to blast a hole in Noah's face. "People shouldn't fuckin' have kids they don't want. You thought you were special? You thought you were gon' be special? You thought my ma was gon' want yo' ass? She don't want no kids either! She don't want you, she don't want me . . ." He was beginning to cry as he started to speak in fragments, no longer conscious of what he was doing. "Years of this . . . we all fucked up . . . It's fucked up, man . . . It's fucked up!"

Noah eventually stopped struggling against Mikey's embrace, but Mikey continued to squeeze with increased energy as he unleashed his emotions. Over his own sobbing and erratic statements he was deaf to the sound of the front door bursting open and the trotting of feet as armed officers hurried down the hall toward the bedroom.

"Drop the gun and put your hands in the air!" the first officer on the scene demanded. His gun was trained on Mikey's shoulder as he spoke with authority.

Two other officers filed into the room with their guns on Mikey as well. No one moved.

Mikey looked up in a daze at the guns staring back at him. Suddenly, it occurred to him that he was in a compromising situation. He looked down at Noah's still body and the stunned look stuck on Noah's little blue face. The child's eyes didn't blink at all.

"Put the gun down and raise your hands!" the lead officer repeated.

Mikey began to panic at the realization of what was going on. "Oh fuck," he mumbled. "Fuck fuck fuck." He released his hold on Noah's neck and stared in shock at the child underneath him, but he failed to put down his gun.

"Come on, son," the officer encouraged in his strong baritone. "Don't make an already ugly situation any worse." He tried to imagine what thoughts were running through the assailant's mind and could only think of two things; either this guy was going to try to shoot it out with them or he was going to turn the gun on himself.

Mikey shook his head. He couldn't go to jail. He'd heard stories of what they did to some dudes in jail, especially those who were accused of abusing children. If word ever got out about what he'd actually done to Noah, then he definitely didn't stand a chance behind bars. He knew his mother would never support him once she found out what had happened here today. He stared at Noah and cursed the child's existence. If his mother had never brought him here, then none of this would have happened. He blamed his mom for making him so fucked up in the head over the years, and Noah for tempting him to do things and feel things he never wanted to give in to. Now, here he was with the police threatening to impair him if he didn't drop his piece and surrender quietly.

"Come on," the officer encouraged once more. "This doesn't have to go the way you're trying to take it, son. Take the high road here and drop the gun."

Mikey pulled the pistol away from Noah's face and looked into the officer's eyes with tears stinging his own. He couldn't do it. He couldn't be the obedient perpetrator that the officer wanted him to be any more than he could be the perfect child his mother had wanted him to be despite the imperfect things she and his father had done to him. He was the monster they'd created, and the truth was that the world would be a much better place without him and the havoc he seemed to create in everyone's life. He raised his gun to his head. Every heart in the room dropped as they all realized what was about to happen next.

"Think about this, son," the lead officer said, his strength breaking as emotion began to set in. "Think about this."

"I already have," Mikey replied.

"Ma'am, stop! Stop!" an officer snapped at her as she grabbed Olivia and pulled her away from the front door of Ms. Mae's house. "You can't go in there. It's a crime scene."

"I need to get to him!" Olivia snapped back. "I need to get to Noah. I placed the 911 call. I have to get him."

"There are officers inside trying to contain the situation. Now, you're just gonna have to be patient and let us do our job."

"I'm so sick of everyone telling me about doing their job! If everyone was doing their job to begin with, none of us would be happening now!"

The female officer had no clue what the woman was talking about, but she was also in no mood to argue with a disgruntled citizen. "Listen, lady . . . I'm gonna need you to step down off the porch and—"

A gunshot resounded from the back of the house, cutting off the officer's statement and getting everyone's attention on the outside.

Olivia gasped. "Noah!" She broke free of the officer and pushed her way into the home with the woman fast on her trail.

"You can't go in there! It isn't safe," the officer hollered after her.

"Noah? Noah?" Olivia called out as she ran through the house frantically, not caring about the danger she was running into.

She reached the open door of Ms. Mae's bedroom just as the female officer grabbed her by the wrist.

"Ma'am, I'd hate to arrest you but—"

"Please step back," the lead male officer spoke as he held a bleeding man by the wrists and handcuffed him. The officer began to read the man, whom Olivia assumed was Mikey, his rights as another officer called over the radio for an ambulance.

"Noah?" Olivia cried out, trying to peer past the commotion in search of the boy.

"Please contain her," the male officer spoke to his female counterpart as he began to usher Mikey out of the room, down the hall, and out of the house.

Once the other officers filed out, Olivia snatched away from the female officer once more and stared in disbelief at the body on the bed. Her initial thought was that he'd been shot. Blood splatter was on the bedspread beside him, but nothing covered his body. Olivia walked over to the bed with her hand over mouth and her tears dripping down upon it. "Noah," she whispered as her eyes fell upon his unmoving, lifeless body. She could see the bruising already evident around his neck. His eyes remained opened giving him a shocked expression. She moved closer and stumbled over the receiver resting on the floor. Olivia remembered the initial fear in his voice when he'd first called her. It had only taken minutes after that for Mikey to extract the life out of him.

Olivia climbed onto the bed, reached over, and used her index and middle fingers to close his eyelids. Her heart was shattered beyond repair. She was speechless as she sat staring at his body, wondering how things could have been different if she'd gotten there sooner or if she'd fought harder, earlier, to remove him from the home. No one had listened to her or taken her seriously until recently. Just when she'd gotten the Office of the Inspector General to investigate the Department of Family and Children Services, just when she'd gotten word that a fire had been lit under social services' ass and the investigation against Ms. Mae was about to be reopened . . . this happened. It was too late. Everything she strived for, all of her efforts were now pointless. The one thing she was trying to avoid had occurred nonetheless.

"Ma'am, we need you to leave the room," the female officer stated gingerly, now feeling sorry for Olivia upon witnessing her emotional connection to the deceased child.

Olivia looked up at the woman and felt herself growing faint. "I made him a promise and I broke it," she told her. "I didn't make it in time. I . . . I didn't make it."

The officer put her arms around Olivia and led her out of the room as a paramedic seemingly came out of nowhere and covered Noah's body to await the coroner who was on his way. It was over, and Olivia had never felt so distraught and useless as she did in that moment.

Chapter 16

Olivia hadn't left her house since the day of Noah's small funeral. In attendance were only her, Daysha, Shanice, a representative from social services, and a few kids from his class and their parents. Ms. Mae hadn't attended because she'd recently been arrested for the part she played in abetting a child abuser. Mikey's futile attempt to shoot himself that day had led to one of the officer's placing a bullet in his thigh, which had impaired him enough to drop his gun so that the lead officer could detain him. Upon being taken into police custody and questioned, Mikey had sung like a canary, telling the investigators how his mother knew what was going on, what she and his father had done to him as a child, and what she herself had done to Noah from time to time. Neither mother nor son would be getting out of jail anytime soon.

Noah's funeral was the most depressing moment of Olivia's life for many reasons. She'd paid for everything; his coffin, his burial plot, even the suit he was buried in. It was the very least she felt that she could do, considering that she felt like a failure. That was three weeks ago. Now, she was content with drinking rum and researching articles highlighting the astonishing number of deaths of children in DFCS custody. Her obsession with that research catapulted her to look up statistics about childhood sexual abuse. She'd done so before, but now it felt as if she needed to know all there was to know.

She needed every bit of information available, but most importantly, she was searching for the reason of why the epidemic was so widespread and vastly growing but so unspoken of.

In her reading, she discovered something she'd missed due to cutting herself off from the outside world aside from her newspaper and Internet. Olivia sat straight up in her chair as her eyes quickly read over the article detailing the vice president of the United States' initiative to combat sexual abuse on college campuses.

"What the hell?" Olivia spoke out in the silence of her office. It wasn't that she didn't applaud the White House's attention to the fact that sexual abuse was running rampant within the nation. It simply appalled her that their research seemed so outdated, and that it wasn't clear to the administration that by the time most of the female college students they were targeting reached college age, the majority of them would have already experienced some form of sexual abuse as a child. Never mind the fact that it wasn't only females that were susceptible to sexual abuse, but males too.

Olivia was hot. Memories of Noah's frail body and thoughts of the pain he'd experienced at the hands of Mikey infuriated her. Flashbacks of her own father traumatizing her so badly that she'd been forced to turn away from her family while trying to erase any memory or connection that she had to them, even changing her own name when she'd gotten of age. But no matter what she tried to do, memories of who she was . . . Flashbacks of Kennedy being abused over and over continued to haunt Olivia Collins, the healed individual that she wanted to be.

Only she wasn't. She wasn't any more healed now than she was when she was Kennedy Henderson screaming and crying for her life while enduring the abuse her father joyously inflicted upon her.

Taking a swig of the straight shot of Bacardi in her glass, Olivia opened up a Word document. She'd made Noah a promise that she'd fix things. Although she hadn't been able to save him in time to spare his life, maybe she could do something that would correct the epidemic and save yet another child. As her fingers began to type, her phone rang. She ignored it, not even looking over at the caller ID to see who it was. She recognized the ring tone as Kasyn's. He'd been calling frequently since Noah's funeral. Eventually, she'd call him back, but right now, she was busy trying to do exactly what he'd told her to do. He'd been right. How could she help Noah if she couldn't even help herself? It pained her to know that so many children were out there in the world experiencing the same hurt she'd been privy to in silence. By attempting to do something about it, she'd be helping children she'd never met while also helping herself by being honest with the world about what she'd experienced. Who knew, maybe sharing her testimony and putting her heart into an initiative to combat childhood sexual abuse would prove to be a healing experience for herself as well as others.

Twenty minutes later, Olivia sat back and reread her draft, wiping the tears from her eyes.

President Obama & Vice President Biden
The White House
1600 Pennsylvania Ave NW
Washington, DC 20500

Dear President Obama & Vice President Biden,
I was sexually abused by my father. I was four-teen at the time. Now I am thirty-one, but the pain of the occurrence has never left me. I am author Olivia Collins, and I am decidedly living a mission

of promoting sexual assault awareness. Here's why I'm writing to you: I am dismayed by the lack of support and assistance sexual abuse victims get from law officials and the community pertaining to their claims, as well as the lack of support young victims get from communities, including their families, as if they have no right to be protected or no credibility to be believed. No one deserves to be sexually abused—period. I don't have to tell you that sexual abuse is one of the most underreported crimes in our nation. I've followed your Task Force initiative to Prevent College Sexual Assaults. While I commend the initiative wholeheartedly, I feel as if something is missing. The most typical type of account I hear of often is child sexual abuse with a parental predator. Because the abuse is inflicted by someone the victim knows personally, someone of authority in the victim's life, they or their non-predatory parent overlook the incident(s), don't act on it, and fail to get officials involved in order not to upset the family. This is one reason why this crime is so underreported.

Additionally, our society doesn't want to believe that this type of epidemic is plaguing our nation. The Rape, Abuse, and Incest National Network (RAINN) states that 44 percent of female victims were first raped before the age of eighteen. That's close to half of sexually abused females in general! The CDC's 2012 study shows that 42.2 percent of all female victims were first raped before the age of eighteen and 29.8 percent were first raped between the ages of eleven and seventeen. These victims were not college students. The CDC's 2012 study goes on to say that 37.4 percent of college students (only) were first raped between the ages of eighteen and twenty-four. What this says to me is that the nation's toughest sexual abuse issue and most prominent target victim group is adolescents. My question is, what can the White House do to help lessen the increasing number of abused children?

As a forward thinker, I don't just come to you with questions and complaints. I also offer solutions! As a child sexual abuse survivor, I only wish that programs or resources were readily made available to me to help me break free from the abuse of my father. My suggestion is to arm both parents and children with information. Children, adolescents, and teens need age-appropriate references that they can draw from when facing such traumatic ordeals. Things like posters in schools displaying national and/or local hotline numbers, on-site individuals who are thoroughly trained to recognize the signs of sexual abuse and act accordingly, inclusion of sexual assault prevention measures into health education and/or sex education courses, and national commercial campaigns geared toward children providing hotline numbers. Children need to feel safe and have a sense of security when reaching out for help. I would be more than honored to work with a team to help put these types of across-the-board, national help aids in place so that I will never again have to hear a story about a child calling for help and screaming, but only after things have gotten completely out of control.

We have a duty to protect our children from damaging occurrences which may affect them physically, psychologically, socially, emotionally, and educationally. Please find enclosed my bio and *the data I referred to in this letter. It is my sincerest hope that my concerns will be addressed and that, whether or not my ideas will be acted upon, something will be done to protect our nation's children.*

Thank you in advance for your support.

Respectfully,

Olivia Collins

Olivia smiled through the tears. "I made you a promise," she said aloud. "And I'm sticking to it." Even if it took the remainder of her natural life, Olivia felt strongly that kids like Noah had rights, and it was her responsibility to protect them. She sipped from her glass once more as she hit print on her screen.

Printed in the United States
by Baker & Taylor Publisher Services